Praise for S

"McDowall has a true talent."

"The definition of a page turner."

"Stands shoulder to shoulder with other authors in this genre."

"Powerful. Insightful. Real and gripping."

"Every piece of the puzzle slots together to create the perfect masterpiece."

"A great example of plot, pace, and characterisation."

Other titles by Stewart McDowall

Detective McQueen series

#1, The Mind Hack
#2, The McQueen Legacy

The McQueen Legacy

Stewart McDowall

SRL PUBLISHING

SRL Publishing Ltd
London

www.srlpublishing.co.uk

First published worldwide by SRL Publishing in 2025

SRL PUBLISHING
THINKING DIFFERENTLY, DELIVERING CHANGE

Text copyright © Stewart McDowall, 2025

The moral right by the author has been asserted in accordance with the Copyright, Designs, and Patents Act 1988.

ISBN: 978-1-915073-42-6

1 3 5 7 9 10 8 6 4 2

This book is sold subject to the condition that it shall not, by way of trade or otherwise, be reproduced or transmitted in any form or by any means, electronic, mechanical, photocopying or otherwise, without the prior permission of the publishers.

No part of this book shall be used in any manner for the purpose of training artificial intelligence (AI) systems or technologies.

SRL Publishing and Pen Nib logo are registered trademarks owned by SRL Publishing Ltd.

This book is a work of fiction. Names, characters, places, and incidents are either a product of the author's imagination or are used fictitiously. Any resemblance to actual people, living or dead, events or locales, is entirely coincidental.

A CIP catalogue record for this book is available from the British Library

SRL Publishing is a climate positive publisher offsetting more carbon emissions than it emits.

Your legacy is every life you touch
Maya Angelou

One

As soon as she began speaking, McQueen knew she was lying. Maybe it was in the little cough to clear her throat or her general tone and body language, or perhaps it was something less obvious that his training and experience had flagged up to his subconscious. The off-key music of lying? Whatever it was, he was certain that what she was saying wasn't the truth, the whole truth, or anything like the truth. Sometimes you have to trust your human instincts, see the whites of their eyes. There's a good reason why the lie detection results of polygraph machines aren't admissible in court, even though their shocking lack of reliability doesn't seem to trouble the name-and-shame day-time TV shows.

As a forensic psychologist and criminologist now turned private detective, McQueen had spoken to a lot of very good liars in his time, a few of them had completely fooled him, but not this one.

'It's absolutely outrageous,' she was saying. 'I didn't steal that money.' And then she said it again, this time

The McQueen Legacy

reaching out to tap the syllables on McQueen's desk with her bony finger. 'I. Did. Not. Steal. That. Cash.' She leaned back again. 'Oh, they'll make up some nonsense, false accounts but I had nothing to do with it, so that's why I'm here. You're a private detective and I need you to work with my solicitor to prove I'm innocent. It's terrible, Mr McQueen. I worked for them for years. Day after day. And now I'm being victimised and made into a scapegoat. But I've kept the evidence, I've got a computer memory stick with all the spreadsheets on it.'

McQueen sat back in his chair and looked her over carefully. He'd read the briefing sheet his assistant, Sekalyia, had prepared for him which summed-up Mrs Bolton's case. She was an aging company bookkeeper who had worked for a successful multi-national firm called Summertown Industries for many happy years, until they'd discovered a two-million-pound hole in their accounts and decided that she was the thief. Sitting there with her short grey hair and friendly eyes, she looked every inch the trustworthy grandma. She was clutching a large mustard-coloured shopping bag on her lap and was fiddling nervously with the strap. He wanted to believe her, he really did, and so would a jury, but he hadn't seen the prosecution's evidence yet, although Sekalyia's note described it as "compelling".

Whether she was lying or not, McQueen didn't want this case. A big part of it was going to be tedious number crunching. Forensic accountancy wasn't his specialty, which would mean he'd have to outsource that aspect of the work and he'd be left interviewing her colleagues and acquaintances. He'd have to spend endless hours trying to piece together a glowing character reference while at the same time attempting to point the finger of suspicion at someone else. McQueen wasn't sure why Sekalyia had let this one slip through the client-vetting process, probably felt sorry for the old lady and her sob story, but McQueen had already decided to let the kind old woman down gently.

'Mrs Bolton,' he said. 'Something like this could take a lot of time. Many painstaking hours and, to be frank with you, you've seen my rates.' He smiled and shrugged apologetically. 'This could get very expensive for you and it wouldn't be fair for me to—'

But the seated woman didn't let him finish, she held up a crinkly hand to dismiss his concerns.

'Oh, you don't need to worry about the money,' she reassured him. 'That's not going to be a problem. And if it works out as a little more tax-efficient for you…' With surprising dexterity her hand dipped into her bag and came out with two large bundles of twenty-pound notes which she tossed onto McQueen's desk with a thud. 'A good faith retainer,' she added. The word that immediately forced its way into his mind from Sekalyia's notes was *compelling*. He looked her straight in her slightly watery but unblinking eyes and then he stared hard at the money, trying to give it the respect it deserved. He didn't ask where she'd got her hands on that kind of cash, he didn't really want to know. Above him he could feel the weight of his accountant's expectation pushing down on him and could almost see the unpaid bills being waved in his face.

'It's okay,' he said after a long pause, 'you can put that away. I'm sure you have other important uses for it.' She kept her eyes on him as she plonked the stacks back into her bag. He wanted to tell her he just wasn't interested, that he didn't believe her story and she had very little chance of fighting the case, but something was stopping him. He didn't know why but his usual unwavering decisiveness seemed to have deserted him. Based on his clinical training he was a big fan of the medical approach of telling a patient the unvarnished truth. Better to be upfront with bad news than to nurture false hope. But for some reason today, watching her fiddling with her bag as she fixed him with an almost-pleading stare, he just couldn't do it. Instead he took the coward's way out.

'Listen, Mrs Bolton,' he said attempting a reassuring tone. 'I'm going to speak to my colleague, we'll review the case and the evidence and then I'll get back to you. I'm not saying I'll take the case, but as I say, we'll be in touch.' He stood, smiled, and then moved towards the door hoping to usher her out. Mrs Bolton stayed seated.

'But do you believe me?' she asked, an annoyed tinge to her voice. 'Because if you don't believe I didn't steal their money there's no point to this.' It was unsettlingly blunt and McQueen felt cornered. The politician's answer to the question would have been to not answer the question. To avoid committing and loop back to, "it's too early to say" and "we'll review the evidence", but McQueen took the other gutless route favoured by politicians the world over.

'Of course I believe you,' he said in a confident voice.

After the woman and her bagful of money had gone, McQueen went into the adjoining office and flopped down onto a small sofa that was across from Sekalyia's desk. He was fairly clueless when it came to office furnishings or any other kind of furniture for that matter, so the couch had been her idea, a touch of comfort for any traumatised clients. There was also a box of tissues on the desk. Patiently he watched and waited while she finished typing, knowing better than to break her train of thought while she was in full flow.

Although McQueen had an ex-wife, he had no children but he was still able to recognise that his feelings towards Sekalyia were paternal. He felt warming pride at her every achievement and stinging pain at her occasional missteps. Straight out of university Lia, as everyone called her, had started as his office manager but with her ambition and talent it hadn't taken long for her to also become his assistant and co-investigator. Initially he had simply valued having someone with a different perspective to listen to his theories as he picked his way through the vagaries of any challenging cases. She had her own opinions and a confident voice that was more than prepared to tell him if he was talking nonsense. He had started to rely more and more on her youthful insight and reasoning until she had become an integral part of his work. Sometimes she saw things he hadn't even seen or perhaps hadn't wanted to admit. There was also the fact that, on one occasion, she had risked her own life to save his by driving her car at a gunman. It was an incident they rarely discussed but of course neither of them had forgotten.

These days Lia worked a few of their cases by herself, but at the same time she was still the perfect first point of

The McQueen Legacy

contact for the prospective new clients that came in. Like a one-person triage department, she quickly assessed the merits and risks of their problems as they arrived and decided whether they would interest McQueen. In short, she decided which ones needed immediate detective attention and which could be sent home with a paracetamol and a pat on the back. Her instincts were usually impeccable, that's why McQueen was curious to know why she thought the Bolton case was worth pursuing.

When she'd triumphantly tapped the keyboard to end her email Lia swivelled in her chair to face McQueen. She held up her hands in surrender, she knew he'd been waiting to ask her about the Bolton woman.

'I know, I know,' she said apologetically. 'Looks like a terrible job. Mountains of boring spreadsheet work, I mean she even left me her precious memory stick.' She smiled and showed him the small object, its silver casing glinting in the light. 'We'd be facing off against the well-funded legal experts of a hugely powerful organisation. Trusting the word of a single elderly woman. And I know you're wondering why I thought this might be something for us.' She grimaced and shrugged her shoulders, 'What can I say, David and Goliath?'

'I get it,' he said, nodding. 'The hero complex, helping the old lady across the street, but Lia, what makes you think she's telling the truth?' All playfulness dropped away from Lia's demeanor as she straightened in her seat and pointed at the door that Mary Bolton had exited.

'Oh, she's telling the truth, McQueen,' she said, 'That woman isn't lying, I'd stake my career on it.

Two

The meeting was about to start and Tania was squirming a little on her chair. There was a vibe in the air, something testosterone-fuelled and faintly dangerous, and it was making her feel uneasy. In contrast, next to her, Richard was almost bouncing in his seat, a barely supressed grin on his face. Even as they'd pulled into the carpark he'd said, 'You're going to love this,' although based on the online videos of the great man he'd already shown her she strongly doubted it. She'd managed to smile and nod as if she hadn't already made her mind up.

Richard was the only reason she was there. It was her attempt to show interest in the things that interested him, she was making a sacrifice in support of their relationship and all she could do now was see it through. Things had been a little rocky between them recently, especially since Richard had lost his job again leaving her as the earner in the household. It was the third job he had lost in a year. They'd all been great-sounding sales positions except that the basic salary was minimal and the attractive bonuses were reliant on achieving unattainable targets. Or at least that's how Richard had described them. Easy jobs to get and even easier to lose. Fortunately, in financial terms, Tania's career was going very well although that did nothing for their domestic tension. She'd been in banking since leaving university and year after year her diligence and hard work had been recognised and rewarded. She was on an upward swing which seemed to be making it hard for Richard, whose own pendulum was decidedly south-bound.

The hall was in a small rural community centre in a north Yorkshire market town outside York, a popular public space for hire that regularly hosted a diverse range of community gatherings from council meetings to formal wedding celebrations and raucous ceilidhs. A solid, stone-built structure that had once been the village school and had witnessed much in its hundred-odd years but was about to see something new.

The uncomfortable chairs were arranged in rows all facing the low-level stage which was still completely empty. She'd expected a lectern or projector screen but there was nothing, which for a thrilling second made her hope that perhaps it wasn't going to happen. The echoey room was bumbling with an excited murmur punctuated by occasional coughs. As casually as she could, she turned her neck to look around her and wasn't surprised to see the audience was ninety percent male and aged between twenty and forty.

At exactly eight o'clock a man walked forward from the back of the room and all heads turned to watch him enter, including Tania's. He was about thirty years old, handsome, with a neat short blonde haircut and a prominent forehead that shone slightly in the lights. He was wearing a white open-necked shirt and light-coloured slacks and a small black microphone headset curved round to the side of his mouth. His look put Tania in mind of someone about to announce the exciting launch of a new mobile phone or software release. She easily recognised the man from Richard's videos as he strode purposefully to the stage and turned to face his audience who had already started clapping their appreciation, their restlessness turning to excited anticipation. The man clasped his hands together in front of him forming a finger pyramid which he then pointed into the front row. He wasn't smiling, there was no manufactured warmth or false friendliness. Without preamble he launched right into it.

'I'm Zach Lindley,' he said in a non-discernible accent booming through the speakers that Tania had only just noticed at each side of the hall. 'But you already know who I am or you wouldn't be here. And yes, I'm here to talk to you tonight about those other people.' He paused and scanned the room, many of the heads in front of Tania were nodding. 'Yes, the ones who lie and cheat and steal,' he continued. 'The ones who don't get caught. The ones who always win.' He threw his arms wide to encompass the whole room. 'And then there's us,' he said. 'The good people who always lose. We can't compete. They are better at this rigged game than we are because they invented the game.' He unclasped his hands and held up a finger. 'And before you ask, no, I don't believe in karma. There is no reckoning. There is no natural levelling up. There is no justice. And what about traditional religion? Well, I'm here to tell you that the ones who believe in God, that's why they believe in God, so they can con themselves even if they don't get to see it in this life there is still punishment for the bad and reward for the good. But let me tell you very clearly, here and now, that's not what I believe.'

There were mumblings in the crowd of "that's right" and "yes!". Zach was pacing now, trying to make fleeting eye contact with as many people as possible. He fumbled in the back pocket of his jeans and brought out a piece of paper which he carefully unfolded. He held it aloft. 'It was when I got this, I knew. It doesn't really matter who it came from, all that matters is it was my thousandth corporate rejection. That's when it all became clear to me. It was at that point,' he raised his finger heavenwards, '*That* was when I realised, qualifications don't matter. Hard work doesn't matter. Intelligence doesn't matter. Talent doesn't matter. I *knew* then that no matter what I did it was never going to happen for me.' The heads that had been nodding were now bobbing enthusiastically, his words resonating and causing the human waves.

'The system has been set up to *stop* people like you and me from achieving our dreams. They have it all sewn up.' He was smiling as if this was a funny idea, but it was an acid-bitter smile. 'They mock you. They tell you to chase your dreams, to never give up, and then they sit back and laugh and laugh and laugh at your stupidity as you batter yourself into a bloody pulp against the invisible walls they have already put in place to protect themselves and their own kind.' He stopped walking the stage and waited until he was certain everyone was ready for his next words. 'And how dangerous are they, these others? The ones who are blocking you? Well, I have the evidence and I can tell you they have been murdering people and getting away with it. They own the authorities and they own the police. If you step out of line, they will kill you.'

Tania had to supress a giggle and she turned to Richard so they could share a laugh at the self-pitying pomposity of it all, but her boyfriend's eyes were wide, his face rapt, smiling as if he'd just heard from God himself. Looking at him submerged in this other world she suddenly felt very lost. She reached over and shook Richard's arm.

'Toilet,' she said, as she stood and squeezed past him. He hardly seemed to notice and neither did the other three men she had to get past on her way to the aisle, their total focus was on the man who was tapping into their hurt.

Tania waited an hour for Richard in the car. When he came out she'd already prepared an explanation of how she'd been feeling sick and hadn't wanted to spoil the meeting, but her excuse wasn't required. Richard was too hyped up to even ask her.

'That guy knows,' he said, sliding into the passenger seat. 'He's absolutely on it.'

'I'm sorry I missed it,' she said quietly. 'So what was his point?' For the first time Richard turned to look at her, an incredulous scowl on his face.

'His point? Did you even listen? That man is a genius and you're asking what his point was?'

'Yes, what was his answer to all his problems, apart from blaming everyone else and charging fifteen quid a ticket to do it? I assume he had an answer?'

Richard turned away and stared out of the window. 'It's always about money with you, isn't it?' he said. 'Zach said there'd be negative voices,' he added, his voice getting louder, 'and they often come from the ones closest to us.'

'I'm not being negative,' she answered, starting to feel anger rising, 'I'm just asking a simple question.' But Richard had already shut down, it was the same whenever she tried to find out exactly what had led to his latest sacking.

'Let's just go home,' he said, 'but I'm telling you now there's another meeting next weekend and I've booked a place. It's the whole weekend and it's at a retreat.' She had started the car and had been pulling out of the carpark, so was slightly distracted, but then the information filtered through.

'Next weekend? But you know that's when I've got—'

'You're not invited,' he interrupted, still staring out of the window. 'I'm going on my own.'

Three

Darkness was slowly embracing the office, casting its gloom into the corners, turning the gentle glow of McQueen's computer screen into a dazzling portal that wanted to lead him straight into the pain of his clients. People only turned to a private investigator when they had exhausted all other possibilities, when their suspicions were no longer bearable, or their suffering had been ignored by the rest of the world. McQueen saw his primary role as emergency pain relief. Often that pain was mental, sometimes it was physical, and from time to time it was both.

When McQueen had given up the relative security of his position as a respected forensic psychologist and criminologist, it had been with the best intentions. Naïvely he'd thought he could do more for the world by chasing actual murderers than teaching students about their possible motivations. He recognised that belief now as part of his own fantasy hero complex.

His gradual transition into hands-on crime fighting had started when on a couple of occasions he'd been asked by the local police to produce psychological profiles of possible suspects. Taking the pattern of events surrounding a criminal incident he'd had to translate that into the possible age, job, or habits of the unknown suspect. It was a challenging task that brought theory into the harsh realm of real life, and it came with responsibilities. Get it wrong and you could lead an investigation down a blind alley, but get it right and it could be a useful tool. Fortunately, McQueen had been very good at the task. One of his character profiles of a serial rapist had been so accurate that it had helped the police to narrow their search and track the guy down in days. Based on the evidence seen in the guy's previous attacks, McQueen had been able to predict where and when he was likely to strike again. A policewoman in plainclothes, that on McQueen's suggestion included an ankle length dress, had done the rest. The win was a professional buzz for McQueen and it had given him a taste for the gritty realities of life and the thrill of the hunt. Unfortunately, his mid-life career shift had not gone down well with his then wife, and coupled with the way he was drinking at the time had resulted in the end of their marriage. He regretted the hurt he'd caused to his wife but not the change of career.

Since leaving academia and the insular world of books and students, McQueen had helped to bring to justice five different murderers who, between them, had been responsible for the deaths of at least thirteen people, probably more. On the back of his victories, McQueen had gained a certain level of tabloid fame and even turned up on TV a few times. In the early days of his one-man agency it had been a struggle to find interesting clients, but after his famous triumphs they started to come looking for him.

However, there had always been something that had eaten away at McQueen ever since catching his first killer. It was obvious but inescapable — bringing to justice was not the same as bringing victims back to life. Victims' families could feel some semblance of closure, but their lives were never the same. Stopping a murderer before they ever killed had to be the goal.

McQueen got up from his desk and walked across to the window to look down on the empty carpark, the very place where he had once been shot and where Lia had saved his life. He turned away from the window and then, to avoid the glare of his computer, he went into Lia's empty office. She had gone home hours before to her boyfriend, Carl. She'd done enough late nights at work to cause some domestic friction and even though Carl had time-consuming work commitments of his own, they'd both agreed to schedule at least one night a week when they ate together. Tonight was one of those nights.

On the screen McQueen was avoiding were the graphic details of his most recent cases, one in particular which had ended badly in his eyes. A murderer called Sutton had eventually been taken down, but the wife and three children of his final victim would never see their father alive again. Crossing the office he went into the bathroom. The overhead light reluctantly flickered into life and he was confronted by his own image.

'You're losing it, McQueen,' he said as he studied the tired eyes, the sagging face, the expression hovering somewhere between mild panic and defeated resignation. Where was the old confidence and swagger? He saw none in that look. He ran his fingers through his hair, massaging his scalp as he did so, trying to squeeze out the doubts that had begun to plague him. Was the brain inside his lumpy skull still up to it?

'Too many wrong decisions,' he said quietly, 'Too many mistakes.' He sighed and turned away from the brutal honesty of the mirror.

Back at his desk he was about to shut down and leave the empty office to go home to his equally unoccupied flat when an email pinged in. It looked like spam. It said it was from *Intrusive* and when he hovered his cursor over the name to reveal the details of the sender it only said *intrusive.thought@empty.com*. The subject line also said *Intrusive*, someone obviously had a point to make. He stared at the words for a second and mused on the idea that all emails were intrusive by their very nature, forcing their way uninvited into your life. As he paused, his mind floated free for a couple of milli-seconds before suddenly a mental connection was made through the miracle of human synapses as they linked to a faded memory. Before he'd even clicked his mouse to open the email he could feel a faint panic rising. When he'd finally read the short message he closed his eyes and let his head slump forward as if gravity had finally won the lifelong battle against his neck muscles. With his chin on his chest he breathed in deeply. He instinctively followed the calming advice he had given to so many others. Breathe in for four seconds, hold for four more and then breathe out for the same count. Eventually, when the anxiety had subsided he straightened up and forced himself to read it again.

Dear GREAT AND WONDERFUL Doctor McQueen, please help. I'm having these terrible intrusive thoughts. They are hounding me. I keep imagining that I am going to kill you. I'm afraid to be around knives because I feel sure that if I picked up a knife I would STAB you. I can visualise it, it's very clear, it terrifies me.

Is this dangerous? What do you think? Is this something I should be worried about, I mean you're the doctor, right?

The message wasn't signed but it didn't need to be, McQueen knew exactly who had sent it. An echo from the past, an unwelcome visitor who had never really gone away. If he was still drinking, this was the time when he'd have been reaching for the bottle in his bottom drawer, an emotional crutch that would inevitably collapse under him. These days there was no whisky waiting in the desk to trip him up, not because it might have been a temptation but because he knew he'd never need it again. What he had instead, was the brutal pain of facing his problems straight on and the intrusive email was just such a problem.

Four

'You know the rules. The deal is no work and no screens tonight.' Lia was pointing at Carl's open laptop on the kitchen table. He nodded and closed the lid immediately.

'Actually, it wasn't really work,' he said. 'It's just some YouTuber all the guys in the office have been talking about that I wanted to check out. I thought he'd be one of the usual idiots but it turns out he talks a lot of sense about stuff. A few of the guys have been talking about going to one of his meetings, they wanted to know if I was up for it...' then he tailed off. Lia wasn't really listening to his explanation and he knew it didn't matter what he'd been doing, a deal was a deal.

They sat at the table to eat the homemade vegetable curry, one of Lia's specials. It was another date night rule: no slouching in front of the TV balancing trays on their knees as they did most nights. Sit at the table, eat, and talk to each other, a simple little recipe to make sure they didn't lapse into an indifferent boring routine.

As they ate, they talked about some of their upcoming

family events but Carl could tell Lia was distracted and he had a pretty good idea why that might be. It was the other rule, no talking shop at the table he guessed she was wrestling with. After a few minutes of watching her chase a piece of cauliflower around her plate with her fork, Carl knew they'd have to do some rule bending.

'Okay,' he said with a sigh. 'I was working at my computer for ten minutes while you were cooking, so that buys you exactly ten minutes to get your work worries off your chest.' They both smiled. She didn't need to ask him how he'd guessed, Carl's mind-reading capacity was one of the many things she loved about him. She put down her cutlery.

'It's McQueen,' she said, 'he's just…' she grimaced as she struggled for the right way to phrase it, 'he's just not himself at the moment.'

'How do you mean?' Carl had continued eating but he was listening.

'Things seem to be getting to him much more than they used to. Much more than they should.'

'Like what?'

'Well, I told you about the Sutton case?'

'Yes, sure, you helped to catch that psycho and now he's in prison. End of story.'

'Yes, it should have been the end, a job well done, but McQueen's been beating himself up about it. He's convinced all the signs and clues were already there and if he'd been a bit faster he could have prevented that last murder.'

'And could he?'

'Maybe, but that's hindsight. What's done is done and

he did his best at the time. But it's affecting his judgement. It's like he's lost his confidence. For example, an old woman came in today who is clearly being set-up by her company to take the blame for some missing money and McQueen flat-out refused to believe her, based on nothing more than his gut instinct. I gave him a pre-brief note telling him the evidence was too compelling to be true and he misread it. He thought I was saying it was compelling evidence that she was guilty.'

'So,' he smiled, knowing exactly where this was heading, 'are you going to help her?'

'No, the McQueen agency has declined her case.'

'Okay, but that's not what I asked, I said are *you* going to help her?' Lia took a forkful of food and frowned as if the thought had never crossed her mind.

'Weeeellll,' she said, stringing out the word as if this was an idea that had only just occurred to her, 'to do that I'd need someone to help me with some of the heavy financial analysis. Someone who can crunch serious numbers accurately.'

'Oh, you mean someone who works in finance and knows their way around a spreadsheet?'

She nodded innocently.

'Yes, I suppose so,' she mumbled through a mouthful of curry.

'C'mon, Lia, you're talking about me aren't you?'

Lia checked the kitchen clock. My ten minutes is up,' she said cheerfully. 'Back to date night.' Carl laughed.

'Nice,' he said. 'but I'd have to think about it.'

'I know.'

'I mean I'm up to my ears at work at the moment.'

'I know.'

'And it's not really my speciality.'

'I know.' Lia had nodded along at all his protestations. 'All I want you to know,' she said airily, 'is that she's an old woman, probably the same age as your mother, and she's been seen as an easy target for some unscrupulous corporate thief.'

Carl shook his head.

'My mother? You managed to get my mother into your pitch?' Lia scooped another spoonful of curry onto Carl's plate.

'Did it work?' she asked.

'I'll get back to you,' he said digging into the food, 'but my office is closed right now, I'm on a date.'

Five

Tania was sitting alone on the couch gazing vacantly at the late news even though the various international disasters being brought into her home were washing over her with less impact than a cartoon. As alarming as some of the footage was, she wasn't taking any of it in, it was just moving images and background noise in the quiet living room. The plate with the congealed remnants of a take-away Chinese meal, which she'd eaten without really noticing, lay on the coffee table. Tania didn't need the news, she was preoccupied with a developing story of her own so she grabbed the remote and turned off the TV.

It was Saturday and Richard had gone on his second weekend retreat to a mysterious rural setting in Yorkshire, and once again she had not been included in his plans. She couldn't even speak to him. While he was at the retreat he said he wasn't allowed to have his phone, all delegates had to hand them in at the entrance. They'd been told this was so they could stay focused on the meetings but Tania suspected it was so no rogue video clips could leak onto the internet. It didn't really matter, Richard had only one topic of conversation these days and that centred around his current well-ness guru, Zach Lindley.

There had been some noticeable changes in Richard since he'd been going to the meetings and Tania wasn't quite sure how to deal with them. She couldn't deny he had been more energised and motivated recently, but that energy didn't seem to be directed towards finding a job. He was quicker to anger too, and she'd learned not to question him too closely about his plans, which seemed to be a particularly sensitive subject with him. In an offhand way he'd told her he spent a lot of time researching on the computer while she was out at work, but she knew it wasn't recruitment agencies he was trawling. He was vague about what he was searching for, but she was fairly sure it would be something to do with his new obsession. When she tried to check his search history, it had all been deleted.

From what Tania had been able to pick up from the YouTube videos she'd seen featuring Zach Lindley, the main thrust of his presentations seemed to be around how unfair the world was and how it was only the righteous and good that suffered. It all sounded very childish to her, but the videos only went so far, they were meant to be teasers, bait for the live meetings. Zach Lindley seemed to be bucking the modern trend of putting absolutely everything online, conversely he wanted to get his followers off line and into his lecture halls.

Meanwhile, Richard's activities were starting to drain the joint bank account. It was worrying, he had no income, but it wasn't even the money that bothered her the most, she had savings of her own kept separately from Richard's, no Tania's main concern was she simply didn't understand what was going on. In the language of her work she wasn't able to quantify her exposure to risk, either emotional or financial, and that made her feel very uncomfortable. She couldn't get any real answers from Richard, he was evasive and quizzing him only seemed to make him mad and drive a wedge between them. However, Tania had never been the type of person to let things get too far out of her grasp. Sure, she wanted to be supportive no matter what kind of crisis Richard was going through, but it was getting more and more difficult to sit and wait for the next phase whatever that might be. At heart she was a do-er not a watcher and if she was going to rescue her relationship she felt it was time for her to actively do something. Opening her computer Tania began to do her own research, she knew she needed help, but not the soft wooliness of emotional support or therapy, she wanted hard practical help and she had decided that what she needed was an investigator, someone who could find out exactly what she was facing.

A quick search turned up several private investigator companies and, looking through them, they all seemed to offer similar services. There was the corporate side which included sections such as unauthorised absence checks, injury claim verification, and employee theft. It sounded horrible but then there was the even more awful personal side of the business with the daunting-sounding matrimonial investigations and cheating partner investigations. Tania's eyes scanned through the headings which were presented like a shopping list: surveillance, vehicle tracking, lie detection tests, it was starting to become a depressing blur. All the companies were keen to point out they offered discreet, professional, and experienced services, but Tania was starting to think she was in the wrong place and maybe it hadn't been such a good idea.

The search had also brought up several news articles so she randomly clicked on one she thought was vaguely familiar.

The piece was about a serial killer who had been tracked down by a private investigator called McQueen, who was some kind of professor of forensic psychology or something. She was scanning and not reading in any detail, but she liked the sound of it. Maybe a psychologist would have a good insight into what was going on with Richard beyond the general facts of where he was and what he was doing? There was a link to the McQueen Agency website, so she plunged right in.

The website mentioned several of the high-profile cases the agency had helped to solve, including the murder of a TV presenter called Emma Cullen. Tania didn't remember Emma, but she did have a fuzzy recollection of the story. The examples all stressed how McQueen's forensic psychology and criminology expertise had been essential to the solving of these cases, rather than the cold and pragmatic tracking and surveillance the other companies talked so much about. She was wondering if perhaps her minor problems weren't going to be glamourous enough to be of any interest to this Dr McQueen, as far as she knew no one had been killed yet, but she couldn't escape the thought even that was a possibility.

There was an interactive enquiry form on the site to book an appointment and she quickly filled in her contact details. There was a large section with room to explain the reason for the request. She started to type into the space but after a few sentences she stopped and erased it all. There was a big part of her that was resisting the idea of spying on her partner, she knew she was crossing a line and could even be seen as paranoid, controlling behaviour in itself. A thought went through her mind that maybe *she* was the problem, but quickly kicked that nonsense into touch. She wanted to think that what she was doing was about more than simply grubby sounding hidden bugging devices. And she had another pressing reason to find out where her relationship was heading to, but it was yet to be confirmed.

She thought hard for a few seconds and then wrote the two words that summed up all her concerns: *Dangerous cult*. Without giving herself the chance to change her mind she pressed the button and submitted the form.

She felt some satisfaction in the feeling that she had started a ball rolling, but there was also the nervousness of not knowing what damage it might cause on its path. In truth, she didn't really expect to get any response from the agency but it was almost a test, if they weren't interested then perhaps she should leave it alone.

She would have liked a comforting glass of the white wine that was cooling in the fridge, but knew she shouldn't, not now, so she made a cup of tea instead.

Six

'Come on, McQueen,' said Lia, her impatience finally getting the better of her. 'What the hell is the matter with you? You've been brooding on something for weeks. Surely it's not still that Sutton thing?'

McQueen shook his head. 'Not really,' he replied, 'even though that does still bug me. I should have seen it all quicker. I had all the clues, I just wanted to be sure.' He sighed heavily. 'But I didn't and that's that. Nothing I can do now.'

It was lunchtime and they were sitting in the same Italian restaurant they visited every Wednesday. McQueen had made it a habit to buy lunch for Lia once a week, partly to show her some well-deserved appreciation but also to get them away from the office, the clients, and the computers. In the informal comfort of the restaurant they could usually get to the bottom of anything that might be bugging either of them. Sometimes it was trivial stuff like his lack of dedication to cleaning the office microwave after a messy snack, and sometimes it was more serious such as clients who still hadn't paid their bills. They'd been a good team so far and McQueen didn't want to jeopardise that closeness.

For her part, Lia was wondering if McQueen was going to bring up her interest in Mrs Bolton, the accused embezzler. Lia had been honest with her boss telling him she had not given up on the case and she and Carl were still looking into the details. The idea was that if they found out anything worthwhile, McQueen might reconsider taking the case on officially. Carl had made some progress with the mystical spreadsheet figures, and he'd uncovered some 'financial anomalies' as he called them. He'd said there did seem to be a lot of cash coming into the business, more than would be expected, but he was still a long way from any kind of conclusion. Lia had started to talk to some of Bolton's ex-colleagues to try to get a feel of the culture of the company she'd worked for. This was all being done largely in their own time and Lia was trying not to let it impact her other agency work, but of course, inevitably there had been some cross-over and she was sure it hadn't gone unnoticed by McQueen.

'So, if it's not Sutton what is it?'

McQueen was clearly uncomfortable and struggling with something he didn't want to say so Lia kept quiet and let the silence work its forceful magic. As she waited patiently, she studied his craggy features and the neatly cut white hair. He'd told her previously his hair had been that colour since his early twenties and consequently to many of his friends he'd never seemed to age, he'd always looked older than his years.

Eventually he took a deep breath and she knew he was ready to open up.

'You know about intrusive thoughts, right?' he asked. 'Those awful ideas that pop into your head and seem to be telling you to do some terrible thing? A thing you would never, ever do in real life?'

Lia nodded, 'Of course, we've talked about them before. Like suddenly thinking of pushing your friend off a cliff just because you are standing near the edge together.'

'Exactly. Or imagining driving into the oncoming traffic at night. It's usually something that flits across your mind and then is gone. You are never going to act on those thoughts, but it can be disturbing when they occur. It can make you question yourself.'

'So is that it?' she asked as she began to crunch on a bread stick. 'You've been having intrusive thoughts of strangling me when I get in late?' They both laughed, but McQueen's chuckle was strained.

'For some people,' he said slowly, 'intrusive thoughts can really become a problem. These poor people become so disturbed by these horrific ideas that are forcing themselves into their minds, it starts to dominate their lives.' McQueen had ordered a salad, but it didn't look to Lia as if he was going to eat it. He pushed his plate to one side and continued his story.

'As you know, before I became a private detective I was lecturer. One afternoon one of my mature students came to see me after the class. She was very upset, crying and everything and I could see it had taken a lot for her to speak to me, so I sat her down, got her some tea and let her calm down. I thought she was going to tell me she was struggling with the work. You know, ask for a deadline extension or

The McQueen Legacy

something? But no. She said she needed some advice and she didn't know who to turn to, but as I was a psychologist, she thought I was a good place to start.'

McQueen paused and took a sip from his carbonated water, the only drink he ever ordered. Lia had been taught some basic interview techniques by McQueen and now she was using them on her teacher. Rule one, when a suspect begins to talk, let them talk, don't interrupt or break the flow, you may never get it back again, so Lia sat silently as McQueen unloaded.

'Now, understand this, Lia, any medical practitioner will tell you what they dread the most is being approached out of hours. You need a professional distance with any patient, the whole situation is fraught with risk. I've seen a surgeon friend of mine turn away from the side-line at a kids' football match after an injury because he didn't want to get drawn in. So, I was reluctant to get involved, but the woman was distressed and I couldn't ignore that. I wanted to help. It turned out the woman's husband was a builder but he'd been unable to go to work because he had developed a problem with hammers.'

'Hammers?' Lia wasn't sure whether to smile or not. She was breaking rule one, but she couldn't help herself. 'What do you mean, a problem?'

'I know it sounds ridiculous but he couldn't bring himself to touch a hammer, in fact he couldn't stand to be in a room with one.' Lia was right on the edge of laughing out loud but something about the seriousness of McQueen's face made her fight it off.

'Right, I can see how that would be a bit of an issue for a

builder,' she said trying but failing to lighten the mood a little.

'He told his wife that ever since his baby son had been born, he'd been having hideous intrusive thoughts that he would pick up a hammer and smash the baby's head.'

'Wow, so what did you tell her?'

'You have to understand I was never a clinical psychologist, I was a *forensic* psychologist, I specialised in crime and the people who commit crimes. Clinical wasn't my area. But of course I had done some general training early on and I did know the basics, so I told her that her husband needed to get some therapy. He needed to see a qualified clinical psychologist and that he would probably be able to overcome it.'

Lia studied McQueen as he sat across from her, and if she wasn't mistaken his eyes were slightly moist. She looked closely at his face searching for clues as he looked down at the untouched plate.

'That's all I should have said,' he continued. 'I should have left it at that. But I was young and cocky so what I also told her, to reassure her and to make her feel better, was that she had absolutely nothing to worry about. That no one ever acted on their intrusive thoughts and that she and the baby were safe.' He stopped talking and closed his eyes. He was breathing hard through his nose, clearly fighting back the tears. She knew McQueen well enough, she had seen him in enough stressful situations to guess what was coming next. She should have waited and let him speak when he was ready but the question was too powerful to stay unasked.

'He hurt the baby, didn't he?' she said softly. McQueen

nodded.

'He killed the baby,' he said in a flat monotone, like a computer giving an emotionless factual answer. Lia was shocked, but immediately switched into protective mode.

'It wasn't your fault. You couldn't have known,' she said.

'No, I couldn't. It turned out he had much bigger problems than intrusive thoughts, he was mildly psychotic, he was taking mind-altering recreational drugs and there were a number of other factors, but it didn't change the fact his wife blamed me. She was distraught and in blind pain. I was the only one she'd spoken to about her worries and I'd told her she didn't need to worry.'

'Like you said, you were just trying to make her feel better.'

'Making people feel better is not always the right option, Lia, that's the short-term weak option. I didn't know the full situation so as a professional I should have told her to get specialist help and kept my mouth shut.'

Lia could see how awful it must have been and how badly it had affected McQueen, but she couldn't quite understand why it was such a hot issue now. He'd never spoken about that incident before, so she was guessing something had triggered his current reaction.

'Okay, but this was all quite a few years ago, right?' she asked, questions crowding her mind. 'So why are you suddenly dwelling on it now?'

McQueen sat back from the table and looked at Sekalyia, a young, bright, talented woman who, under his wing, had quickly become a formidable investigator. From the moment she had come into his office to apply for the admin job, he had been impressed by her on so many levels. One of her biggest strengths was that she always cut through the confusion and asked the right questions, just as she was doing now.

'I'll show you the email when we get back,' he answered, 'but last week I think she got in touch. The wife. Her name is Judy, by the way. She was Judy Mason when I first knew her but she went back to her maiden name of Judy Greene.'

Lia pushed aside her own uneaten food.

'C'mon,' she said taking the coat from the back of her chair. 'Show me.'

The restaurant was a ten-minute walk from the office so they were soon back in front of McQueen's screen. He opened the email he'd received from Intrusive and let her read it. He watched her expression change as she scanned the message. ... *I'm having these terrible intrusive thoughts... if I picked up a knife I would STAB you*.

'Okay,' she said after finishing the email, 'there's no name, but that's a death threat and we should inform the police.'

McQueen smiled for the first time.

'C'mon, Lia, you know how many death threats I get on a monthly basis, that's not even a bad one. It's a soft inferred threat. And I can't even prove who it's from. I'm not going to the police with that. They'd laugh me out of the station.' But Lia's concern was not assuaged by McQueen's seeming calmness.

'What about talking to Tracey, maybe she can find out who the sender is?'

McQueen had experienced what could be termed 'a difficult relationship' with the local police in Leeds ever since he had started his agency. Most private investigators were ex-coppers themselves who could rely on their old pals on the force for inside information and the odd friendly tip-off. They also benefitted from the turning of a blind eye from time to time when they sailed a bit too close to the legal wind. No one wants to see an old mate get into bother, especially if that old colleague might offer you some lucrative work once you hit fifty-five and you are no longer needed by the force. McQueen on the other hand, had never enjoyed those luxuries and in fact had found himself declared a suspect on more than one occasion. Added to that was the fact he had shown failings in their incompetent investigations a few times, the result was the police just didn't appear to like McQueen, or his agency, at all. He was seen as an amateur sleuth, an academic who had got lucky a few times. On the whole the police treated him, at best, as a meddling nuisance and, at worst, a criminally obstructive dilatant. A painful thorn in their sides that had to be plucked out and disposed of.

The one exception was Detective Tracey Bingham. She had always considered herself an outsider in the police force and, for that reason, had seen past the limitations of the old-boys club network to reach out to McQueen when she had needed to. But it wasn't a one-way street, the support was mutual and Tracey had come to McQueen's rescue more than once. They had become friends and had ended up sharing some of their most dangerous and scary moments. She was the only police officer he trusted and in fact he had even asked her to join him in the agency as his partner but she'd wisely chosen to stay in the force. She was a busy woman and he wasn't about to trouble her with one slightly disturbing email.

It wasn't the talk of stabbing that had got to McQueen anyway, it was the emotional baggage the email had dumped into his inbox. He knew all the reasons why it shouldn't have hurt him so much, and he was aware of what he would have said to someone else who was in his position, but it was yet another example of the difference between theory and reality. His rational mind knew perfectly well that he couldn't be held responsible for the tragic actions of a psychotic man, but still deep down he couldn't escape the gnawing guilt.

Seven

The argument had started over whose turn it was to cook, but they both knew that wasn't really what it was about. Like most domestic disagreements, the original ignition point of the hostilities wasn't the root cause, it was just the way in. Even though there was nothing actually bubbling on the hob yet, there had been something brewing between them for a while. She could trace it back to that first Zach Lindley meeting.

Normally Tania would have just let it ride, she'd have got on with chopping the onions and swallowed her disappointment along with her pasta, but even though she hadn't heard back from the McQueen agency yet, since making the enquiry she had been feeling bolder. The mere process of putting down her details online had forced her to focus on her fears and confusion and that, in turn, had made her angry.

'I'm just saying that I'm the one who has been at work all day,' she said, banging the pot down on the chopping board and picking up the large kitchen knife. 'I'm tired and it would have been nice if you had found the time to start the meal.' She cut open the net bag and several onions spilled out. She chose the largest of them and sliced through it with force.

Richard looked up from his phone but didn't put it down.

'What? So, I'm your servant now am I?'

'I never said that, but the thing is I cooked last night and the night before and I just feel like it might be your turn?'

He was smiling in that mirthless nasty way that bullying teachers often use.

'Just because you've been lucky, lucky enough to land a cushy job, which you don't righteously deserve, I'm supposed to drop everything and wait on you hand and foot?'

He wasn't yelling, but his calm acidity was somehow worse.

She stopped chopping and blinked. It was like hearing an out of tune piano, discordant and strange. The, *don't righteously deserve* comment was something new.

The demands of her job were something he knew very little about, he'd never really been interested enough to ask before, although he'd been happy enough to accept the rewards her salary allowed them to enjoy. *Deserve* didn't come into it, she had earned the respect of her peers and, through hard work and diligence, had carved out her career in a male-dominated industry. She was proud of what she'd achieved but she didn't brag about it, she'd never tried to belittle him and she didn't need his or anyone else's validation.

The McQueen Legacy

The two of them had argued in the past, of course, and as is the way of disputes things had been said in the heat of the moment that should not have been said, but that strange phrase, *don't righteously deserve* just didn't sound like Richard at all.

'What do you mean I don't righteously deserve my job?' she asked, the anger showing in her voice.

He shook his head as if baffled by her ignorance.

'Amazing,' he said, 'how blind the obscenely lucky can be to the struggles of the rest of us.'

There were so many things she could have said and so many she desperately wanted to say, but she hadn't quite reached the point of no return yet.

'Is this one of Mr Lindley's theories, by any chance?' she asked, unable to keep the sarcasm from seeping into her voice. 'Jobs should only go to the righteously deserving? And I suppose that's anyone who turns up to his meetings?'

He stood up and walked towards her.

'Let me ask you this. What will you do when A.I. takes your precious job, Tania? Where will you be then? What will define you? Where will your economic power be?'

She was genuinely stunned by this latest turn in the conversation and was struggling to make sense of it.

'You mean artificial intelligence? That's why you don't want to cook because of A.I.?'

'Mock all you want, Tania, but I guarantee every single office job in this country will be gone within five years. Did you know that? Were you aware of that?'

Richard was becoming quite animated now and moved closer to her. 'Zach Lindley has seen the plans the government has drawn up. All of us will be surplus to requirements and no longer of any value at all. It's already happening. Zach is the only person who has an answer.'

Tania had put down the knife and now she opened the drawer next to her and casually dropped the blade in before closing it. She had never felt physically threatened by Richard before, it wasn't his style, but this wasn't the Richard she knew and she didn't want to take any chances.

'And what is Zach's answer?' she asked in as calm a voice as she could manage, but he didn't reply. Instead he shook his head and smiled that sickly smile again.

'You think I have nothing,' he said, close enough now that she could feel his breath on her face. 'Because I don't conform to what you think is the only way life can be lived. I don't play the game. But I have much, much more than you think. Because I have knowledge.' He nodded and stared into her eyes so she could see the truth in what he was saying. 'I know things about how this all works and what will happen, and I know how to make it stop.'

In the face of this barrage of nonsense her anger had completely gone leaving her feeling depleted and weak.

'Richard, you're scaring me,' she said quietly, but he took this to mean that she had been frightened by his world predictions, not by his erratic behaviour.

'Oh, you don't need to be scared,' he said softening, and placing an arm around her shoulder. 'As long as you're with me you'll be fine. The tables will be turned. I will be the provider of safety and security when we move to Senby.'

'Move? What do you mean move? Where's Senby? What are you talking about, Richard?'

The McQueen Legacy

'It's a village, not too far from here and that's where we're all going to go. Someone has donated his farm as a base and Zach is setting it up.'

'When is this?'

'Soon. Not yet, but soon.'

Tania felt as if she was standing under a deluge of sand that was slowly burying her. She needed time to think and to process what had just happened. It was all too much to take in but her main survival instinct was to humour Richard long enough to work out what she should do. She had secret knowledge of her own, the most basic and ancient knowledge of all. She'd been waiting for the right time to share it, but this felt like it was as wrong a time as it could be. Still, he had to know. There was a personal development that would change everything for them both and it was making it difficult to handle the crazy things Richard was saying. There was now an invisible but powerful bond between them Richard still wasn't aware of, a complication that added another dimension to their relationship.

Tania was pregnant. She hadn't completely trusted the home test and just to be sure she'd had the result confirmed at the doctor that morning, and she could already feel her motherly instinct to protect her unborn child awakening deep within her. Suddenly she blurted it.

'I don't think we can move,' she said. 'I found out this morning I'm pregnant.' His reaction was strange and not what she'd expected. He pulled her to arm's length and looked at her stomach as if he had suddenly developed x-ray eyes. He didn't miss a beat.

'You sure?'

'One hundred percent,' she answered.

'Well you know what this means?' he said with a grin. 'Even more reason to move, we have to protect the future for our baby.' He gently patted her belly, which as yet showed no signs of swelling.

'Zach's going to love this.'

She couldn't believe what she was hearing.

'Zach? What's Zach got to do with anything?'

'I'm sure it will be part of his vision,' he said. 'Our children will benefit from the freedoms we win. It starts in Senby.'

Tania couldn't believe what she was hearing, possibly the greatest event in her life so far was being examined through the prism of stranger's unspecified 'vision'. She was suddenly weakened and she felt a tear roll down her cheek. He saw it and smiled broadly.

'I know,' he said. 'It's wonderful isn't it?'

Eight

It was a gloomy Leeds morning and the grey buildings that were dotted along the ring road looked drab and menacing as Lia drove to work. A few of the larger ones were converted old mills that must have been even more depressing back when people had to work in them. She thought about the back-breaking, dangerous jobs they must have done and the way people were so grateful for the work they would put up with the odd lost finger. The good old days.

As she pulled into the carpark, Lia could see McQueen's office light was on and guessed he was probably already at his desk. She was late arriving having slept in after spending the night trying to understand the things that Carl was telling her about Mrs Bolton's paperwork. Spreadsheets were a mystery to her. The mere sight of them brought her out in a cold sweat with their oppressively neat little columns and tight boxes with their hidden complex algebra. Sum all these and divide by those at the click of a button. The numbers danced and morphed for her and the harder Carl tried to explain the worse it got. He would point at a series of figures and say, 'You see?' and she would inevitably reply, 'Er, no.' She had given up pretending to understand and she just waited patiently for his conclusions.

'This can't be right, can it?' he said at one point staring incredulously at a number in bold and she replied,

'Can't it?'

Exasperated he shook his head and pointed again at the screen as if it would all become clear to her now that he was pointing so energetically. It didn't help.

Even though she was adding no value to his research she sat with him because it didn't seem fair to leave him alone to do it. After all it was his precious free-time and it wasn't even his homework, he was doing her the favour.

Eventually after hours of watching him check and recheck she looked at the clock which was on its way to 1a.m. and said, 'Carl, I don't really understand, but I can see you're getting agitated so could you sum it up in one word? Remember, explain like I'm a five-year-old.'

He collapsed back into the cushions of the sofa and rubbed his eyes. 'I don't want to make any false assumptions because it's a big, serious statement,' he said tiredly. 'And one word isn't going to do it, but two words might.' She waited expectantly.

'Money laundering,' he continued. 'It looks to me like Summertown Industries has been cleaning up cash for someone. The money that's missing seems to be covering for a shortfall. It's only my opinion and I probably couldn't prove it, but that's what it looks like to me.'

'Right,' said Lia, 'and I may be crap at spreadsheets but

The McQueen Legacy

this much I do know, where you've got money laundering you've got criminals.'

'Yep.'

'And Mrs Bolton, do you think she's involved?'

He shrugged and opened his palms to the ceiling.

'Look, this Mrs Bolton was the company bookkeeper. She's not a qualified accountant, her role was to keep track of the money coming in and the money going out. It was essentially an admin job, and if the money coming in was a pile of untraceable cash, I guess it wouldn't be that difficult to pocket a little here and there? You remember the famous Mexican drug lord, El Chapo?'

'Of course, but if you're going to tell me that she was Britain's answer to El Chapo I'm not going for it.'

'No, listen to me, what I'm saying is that at the height of his power in the Sinaloa cartel they were generating so much cash they didn't know what to do with it, so they were burying it in huge secret holes in the forest. They didn't want it found by the authorities but they accepted a ten percent loss on every buried batch. You know why? Eaten by rats.'

'Rats?'

'Yep, rats don't know much about currency it was just paper to them.'

'So are you saying that Mrs Bolton could be one of the nibbling rats?'

'I don't know, Lia. These are just cold figures on an uncaring spreadsheet. Who knows who knew what, but I think that's your department anyway.'

When Lia had climbed the stairs and buzzed her way through the security door she could see from the outer office that, sure enough, McQueen was at his desk. She said good morning, walked into her own office and threw her bag behind her seat. She was painfully aware she had plenty of basic admin to get on with which was going to be her task as soon as she had a cup of coffee in her hand. She had been letting the boring stuff slip since she'd started looking into the Bolton case, but she also knew that some of the dull things she had to do were an essential part of the smooth running of the agency.

'Lia, can you come on in for a second?' called McQueen. She walked through the open door and saw that he'd already made her a coffee in her favourite mug which was sitting on the edge of his desk.

'Please sit,' he said, motioning to one of the chairs which were used for client meetings. 'I made you a coffee, it should still be warm.' This felt like it was going to be a serious discussion and Lia was already lining up some answers which she liked to think of as solid reasons rather than lame excuses. There were some invoices that hadn't been sent yet, which was entirely down to her.

They sat in silence for a few seconds as she sipped her drink which was barely warm, a subtle indicator of how long it had been waiting for her.

'Sorry I was a bit late this morning,' she said. He waved away her apology before she could get into it.

'You don't need to explain,' he replied. 'The only time you are ever late is when you've been working late on a case. We have trust here,' he said indicating with his hand

The McQueen Legacy

that he meant both of them. 'When we lose that, we'll call it quits.'

'Okay,' she said. 'In that case what do you want to talk about, because I've got a lot on?'

'Two things,' he said. 'One, I want to give you another urgent task, something that's going to benefit both of us.' Lia thought about all the things she had to do that day and the thought of another one being added to the list was less than thrilling. He could see her expression and he smiled.

'I want you to write an ad, contact a recruitment agency and hire someone to do the office admin.'

'Really?'

'Yep, the time has come, you need an assistant. We've been doing pretty well and a lot of that is down to you. I think you're too valuable to this agency as an investigator. I don't want you to spend your work time doing the drudgery and your free time doing the work that you're so good at.'

Lia was elated and she couldn't hide it.

'Oh, that would be brilliant,' she beamed. 'It really would help the agency, it would, mean I could—' But McQueen cut in.

'It's okay, you don't need to convince me, Lia, I've already decided. But point number two is this,' he said, spinning his screen to show her the online contact form.

'Why haven't you got back to this woman?'

Lia scanned the form that he was showing her, 'Oh, Tania and her dangerous cult? I mean, there's no information. What does she even want? I didn't think you'd want to waste your time on it.'

'Lia, this is exactly the kind of time I want to waste. It's interesting and intriguing, and I'm intrigued. I've already answered her this morning and she's very keen to meet up. Desperate even. She can't get over here so I'm going over to see her at lunchtime today in York.'

Lia was too grateful and keen to get on with hiring a new assistant to argue with McQueen about the cult woman, so she simply said, 'Fine, whatever, in my opinion I think you are probably wasting a whole morning but you're the boss.'

As McQueen spun his computer back round to face him he asked, 'So what about the old embezzler, Mrs Bolton? Any news there?'

Lia was already up out of the seat and on her way to get a hot coffee. 'Funnily enough, there have been some developments, McQueen,' she answered. 'I'll let you know how it pans out.'

Nine

Outside the train station McQueen crossed the busy road, dodged the buses and taxis and then turned left. He'd thought about driving but it would have meant the stress of finding parking in the busy tourist city and he always hated that particular hassle. If anyone had asked he might have said that rather than spend a petrol-fuelled hour in the car, he had taken the train for planet-saving reasons, but it wouldn't have been true. He could also have said using the train meant he could do some work on the journey, but that would also have been a lie. The truth was, apart from the parking, he'd chosen the train so he could stare brainlessly out of the window and let the fields and hedges rushing by take some of his darker thoughts with them. The questions that came to him in the rhythm of the track were simple ones: Who lives on that farm? Who lives in that house? Who works on that farm? Who lives in that house?

York has a lot of history, too much to absorb, and McQueen only knew snippets of it. He was no history buff, but it was hard to ignore the legacy of the past in a place that screamed it out from every nook and cranny. For instance, he knew the small patch of grass sandwiched between the pavement and the road was an ancient cholera burial ground. It even had a couple of the gravestones. Long-forgotten dead bodies of the early nineteenth century passed by anyone heading into the city. There was a faded plaque to commemorate the poor lost souls, but who reads those? As he rounded the bend under the arch of the old city walls, the spires of the world-famous York Minster came into sight above the other buildings. This was another thing he knew about, nothing in the city was permitted to be built taller than the minster. Old York was never going to be New York.

The impressive building was described in the literature as an 'iconic gothic-style medieval cathedral' but McQueen just thought of it as a magnificently massive church that acted as a tourist magnet, with the power to pull people in from around the globe. Foreign tourists visited in coachloads to cross it off their to-do lists and kids were forced on school trips from places like Sheffield to get some medieval history, whether they wanted it or not.

McQueen had arranged to meet Tania at a coffee shop in one of York's quaint little side streets. She recognised him from his website mugshot and, for her part, she was wearing the sky-blue coat just as she'd said she would. She was tall, straight-backed and dark-haired and, although she was wearing minimal make-up, she had a natural glamour about her, something to do with the high cheekbones and arresting green eyes perhaps? Even so, McQueen picked up an air of uneasiness from her quick movements and her wary glances up and down the street, that could even have been fear. The café was a small place, the tables were quite crowded together and it quickly became apparent Tania wasn't going to be comfortable talking to him where they could easily be overheard, so they decided to get their drinks in takeaway cups and walk and talk.

It was an overcast day with only a smattering of tourists milling around and they soon managed to find an empty stone bench. It was on one side of a landscaped grassy area known as College Green. To their left the imposing back wall and windows of the minster towered over them and opposite across the cobbled road, a row of low-roofed cottages, three of them converted into tea shops. On the grass in front of their bench was a stone column with a sundial on top—useless in today's gloom—and at the exact opposite end of the technology spectrum as the Apple watch that Tania kept nervously checking.

As both of them were wearing dark office suits, to any passer-by who could be bothered to notice they looked like two work colleagues taking their lunch together. Not that anyone was noticing, but it didn't stop Tania from scrutinising anyone who came towards them.

As they sat at the cold bench a group of hopeful pigeons swarmed around their feet nodding furiously until they realised this couple weren't going to be dropping sandwich crumbs and flapped away.

'I know it would have been easier to meet in Leeds,' she said. 'But there was more chance we would be seen there so, as I had to come to York anyway to visit a client, I thought it was a good option.'

'Seen? Seen by whom?'

'My partner, Richard. I think he's started following me recently,' she said. 'I keep thinking I've seen him when I'm out. Maybe it's just me being silly and over-cautious.'

McQueen was used to recognising the signs and habits of relationship difficulties. Much of his work in the early days of the agency had been centred around spying on unfaithful partners. That was when he was still trying to establish himself and was grateful for anything bringing in revenue, but he'd been glad to leave the messy side of the business behind. The worst cases had been when there had been no evidence of cheating but still the paranoia had lingered and festered. For men, that often resulted in violence and more than once it had been McQueen's suspicious clients who had ended up in court. He was hoping Tania's case wasn't going to head in that direction.

'It was an intriguing enquiry you sent in, Tania. I'll be honest, the only reason I agreed to meet you was that you mentioned a dangerous cult and I was curious. I haven't had one of those before. Also, frankly, I wanted a day out of the office but tell me about this cult?'

She answered with questions of her own.

'I saw on your website that you're a doctor?' she asked. 'A Doctor of Psychology? Is that a Ph.D.? I have a friend who has a Ph.D. in something to do with butterfly wings. I often joke that she's a butterfly doctor.'

McQueen smiled. 'I know what you're thinking,' he replied. 'Not a proper doctor.' He turned to look at her and she didn't deny it. 'Well, it's true I can't take out kidneys and I've got no interest in looking at anyone's nasty rash,' he continued. 'I'm afraid I was a boring academic. It's all on the website somewhere, I did a degree in psychology, a master's in forensic psychology and a Ph.D. in criminology. I lectured for years and then I decided to get a real job.'

Tania was staring straight ahead, her green eyes focusing somewhere in the distance.

'As part of your studies did you lever earn anything about cults?' she asked.

'Yes, a little bit and they are something I have followed in my own time, whenever they appear on the news, really. It's usually when they are attached to some atrocity or other. There are some strong psychological drivers at play in all cults, and I guess it's those which interest me on a professional level. That's why I'm here, I suppose.'

This seemed to satisfy her and she took a white A4 envelope from her pocket.

'These are some of the details,' she said. 'Basically, Richard, my partner, started to attend some meetings a little while ago held by a guy he'd seen on the internet. Then he started going away at weekends to boot camps or retreats or whatever they are. He's become more and more involved and now he wants us to go and live in some kind of commune. He's started saying some disturbing things and I can't talk to him about it, he gets very defensive.' McQueen turned the envelope over in his hands, but didn't open it.

'And what exactly do you want me to do?'

'Maybe I'm overreacting. I recently became pregnant and maybe the hormones are running riot, but what I'd like you to do is find out about this group. Is it just a harmless support group, a club, or is it sinister? I guess I want to know where this is heading.'

'You didn't say club or group on your form, you said dangerous cult?'

'Yes, that's what I think it is, but I want you to prove me wrong.'

McQueen had heard this statement in various guises many times before. *"I think my wife is having an affair and I want you to prove me wrong." "I think my sister has been stealing money from my mother and I want you to prove me wrong." "I think my husband has killed someone and I want you to prove me wrong."*

McQueen put the envelope in his pocket to be opened when he could give it his full attention. He saw her looking up at the minster and he wondered if she was praying.

'The best stained-glass windows are at the front,' he said. She blinked and refocused on him and he realised she hadn't been looking at the church at all, her mind had been elsewhere.

'I really do have to see a client,' she said standing up. 'Like I say, the details are in the envelope. If you decide to take this job let me know at the email address I've put in there. It's on my work account so Richard has no access to it.'

'I'm taking the case,' said McQueen, the envelope still tucked out of sight. 'I'll be in touch.'

She nodded her thanks, a faint smile escaping her taught features, they shook hands and she walked quickly away in the direction of the city.

McQueen hadn't been entirely open with Tania, he'd inferred he'd had a passing interest in cults but what he hadn't said was as a psychology undergraduate his interest

The McQueen Legacy

had bordered on obsession. From the so-called Manson family to the mass suicides of the Jim Jones death cult, McQueen had been fascinated. He'd read every academic paper there was to read and watched thousands of hours of interviews with victims, cult members, and convicted cult leaders. It was a subject that had steered him towards the branch of psychology devoted to crime. What was going on in the minds of people who join cults and what were the motivations of the people who ran them? They were questions that exposed so much about what humans are and what they are capable of.

McQueen wasn't convinced yet that Tania had a cult problem rather than a bored boyfriend problem, but it was certainly something he was eager to examine. He started to make his way back past the front of the minster, weaving his way past the static figures of tourists with their heads craned back and their camera phones at arm's length. *How many millions of pictures of that house of religion must there be in the world?* he wondered. He stopped to look up at the lovely stained-glass window, it's intense biblical imagery a triumph of medieval devotion. *Some cults have more power than others,* he thought as he headed back across the bridge to the train station.

Ten

It was time. Sekalyia had listened to Carl long enough to know what she needed to do next was speak to Mary Bolton in person. She needed to ask some pointed questions and see her human reactions. This was not something she could do over the phone, Lia wanted a personal connection. It was something she had learned from McQueen, she wanted to see the whites of the lady's eyes. She'd rung and arranged the meeting at Mary's house and the older woman had sounded pleased to speak to her.

'I thought your Mr McQueen didn't want my case?' she'd said when Lia had reminded her who she was. 'Actually, I was going to call you to get my memory stick back.'

'Well, I'm not him,' Lia had replied. 'I only work with him but I'm aiming to change his mind.'

She pulled up in front of the modest semi-detached, red-bricked property and turned off her sat-nav as it repeated for the third time she had arrived at her destination. 'I know, I know,' she muttered under her breath. Over the years she'd had many one-sided arguments with the automated voices both male and female, that usually went along the lines of, "Do you mean this left or the next left?" or, "Are you sure?" and sometimes if she was in a hurry and very stressed, "You are WRONG".

She'd parked on the street as she felt it might be a little presumptuous to stop on the short empty driveway that was inside the gate. People could be funny about such things and she didn't want to start on the wrong foot.

When she pressed the doorbell she heard it ring inside the house and while she waited for the door to open she took in the untidy garden. Lia knew very little about gardening but even to her untrained eye the borders could have used a little care and attention. If Mary had a gardener then they were an infrequent visitor. It was the kind of thing she could ask as an icebreaker once she was inside. There would be tea and there would be biscuits, it was almost guaranteed.

Lia thought she'd heard something beyond the door, but it remained closed so she pressed the bell again and then took her phone out to make the call. Maybe Mary had forgotten she was coming and was busy in the kitchen? Lia's head was down as she scrolled through trying to locate the right number. Suddenly with a whoosh of air the door sprang inwards. The speed of it took her by surprise and she looked up in shock but all she saw coming out of the dark hallway was a blur of black clothing, a hoody, and a mask as someone rushed out knocking her sideways into the wall and then ran down the path. The impact had been hard, she'd felt a solidly muscular shoulder crash against her and there had been no time to avoid it. Her phone had clattered to the floor and she was slightly dazed by the whack her head had taken against the bricks. She could feel a trickle of blood from the side of her head near her ear. She picked up her phone but the screen was a starburst of shattered glass. The escaping person was already gone.

'Mary?' she shouted, as she stumbled into the hall. To her left was the sitting room and looking through the open door, Lia could see scattered papers on the floor. Her first thought was she had disturbed a burglar but where was Mary? Tentatively she ventured inside the room, not sure what she was going to encounter but what she was looking for was a phone, a landline so she could call the police. What she found was the prone figure of Mary Bolton. She was lying motionless in the centre of the carpet, both of her hands were raised to her throat where the sleeve of a blue cardigan was looped around her neck.

Lia's grogginess melted away and she quickly bent to the woman who seemed to be making gurgling noises. Relieved to see she was still alive, Lia immediately scrambled to untangle the sleeve and remove it from her throat. The first step of first aid was always clear the airways, but it usually referred to food blockages rather than ligatures. With the cardigan tossed aside Mary began coughing and gasping deep lungfuls of air and Lia knew that was a good sign. She sat Mary up her back against the couch.

'Have you got a phone?' she asked trying to keep the panic from her voice.

The distressed woman was only able to croak out, 'He was trying to kill me.'

'Where is your phone, Mary?'

'He wanted my memory stick. From work. When I said I didn't have it he tried to strangle me.'

'Okay, let's worry about that later, but right now we need an ambulance and the police. Phone?'

Mary pointed shakily over Lia's shoulder.

'The hall,' she said.

'So what do you think?' asked Carl as he handed Lia a cup of milky tea.

'I think it proves us right,' she answered.

She was sitting lengthways on the sofa in their flat. Her head sporting a nicely swollen, bruised lump, but no bandage. After a long wait in casualty the doctor at the hospital had given her a cursory check over but he'd been bored and unimpressed. He told her she wasn't concussed and that he himself experienced much worse on the rugby field every Saturday. He advised her if she did start to get any severe headaches she should go back to her GP.

'No shit,' she said under her breath.

A different doctor had taken a bit longer over Mary, probably due to her age, but after some tests she too was sent on her way without having to spend a night on a ward. It was a prospect she had been resisting strongly, anyway. They'd said there had been no lasting physical damage, her breathing was normal and Lia had rescued her before any serious oxygen deprivation had affected her.

After the medics it had been time for the police who had taken statements from both of them, but Lia's description of the assailant was fairly useless and Mary's wasn't much better. A youngish man in black clothes, a hooded top, and a face mask.

The uniformed policeman taking the notes had nodded knowingly, it was a description he'd heard a thousand times before.

'These days they know about CCTV,' he said wearily, 'so they dress appropriately.' And then with a slight look of hope he asked, 'Have you got any security cameras in your house by any chance?' but Mary shook her head.

Once the police had finished with their questions they said they would send someone round to check on Mary in the next few days, but they seemed to be about as interested in the whole thing as the doctors had been. They were dismissing the incident as a messy burglary rather than the attempted murder Mary was trying to claim.

Mary was still shaken up by her experience and was reluctant to go home, so she'd arranged to stay with a friend for the night while Lia headed back to her own flat rather then returning to the office. She called Carl from home and even though she played it down, on hearing she'd taken a bump he left work early to get back. When he saw her bruise he winced in empathetic pain which turned to anger when she told him what had happened, but Lia was focused on what it meant rather than the sore head.

'How does someone attacking an old woman prove anything?' asked Carl taking a sip from his own cup.

'It's obvious. Okay, someone is up to something illegal involving money laundering at Summertown Industries where Mary worked. You've looked at the books, you've already seen that.'

The McQueen Legacy

'I *think* I've seen that, but I'm no expert.'

Lia ignored his interruption and carried on. 'Some money goes missing so they try to pin that on an old woman thinking she'll just be found guilty and disappear into the system. Unfortunately for them, she fights back. She gets a lawyer and hires a private investigator. They start to worry it's going to make a stink, that some of their dirty dealing will come to light so they send someone to see what evidence she has and get it back. And then to make sure she doesn't cause any more trouble, they try to kill her.'

'Or it's just a psycho-burglar.'

'No, can't be, Mary told me that he asked for her memory stick. Burglars want money.'

'Ah, right, I see your point. What does McQueen think?'

Lia sighed. It rankled with her slightly that Carl thought she needed help from McQueen, that she couldn't handle it all herself, but at the same time she knew he was right.

'I haven't told him yet. I wanted to have all my ducks in a row before I went to him.'

'And?'

'And now those ducks are quacking,' she smiled. 'It's time.'

She slowly stood up from the couch, testing cautiously to see if she was feeling dizzy. 'But first,' she said checking her watch, 'the most important job of all, probably more important than life itself.' Carl raised his eyebrows waiting to hear what was coming next. 'I need to get my phone fixed.' He laughed and then became more serious. He pointed at her head.

'I've got to say this. This is not the first time something

like this has happened is it, Lia?' They both knew she had faced much worse situations while working for McQueen, life threatening events, she'd even been shot at, but they had decided amongst themselves not to speak about it.

'I'm just saying, do you still think this is the right job for you?'

She raised herself to her full height, Carl was still sitting down so she was looking down at him when she said, 'Carl, I love you and I appreciate your concern and all your help, but let me make this very clear. Do. Not. Start. That.' Carl sighed and shook his head. 'There is something practical you can do for me, though,' she added in a softer tone. 'Something that would help my personal security?'

'What's that?'

'Lend me your spare phone until I get this fixed?' she said, holding up the shattered handset.

Eleven

McQueen needed silence so he closed the door to the outer office shutting out the sound of Dan's phone calls and his furious typing. Dan was the new admin assistant who had been interviewed and hired by Lia who seemed to be working out just fine. It had been a progressive management double-win for McQueen, on one hand he had been able to show he completely trusted Lia's judgement and at the same time he had saved himself the boring hassle of getting involved.

Dan had already earned his keep, for a fairly inexperienced person he had a winning way with debtors, and a couple of long overdue invoices had finally been paid after some persuasive but insistent phoning. Even though the agency seemed to be doing well, and McQueen's media profile was good, as with any small business cash flow was always a concern. Lia's move into more investigative work had meant quite a few mundane office jobs had fallen by the wayside, but Dan seemed to thrive on the mundane

McQueen had laid out the pages from the envelope Tania

had given him. There were lists and handwritten notes. Some lines were in quotation marks, denoting disturbing statements that her partner, Richard, had allegedly made. "Spilled blood is the only lubricant that achieves real change", was one that stood out. Tania had also provided a couple of pictures of Richard. McQueen picked one up and scrutinised it. A dark hired, good-looking young man with a faint hint of Tom Cruise about him. Amongst the lists were some links for Zach Lindley YouTube videos and with the door now closed McQueen was about to dip in. The first link was titled "Luck".

The video image opened on an extreme close-up of a man's face, a guy of about thirty-five, he was staring straight into McQueen's eyes.

'Hi, I'm Zach Lindley. Have you ever been told that you make your own luck? Of course you have. Usually you'll hear that after you've had a dream cruelly snatched away from you. And if you dare complain someone is ready to tell you to stop moaning because you make your own luck. Have you heard that? Well let *me* tell you it's a lie. A big, bad evil lie designed to make you feel like a loser.' The camera pulled back a little to reveal Zach Lindley's head and shoulders, and that he was wearing an open-necked white shirt. He carried on.

'The saying you make your own luck was invented by one of those very lucky people, who has had it all handed to them on a plate. They've been spoon-fed their whole lives. But they want to take credit for all the good luck they've had. They don't want to admit they've been lucky, they want to say *they* made their own luck.'

The McQueen Legacy

Now the video pulled right back to show Zach standing on a darkened stage. It looked like one of those TED talks. You couldn't see the audience, but Zach was walking confidently across the space and then he pointed at someone in the front row.

'But tell that to the child born with brain damage. Hey kid, sorry, but you made your own luck. Tell that to the person living in a warzone. Hey, sorry dude, but it's your fault because you shouldn't have been brought up here.' Zach had crossed the stage to point his accusatory finger at someone else. 'Tell that to the wife of a man who works hard every day of his life only to drop dead of a heart attack. Sorry, honey, you made your own luck when you married this loser.'

He had returned to the dead centre of the stage and the camera was slowly zooming in again. 'They want you to feel like a lazy, unproductive loser. They want you to blame yourself and they never, never want you to question the random luck that got them their wealth and power. They want you to think they are better than you. But they are not. They are not better than you.'

Zach was pointing directly at the camera and at this point the video abruptly stopped and the screen was filled with contact links so you could book to attend one of Zach's live meetings.

McQueen smiled to himself. 'You've got a point, Zach,' he said aloud. He clicked on another one of the videos that had a very similar message delivered in the same style and finished with the same links to the meetings. The next title simply read, "A.I." This one started with the same enlarged face and Zach saying, 'Hi, I'm Zach Lindley, let me ask you this, what will you do when you lose your job to artificial intelligence? A.I. will take your job, there is no doubt about that, and I'm not talking about in ten years I'm telling you *it is happening now*. The speed of development of this lethal technology is exponential and if we don't act today there will be nothing left for us humans to do.

'You can spend every minute of your life in the gym if you want to, you can eat your protein and take your steroids, but you will never be as strong as a lion or a gorilla. Humans are at the top of the animal kingdom for one reason only, we are the most intelligent. But what happens when the machines are the most intelligent? Not by a small amount, but by factors of millions. Computers are designing themselves now and no one is going to stop them.'

McQueen skipped to the end of the piece and again it ended before any possible solutions were explained other than attending a Zach Lindley meeting. McQueen was well aware of the anxiety surrounding A.I. and of the terrified emotions that it could stir up. A pattern was emerging from the YouTube offerings, Zack clearly liked to promote dissatisfaction, which of course was a powerful motivator. There were ten more videos to watch and McQueen was wondering if there would be any on fake moon landings. He was about to click the next link when there was a knock on his office door.

'Hello?' he shouted, and then Dan's face appeared.

'Er, Dr McQueen, there's someone downstairs outside at the security entry who says you'll want to see her.'

The McQueen Legacy

'Dan, sorry, I don't know if Lia mentioned it but there's a procedure for walk-ins off the street and—'

'Yeah. I know about the procedure, it's just she said she had the password and that if I gave it to you you'd let her in.'

'Okay, what was the password?' he felt like he was playing a child's game.

'Intrusive?' That's the word she gave me—intrusive.'

McQueen closed his eyes and tipped his head back and then quickly straightened up.

'Buzz her up,' he said.

McQueen had been advised by his lawyer many years before to never engage with Judy Mason as she was known then, the grief-stricken mother of the dead baby. To never speak to her except through a legal representative, to never accept any liability or blame for her husband's actions, to never apologise, which could imply guilt, or even to be in the same room as her. It was sound legal advice but it didn't sit well with him. He had built his career on talking to people, on getting to the causes of their problems and then resolution through dialogue. With all the legal considerations put aside, the fact was the guilt was there, like a hovering cloud and he felt it. He had told Judy she didn't need to worry about her husband's intrusive thoughts and in this very rare and unusual case he'd been wrong. The correct response would have been, "I don't know anything about your husband, so I can't say."

He had got many things wrong in his life, personal and professional. He had wrecked his marriage through drinking and his selfishness pursuit of the fantasy of becoming a crime fighting hero. Had the drinking started after the tragedy of Judy's baby? He couldn't remember but when he had become a private detective some of his mistakes had almost cost him his life. And not just his. On one occasion his bad judgement had led to a good friend having his legs broken by gangsters after trying to do McQueen a favour. That had been awful but for some reason, the few reassuring words he had spoken to Judy weighed on him more than any of his other missteps. It was like a seed. Some seeds never germinate, they lie like inert gravel on hardened ground, but others manage to take hold, they send down roots and begin to grow until they choke everything around them.

Even as he asked Dan to show Judy into his office he knew he was probably making another mistake, but he felt powerless to stop himself. He felt he owed her something, this poor bereaved mother. Even after all these years if she was going to scream and shout and swear at him he felt he owed her that chance. In fact, deep down it was what he wanted.

Judy came into his office, she was offered a cup of tea by Dan who had no idea of the history and enormity of what he was witnessing, but she shook her head and he left closing the door behind him.

She sat in the chair opposite McQueen and they looked at each other for a long time. She was older, of course, but he could still see the person she had been when she had sat in his lectures. Her clothes were neat and tidy, her hair brushed and arranged with care. Her hands, clasped in front of her carried no wedding ring and her fingers were clean, no dirt under the finger nails. Automatically it crossed his mind that it was unlikely she was living on the streets as a drug addict. Although he hated himself for doing it, it was the kind of assessment McQueen couldn't help making, it was part of the job. He was trying to work out exactly how many years it had been, but then she spoke. There were no hysterics or screaming, her tone was very calm and measured.

'She would have been twenty-one next week,' she said. There was no need to ask who she meant, but she was determined to make him see the person. 'Katie. Katie would have been twenty-one. And he is out now. Free. All better, apparently. He tried to get off with a plea of diminished responsibility, the insanity plea but the jury saw straight through that. Taking drugs is a choice, but they couldn't give him life.' McQueen was no longer thinking about the sensible legal advice he'd received two decades earlier.

'I'm so terribly sorry about what happened,' he offered.

'Twenty-one years too late with that apology,' she snapped back. It was a tricky area for McQueen, he wanted to express his sorrow but he didn't want it to sound like he was apologising for something that wasn't his fault.

'The lawyers banned me from contacting you because it wasn't my fault.'

'Wasn't your fault?' she sneered.

'What is true is that I should have only told you to seek professional help, but I had no idea how ill your husband—'

'You said there was nothing to worry about. You were a Doctor of Psychology and you told me not to worry about silly old intrusive thoughts. You said there was absolutely no chance in hell that he would do anything. You said I was being stupid and hysterical and acting like a neurotic woman.'

This was not how McQueen remembered it, he was certain he would never have said those things, but he didn't want this meeting to turn into an argument.

'I'm sure I didn't,' he said calmly. 'I never thought it so I wouldn't have said it, but it's been a long time.'

'Are you saying I'm lying?' Her eyes had narrowed.

'No, I'm saying you were under an unbearable amount of stress at the time and memories can become unreliable over the years.'

She was staring at him as if she was examining something she couldn't comprehend, like a strange sea creature or an alien. She breathed deeply for a few seconds. Eventually she said, 'You've become famous, Doctor McQueen. That's nice. People think you're a hero.'

He shook his head.

'No. I've helped the police to catch some criminals, that's all.'

He'd already decided not to mention the email she'd sent to him under the name of Intrusive, it would serve no purpose to put her on the spot, but he recognised the mental process she'd been going through. The email had been the first step as she built up her courage and enough confidence to speak to him. And now she'd got bolder and she'd made the move to come and see him, the question was what was the next step going to be? He wanted to de-escalate the situation, so he didn't want to make any accusations that could lead to more conflict. Although he wanted to know why she was really there, what she wanted and what she hoped to get from him, he was waiting for the right time to ask her.

'Catching criminals? So you must know a lot about knife crime?' she said in the same unhurried tone, 'It's very fashionable these days, isn't it?'

He remembered what she'd said in her email and the reference to stabbing him. 'The consequence of all this knife crime on the streets is that ordinary people find it harder to buy knives. I mean a kitchen knife is just a useful tool, like a hammer.' She stopped and let the hammer reference lie there before carrying on. 'But they really scrutinise you when you buy a knife these days.'

For the first time, McQueen noticed the brown leather bag over her shoulder. She swung it around, reached into it, and removed a blue handled kitchen knife with a blade about eight inches long. The knife was still sealed in its hard plastic covering, it looked brand new.

'I bought this the other day,' she continued. 'I'm clearly not a teenager and I didn't have to prove my age, of course, and I guess I don't look like a criminal or a terrorist, but I still felt they were kind of judgmental in the shop where I got it. Like they were trying to work out if I was about to go on the rampage in the street?'

McQueen didn't flinch. He had already decided it would take enough time for her to remove the packaging for him to get the weapon away from her if he needed to, but he was also fairly sure he wouldn't need to. If she'd wanted to stab him she would have had the knife ready and she'd have hidden it until she could get close enough. However, he had been wrong before. It was time to change the flow of the dialogue.

'What do you want, Judy?' he asked. 'Why have you come here after so long?'

'I want nothing,' she said with an airy smile, dropping the knife back into the bag. 'Except I just wanted to catch up. My life stopped twenty-one years ago, Doctor McQueen. Yours went on, his went on, but mine stopped when Katie's stopped.'

'Judy, I think you need help. Grief is a type of trauma and I can recommend some excellent people who you could talk to. I've been through therapy myself for post-traumatic stress disorder, it helped me and it can help you.' It was true McQueen had sought professional support himself when the things he had seen and the close calls he had experienced had started to break into his every dream. He knew what it was like to feel that there is no escape from the thoughts that are haunting you, and he also knew his personal battle wasn't over.

'You and your psychologists and psychiatrists and god knows what? P.T.S.D.? That's what you do, you give it a name and some letters and then it's treatable? You don't understand, Doctor McQueen, I listened to a psychologist once, I trusted him and then my life stopped.'

She got up from her chair.

'It's been lovely to see you again,' she said. 'I'm thinking of stopping in to see my ex-husband, too. Who knows, I'll see if we can patch things up? Maybe we can get back together?'

McQueen stood up, too.

'Don't do anything stupid, Judy,' he said. 'No matter what you do you can't bring her back, but you can still ruin your own life.'

'What do you mean? Ruin? Ruin a life that stopped twenty-one years ago?'

She started to leave.

'Maybe I can help?' he offered. 'Let me help you.'

'You are the very last person who could ever help me,' she said. 'And by the way, her name was Katie.' She bustled on through the outer office, past Dan who looked up from his typing with a bemused half smile, and then she left without stopping to hear another word.

Twelve

'How's the head?' They were sitting in the Italian restaurant and Lia was about to take McQueen through the details of the Mary Bolton case.

'It's okay,' she replied giving the still tender side of her head a gentle rub. 'No headaches, no more than usual, anyway.'

While they both picked at their salads, Lia explained what Carl had discovered in Mary's spreadsheets and his suspicions of corporate money laundering. In a well-constructed, persuasive narrative she linked it all back to the raid on Mary's house in the same way she had for Carl.

McQueen seemed to be listening while he munched his way through lettuce and rocket leaves but, in fact, was finding it hard to focus on what Lia was saying as his mind kept returning to Judy Greene and her impromptu visit. It was something he hadn't told Lia about and for now he wasn't going to, there was someone else he wanted to talk to first. He wasn't frightened by the veiled threats but he felt it was worth discussing them with Detective Tracey Bingham so he could get her official police viewpoint.

The McQueen Legacy

'Okay,' he said trying to rerun in his head what Lia had just been talking about. 'So you think whoever has been stealing money from Summertown Industries has now tried to kill Mary Bolton?'

'That guy was after the memory stick and then he wanted to shut her up.'

'Kind of messy, though,' said McQueen. 'If he had killed her with her own cardigan, it's clearly not going to be seen as suicide, surely that would have brought on more police attention, not less?'

Lia shrugged and spiked a small tomato with her fork. Salads were a Wednesday concession to eating healthily for her, but the amount of oily dressing and cheese on this particular plate probably cancelled out any of the health benefits. 'Perhaps they were going to move the body afterwards?' she offered as an explanation. 'If she had just completely disappeared everyone would have thought the guilty woman had fled?'

McQueen didn't seem convinced, but Lia pushed on anyway.

'Look, I've already done a lot of the groundwork, Carl has looked at the books and I've been speaking to Mary's old work colleagues—'

McQueen cut in.

'And they say she is a fantastic person, as honest as the day is long who wouldn't steal a penny from anyone. Am I right?'

Lia ignored his flippant sarcasm.

'Yes, they do,' she said defiantly. 'So let's be clear, I'm asking if I can tell her the McQueen Agency is officially taking on her case? Can we get her on our books? It will really help her to trust me. The client privilege will be in place and she might open up even more knowing that it's all legally confidential.'

Lia could have sworn that McQueen wasn't actually listening and it was starting to annoy her but then he plonked down his knife onto his plate.

'Look, I'm sure you're going to do the work anyway, Lia, so tell her whatever you need to tell her.'

'Officially?'

'Yes, officially.'

This time he wasn't speaking sarcastically, but Lia still felt she somehow wasn't getting McQueen's full backing.

'You know what I really think?' he said rubbing his chin thoughtfully as she shook her head. 'I think to really enjoy an Italian meal, even if it's a lunchtime salad, you need a nice glass of red wine.'

Thirteen

Tracey didn't like to be seen talking to McQueen, not at the station anyway. Amongst her police colleagues it was considered bad form to talk to any private investigators let alone one who had managed to highlight police failings on a number of high-profile cases. In general, all private detectives were considered to be irritating amateurs who did nothing but get in the way of professional law officers. The only ones who were mildly tolerated were ex-coppers, but only if they kept out of the way and stuck to the civil matters and family disputes the police didn't want to be bothered with. McQueen had not stayed within those unseen boundaries, he'd poked his nose into their business, he'd taken on murder cases, and he'd been successful. It hadn't gone down well, especially as he always generated a lot of publicity for himself.

Tracey did not share that general view, she valued McQueen's input, he'd helped her to solve cases she might not have solved and, to her, they were all on the same side. However, she knew better than to ruffle the feathers of those around her and didn't know when she would need back-up from her colleagues, so she kept her meetings with McQueen low-key and off-grid. Why rock the boat? What that meant was sometimes when she was off duty and walking Charlie, her black Labrador, after a text message she would happen to bump into McQueen.

The dog saw him before Tracey did and romped over to welcome the familiar figure. Charlie was unaware of the issues surrounding McQueen's professional image, he was just pleased to see an old friend in the way that only a dog can be.

'Mud on the trousers,' said McQueen when he had fallen in walking beside Tracey. Charlie had finished greeting him and had taken off to chase his ball. Tracey glanced down at the paw marks on McQueen's legs.

'Sorry about that,' she said. 'It'll brush off when it dries.' They walked on, the grass in the field was long and quite wet and while Tracey was dressed appropriately, McQueen was regretting not putting on some wellies.

They wandered slowly over the open space of Roundhay Park, as they had done many times before and McQueen told Tracey his story. He started with the words of reassurance he'd given to Judy Greene while he was still a lecturer and the resulting tragic outcome. Then he told her about the recent email from Intrusive followed by her visit to his office. He went over the difficult conversation they'd had and how the knife had made an appearance. He kept the account as short as possible and he didn't stray into the tide of emotion the encounter had released within him. He kept it as factual and as unemotional as possible; he wanted an independent professional legal opinion, not a comforting

The McQueen Legacy

pep-talk so he didn't want to come across as yet another whining victim.

When he had finished, Tracey stopped walking and turned to look him in the face. He might have been trying to hide his feelings by wrapping them in factual language but he hadn't fooled Tracey. 'I can't believe you are beating yourself up over this,' she said. 'It wasn't your fault. If we took it personally every time a deranged person did a despicable thing, we wouldn't be able to do our jobs. You tried to help a woman and something beyond your control happened. There's only one person to blame and that's the perpetrator.'

'I know, I know. On paper I know, but still a part of me can't help thinking that I could have done better. It's been happening a lot lately, it's the same as the Sutton case.'

Tracey knew all about the case of Patrick Sutton, the security guard who had killed three separate office workers. On the face of it he had been helping them with their enquiries, using his local knowledge to give them insight, when, in fact, he had been using his privileged position to commit the crimes. She had been there when they had finally arrested him after a tip-off from McQueen.

'Look, you helped us to get him. We were holding the wrong suspect in custody, we'd been heading in the wrong direction and you turned us around.'

'Yes, but I knew it was Sutton who had been killing them. I had worked out his profile and I had pinpointed his address. I knew his job, I even knew his shift pattern. I had enough evidence, but I wanted to be sure, I wanted to be one hundred percent certain. I knew that if I got it wrong your lot would jump all over me. I didn't want to accuse Patrick Sutton if there was a tiny chance I could be wrong because once you point the finger the person might never get over that stigma.'

'Bottom line is we got him,' she repeated.

'But I lacked decisiveness, I hesitated, and while I was dithering another man got killed. I could have stopped that.'

She was shorter than McQueen but she reached up, placed a hand on each shoulder and looked deep into his eyes.

'I don't need to tell you this, McQueen, but we all need to compartmentalise. The job is the job and that goes into one compartment, your life is something else and that goes into a different one. Even James Bond leaves his wetsuit at the door sometimes.' She searched his face to see if this had made him smile, but it hadn't. 'Look, now and then I have to tell Sophie the same thing.' Sophie was Tracey's partner and she worked as a vet. 'Sometimes she'll have a sick animal in the surgery she just can't save. It's very sad and, of course, she loves all animals but if she let it get to her she'd be too paralysed to do anything for the ones that she can help.'

She let go of his shoulders and they stood still for a while side by side watching Charlie as he ran happily not a care in the world chasing birds he was never going to catch.

'She was a baby girl called Katie,' he said quietly.

To break his trance of morbid self-reflection Tracey switched back into practical professional mode.

'Okay, Judy hasn't made any explicit threats,' she said. 'Yes, she's implied things but only very vaguely. You can't prove she sent that intrusive email. You know it's her but you can't prove it. Didn't you say you didn't even ask her about that?'

'No, I didn't.'

'So she came to your office and showed you a sealed kitchen knife she had bought. You know what I'm going to say, it's not a crime.'

'I know that.'

'But, taken with all the other circumstantial information, then it could start to look like a threat. And if you feel threatened you could certainly go to a lawyer. You might be able to get a restraining order to keep her away from you, but that's about all you'll get.'

'What about the ex-husband, she says he's out now, do you think I should try to find him to warn him?'

'What would you say? Your ex-wife wants to see you and by the way she recently bought a kitchen knife? I'd stay well clear of that mess if I were you.'

Tracey kept checking her watch and McQueen guessed she needed to be getting back now to go on duty. As they completed their usual loop they walked towards her car Charlie joined them happily panting.

'One other thing,' McQueen said. 'Just out of interest, have you ever heard of a company called Summertown Industries?'

'I've heard the name,' she replied, 'but I don't know anything about them.'

'Okay, no rumours? Dodgy deals, anything like that?'

She was concentrating on wiping Charlie's paws with a towel in a forlorn effort to keep the back of the car clean, but it was a battle she had lost long ago.

'Nope, why?'

'Unrelated case,' he said. 'Just thought I'd ask.'

As Tracey closed the door on Charlie she turned to McQueen again.

'Are you still doing the P.T.S.D. therapy with Maggie?'

'No, I've lapsed. I don't seem to get the time.'

'Maybe you need to get back to it.'

She was obviously in a hurry to get wherever she was going, but as she climbed into the driver's seat before she could slam the door shut McQueen said, 'Tracey, er, I nearly had a glass of wine last night.' She looked at him and slowly shook her head. She knew all about his previous struggles with alcohol and the chaos it could bring to his life.

'You nearly, but you didn't?'

'Yes, somehow I managed to beat the craving.'

'Then if you beat it last night you can do it again. Just call me if you need to,' she said. 'Any time.'

It was a nice gesture, the kind of thing friends say, but he knew it wasn't true in a practical sense. She was a busy woman, a senior police detective and wasn't available "any time". On reflection he wasn't even sure why he'd mentioned it to her, validation perhaps? To hear it out loud from his own mouth, to reinforce that yes, he had avoided falling off the wagon?

As she drove away McQueen looked down at his sodden shoes and his mud-caked suit trousers. The urge to have a drink had started in the Italian restaurant while he'd been with Lia and it had followed him home to his empty flat. It had stalked him through the night as he ruminated on Judy Greene, baby Katie, Mrs Bolton, Tania and Zach

The McQueen Legacy

Lindley until they all merged into one ominous cloud. In the early hours he had given up on sleep and started watching more of the Zach Lindley videos and, in the loneliness of the night, while cold beers and rich red wines had called out to him, Zach had started to make some kind of sense. He could see why so many people were drawn to the mesmerising mantras and the release from personal responsibility they offered. The message was simple, every single thing that is wrong in your life is the fault of someone else. Like football fans watching their team lose and blaming the referee. It was seductive and comforting to have a scapegoat. By morning his alcohol craving had gone and he had signed up to attend the next Zach Lindley live meeting.

Fourteen

'So where do you think the cash came from?' Lia took a shortbread finger from the plate which had been placed close to her on the coffee table. She considered dunking it in her tea and then thought better of it. Instead, she nibbled delicately at the buttery sweetness being careful not to drop crumbs. These were the good, branded biscuits, not the own-label supermarket variety she and Carl usually bought. Also, the cup was made from thin, unchipped, gold-rimmed bone china; white with a tasteful floral design. It was not the chunky ceramic mug bearing its dark stains and a fast-food corporate logo she was used to. Lia could see she was getting the honoured visitor treatment.

She was sitting with Mary Bolton in the very same lounge where she had discovered the poor woman prostrate and struggling for breath. She had almost certainly saved her life by arriving when she did and that probably accounted for the expensive biscuits.

When Lia arrived at the house this second time and rang the doorbell she had felt a moment of trepidation while she waited for the door to open. She couldn't help standing back from the door step in a piece of involuntary, protective, learned behaviour. She even felt a phantom twinge of pain in her healed head wound. Thankfully, this time it was Mary not a hoody-wearing attacker who opened the door and invited her in. There had been such panic and chaos during her previous visit that she hadn't had time to take in Mary's home, but now she made a conscious effort to absorb the feel of her surroundings.

The house was an old person's home both in furniture and décor. If Mary had really stolen a couple of million she certainly hadn't spent it on the interiors. It wasn't particularly bad, nothing was shabby or worn out, the walls were papered, painted, and clean and the carpet was in good order, but nothing was new. There were a few cheap prints on the walls, a meadow in summer, a seascape, but nothing of any value. The cash had not been splashed on anything Lia could see. At some point, she wanted to get a closer look at the row of photographs in their brown frames standing on the top of the bookcase. She knew from her research that Mary's husband was long dead, but she had a grown-up son who lived in Leeds. Mary's old work colleagues had not been able to tell her much about the son other than that he used to live in Spain and was "the apple of Mary's eye", but as far as Lia knew there was no daughter-in-law or grandchildren.

The hallway with its old-fashioned telephone table and stairs to one side was dark and needed the light turned on even in the daytime. The kitchen, where Lia's offer to help with the tea had been rebuffed, would have been described as in need of modernisation. It was the kind of place that if it were seen by a young couple on an estate agent's website it would leave them thinking they would need to rip everything out and start again.

From the kitchen window you could see out to the back garden which, like everything else, was tidy but unremarkable. It featured a patch of mowed lawn and a clothes line. Mary clearly wasn't an avid gardener.

'The cash?' Mary asked. She was sipping from her teacup but she hadn't taken a biscuit. Lia smiled to herself. Family hold-back as her mother used to call it whenever they'd had visitors. Leave the good stuff for the guests and you might get some after they had gone.

'Yes, I've had someone look at your spreadsheets and he says it looks like there have been large amounts of cash coming into the business that don't seem to be accounted for? Do you know where it might have come from?'

Mary shrugged.

'I was just the bookkeeper, I entered the amounts coming in and going out but, now that I think of it, sometimes I would be told to keep the sources of some of the cash payments off the books.'

'Really? Come on, I mean that's a massive red flag, Mary, even from a taxation point of view. Who told you to do that?'

'I can't recall. Various people, I think. I really can't remember and I don't want to point any fingers.'

'Well, Mary, even if you don't want to you might have to point me in the right direction because the company certainly doesn't have any qualms about pointing an accusatory finger at you.'

Mary nodded but it was as if the message hadn't got through. It was the first time Lia had picked up a slightly odd feeling from the situation, something she couldn't put her finger on. The old woman was sitting serenely and she seemed strangely calm. For someone who had almost been murdered in her own home and was facing a prison sentence for the theft of a lot of money she didn't appear to be as concerned as she should be. Lia wanted to push on with her questions, but she couldn't ignore the atmosphere.

'Can I just say that you seem to be coping very well with it all?' said Lia.

'Why shouldn't I be, now that I've got the A team on my side?' she said. 'Now I've got you and Doctor McQueen I haven't got anything to worry about.' Lia felt her stomach tighten.

'I hope you understand, Mary, that it's still a difficult case,' she said, hoping to manage some expectations. 'The company has a lot of evidence and they'll have good lawyers.'

'Not as good as mine,' answered Mary instantly. 'I've got the best money can buy, plus I have you.'

'Listen,' said Lia, trying to get back to her list which was sitting unanswered on her pad, 'the guy who has looked at the spreadsheets for me—'

'Carl?' said Mary, again her face remained unchanged from the passive sheet that it had been, except for the slightest hint of a smile.

'Er, yes.' Lia stopped checking her notes and looked up at Mary. Something invisible had passed between them; there was a different feel to the air somehow. 'How do you know his name?'

'Oh, you must have told me it before, Sekalyia. He's your boyfriend, he lives with you, he works for a financial consultancy? He sounds nice.'

Lia was confused, she was almost positive she had never mentioned Carl at any time to Mary. In any case, she would not have said his name preferring to keep her personal life away from her professional role, and yet Mary already knew it? Had McQueen been talking to her? It was very unlikely but she made a note to ask him.

'Anyway,' said Lia, trying not to let it derail her while she marshalled her circling thoughts, 'he says it's possible there has been money laundering at Summertown Industries and—'

Again, Mary cut in.

'And with the murder attempt I suffered, which you yourself witnessed, Sekalyia, and then gave a statement to the police about, it all starts to look a bit muddy, doesn't it?'

It was like an electric shock, Lia felt her fingers tingle. It was true, she had given a sworn statement to the police that, in her opinion, a masked man had tried to kill Mary and whether she wanted to be or not she was now part of Mary's story.

'Yes, it does,' said Lia flatly.

'And all you, and the highly respected Doctor McQueen, and my lawyer have to do is stir up enough mud to make it difficult for a jury to see the wood from the trees. How could they be certain enough to convict me? It's all about doubt.'

'Yes,' said Lia again. 'I suppose it is.'

The McQueen Legacy

'If we can cast enough doubt they would have to acquit, that's even if it gets to trial.' Mary held up a finger to show she wanted Lia to wait for a second, and then she got up from her chair and went to the cabinet which was against the wall. She opened the door and took out a wrapped bundle of money. She plonked it down on the coffee table next to the plate of biscuits.

'That's the retainer I tried to give to Doctor McQueen before,' she said, 'but now it's all official, I'm sure it will be more welcome.' She eased herself back into her seat. Lia pushed the money away.

'That's between you and McQueen,' she said. 'I don't get involved with the payments.'

The two women sat for a few moments in silence while Lia thought about what she had just heard and seen. The swirling thoughts were starting to take on an unwelcome shape.

'The last time I came here, when I disturbed the intruder, you knew exactly what time I was coming didn't you?'

'Yes, lucky wasn't it?'

'Yes, very lucky,' said Lia. 'And even though the criminal ransacked your cupboards looking for your papers and memory stick, he didn't find that money, because I'm sure he'd have taken it if he had?'

'No, I was lucky with that as well, wasn't I?'

'It would seem so,' said Lia closing her pad. She felt as if she was a good club level chess player up against a grandmaster and she needed to get away to regroup.

Lia stood up and casually crossed to the bookcase where

she picked up one of the photographs she had been eyeing from her seat.

'Who's this?' she asked, meaning the young man standing next to Mary in the picture.

'That's my son,' she answered proudly. 'Chris.'

'Handsome lad,' said Lia, knowing perfectly well what a mother wants to hear. 'He looks fit and strong.'

'Oh, yes, he is. He goes to the gym every day, never misses a session,' said Mary proudly. 'He used to live in Spain but he moved back recently, he lives in Leeds now.'

'Right,' said Lia looking more closely at the picture. 'And what does he do?'

'Well, as I say he's not long back from Spain, so he's still looking for something. He wants to run his own bar. He's sick of working for other people. As I always tell him you'll never make a million by working for someone else, will you?'

Lia carefully put the photo back.

'Unless you steal it,' said Lia with an innocent grin. She was keen to see the other woman's reaction but Mary didn't flinch, instead she tipped her head back and laughed.

'Good one,' she said. 'I can see you and me are going to be friends, Sekalyia. Same sense of humour.'

Later in the car Lia consulted her notes and sent a text to McQueen.

Just been with Mary Bolton, I'll update you later, but did you ever talk to her about Carl?

About a minute later the reply came back.

Carl? No, of course not. Why?

Thanks, I didn't think so. It's probably nothing.

Fifteen

When McQueen had chosen to give up his previous academic life and become a private detective, he'd done it with a blind confidence that looked to his friends a lot like stupid arrogance. He'd been ignorant but nothing is more empowering than ignorance, the evidence for that is all around us. The first six months in his new vocation had literally kicked that child-like naivety out of him when he'd been caught taking pictures outside a hotel of an errant husband. People often talk about facing a steep learning curve, what McQueen had faced was a vertical climb. In the early days there had certainly been some ups and downs, in fact at times he'd felt like the pilot of a small plane as it dives into serious turbulence. It was a painful mix of, *I'm sure it's going to be fine*, and *I'm probably going to die*.

Faced with the steepest of learning curves it would have been easy for him to give up sleuthing and go back to his old life of lecturing. He'd even flirted with the idea of moving into a media-based role where he would become one of those talking heads on television. It was tempting to join the ranks of the smug experts who rent out their credibility and opinions to documentary crime shows. In the end, though, he'd felt none of those options were right for him, he'd wanted to do something of more societal value so he'd stubbornly clung on to his new career.

Part of his perseverance had come from the need not to be seen to fail, but he'd often asked himself, fail in whose eyes? Who was he trying to impress? He wasn't sure anymore. His wife had long ago married someone else, someone more financially stable, and she'd never been in favour of his new role anyway. In general, he'd quickly lost the thrill of telling strangers at parties what he did for a living, most people thought of private detection as a grubby, sneaky job and although he didn't like to admit it, sometimes it was.

No, what had really kept him going was the knowledge he had genuinely helped some people during the most difficult times in their lives. He had made a difference to those clients and he wasn't prepared to give up that power. It's why he couldn't understand why he was questioning himself so much of late, where had these doubts come from? The triumphs he had achieved were still out there, some of his old clients still sent him Christmas cards and invited him to family events, invitations he always politely declined, but his work was remembered, to a few people it had even mattered. In times of emotional wobble these were the things he had to force himself to remember: the future, the people he was going to help next.

Tania's partner may have been getting drawn into Zach Lindley's group, or cult, or movement, or whatever it was. He was a grown adult and he could do whatever he wanted but McQueen had to find out how bad it could be for Tania's future. She was the client, that was the job, and it was time to put aside all introspection to focus on the task.

McQueen hadn't bothered to give a fake name when he'd registered to attend the Zach Lindley live event. He'd thought about it but he didn't want to risk being embarrassingly exposed by anyone who might have recognised him. Even though it had been a while since he'd been in the papers or on TV, "Hey, are you...?" still did happen from time to time. Besides, he didn't need a cover story, he was just a psychologist at an interesting meeting.

He was met at the door of the village hall by a man with a clipboard who asked his name and then crossed it off the list before standing aside to let him in.

McQueen casually scanned the room to see if he could see Tania's partner but, although she'd included some pictures in the info-pack she'd given him, he didn't see anyone there who resembled the images amongst the sea of young male faces. The hall was full, every seat was taken and there was an expectant buzz of quiet chatter around the room.

McQueen had expected more theatrics than he'd already seen on the dry video presentations, but when Zach eventually walked up onto the small stage it was without fanfare. He didn't thank the audience for coming and he didn't start with an obligatory joke or icebreaker, he was like a headmaster at morning assembly. He was wearing the same simple white shirt he always wore online and McQueen couldn't help thinking, *consistent branding*.

'It is not *your* fault the way the world is, so why should *you* take the blame?' was his opener. Almost every head in the audience was nodding in agreement, and then he launched into it.

'Did you ever lose a job because of someone else's stupidity? A boss who couldn't see your true value? A co-worker who blamed you for their mistakes? An unreasonable customer who lied about you? But do you know why you really lost that job? They fear you. They fear your vision. They fear your intelligence. They fear the things they can't understand and they fear your potential. You lost that job because of their inadequacies. *They* were the problem and *you* took the hit.'

McQueen took a sly look around him at his fellow listeners, saw their narrowed eyes and clenched jaws and he could well believe a good proportion of them had lost more than one job in their lives.

Over the years McQueen has studied many political or religious leaders and they could almost always be described as charismatic. Zach Lindley fitted that template perfectly, but not in a flashy, bombastic way, his was a charisma based on the believable impression that what he was telling you was very important and he was on your side. Though the place was full, it was as if he was talking to each person individually and meant every word. McQueen could see from the rapt attention of the faces around him that they all felt he was only talking to them.

Much of what Zach was saying now as he paced hypnotically back and forth were themes McQueen had heard several times before on his videos. It was a vague mixture of popular conspiracy theories made more convincing by some unrelated but unarguable facts. As Zach moved around the stage McQueen noticed to the right, standing partially hidden in the shadows, there was a man who was monitoring the crowd, watching in the same way a steward does at a football match, his back to the action. Maybe he was a security guard prepared for anyone who might rush the stage? It seemed a little bit heavy-handed and unnecessary to McQueen, Lindley was preaching to the converted and it seemed unlikely that anyone was going to try to stop him. McQueen looked more closely at the man and realised it was actually Richard, Tania's partner. Clearly, he was no longer simply a passive observer of these meetings, he had a role to play even if it was only as a bouncer.

As the speech continued in the same seductive vein the people around McQueen were lapping it up, they were hearing what they wanted to hear, but for McQueen the pitch was still missing one vital ingredient: Zach wasn't offering any answers to the life problems his followers were experiencing, he was pointing them out and then rubbing salt into the wounds. He was stabbing them with their own inadequacies and failings and then twisting the knife. McQueen was there to judge whether Richard was tied up in a dangerous cult but it wasn't clear exactly what the man on the stage was aiming at.

Tania had told McQueen about the proposed move to the farm in Senby and now he started to wonder if these meetings merely served as a rallying cry and recruitment drive to get enough followers to join the cause, whatever

The McQueen Legacy

that might be? Maybe once they were all isolated away from the rest of society that's where Zach's true purpose would become clear?

'So, what is our strength? What can we do in the face of the overwhelming injustice that every single one of you has faced at one time or another?' asked Zach. McQueen sat a up little taller in his chair hoping to finally hear something meaningful.

'From birth there is a linear path, a straight line, that is pre-decided for all of us and it is pre-decided by others,' continued Zach. 'And for their plans to succeed, that path must be followed without interruption. So, what is the most powerful thing we can do?' He gazed around the audience as if waiting for the answer and was met with total silence. No one dared to speak for fear of giving the wrong response. 'We can interrupt that path,' he said. 'We can disrupt at every turn. We can make sure *we* make the decisions, not *them*.'

In a performance setting this would have been the point when the audience would have clapped and shouted out their agreement, but here in the hall Zack's words were met with muttered words like "yes!" and the clenching of fists.

Zach stopped his pacing and stood dead centre of the stage. 'Now many of you have already committed to joining us at our farm retreat. I know you are impatient but we're not ready for you yet, there are some details to be finalised, but let me make this clear, in order to make sure that the only energy we have amongst us is the right energy, participation at the farm is by invitation only. If you are chosen to join us you will be notified and, if you are, I urge you to begin your personal disruption by making that move. What we want is for as many of you to add to our corrective forces as possible.'

Corrective forces? Nice, thought McQueen, Zach was setting up an exclusive club of outsiders who could feel privileged to be insiders at last.

'Remember, you are not crazy. You've been right all along, you are not to blame,' he said raising a finger. 'So let's start putting the record straight.'

When Zach finished he held up his hand, said 'thank you' and exited to the back of the stage. He hadn't whipped the crowd into a frenzy and he hadn't asked for any donations, both of which McQueen had been expecting. There had been no eye-popping, exaggerated remonstrating with the audience, in fact there had been nothing that anyone could point at as deranged or hysterical. McQueen was starting to get a feel of what Lindley's appeal was, he was cutting against the grain of the usual conspiracy theorists and promoting himself as a sensible, credible option. There was no huge outburst of applause or cheering as Lindley walked off, instead everyone stood and clapped, including McQueen.

With the event over McQueen began to make his way out. As he began to push his way through the exiting crowd he was stopped at the door by the man with the clipboard who placed a hand on his arm.

'Doctor McQueen,' he said, checking the list. 'Mr Lindley would like a word with you, would that be okay?' McQueen glanced down at the hand as it lightly gripped his sleeve before it let go.

'Sure,' he said, smiling. 'Why not?' It was a surprising development and McQueen had no idea why he was being singled out, he even thought he caught some envious looks from some of the others as they filed past. He had been wondering how he could engineer a meeting with Lindley without seeming to be too keen but now it had dropped right into his lap. It was the perfect opportunity to ask some questions and he wasn't about to let it slip away. He was guided towards the back of the hall and into a small room. Zach was sitting in a chair and Richard was standing next to him. McQueen was careful not to show any signs he recognised Tania's partner. On seeing McQueen, Richard nodded at Zach and then left along with the man and his clipboard who had led him in, leaving McQueen and Lindley alone. Zach got up from his chair without a smile and held out his hand to shake.

'We're honoured to have you with us tonight, Doctor McQueen,' he said. Noticing McQueen's look of confusion Lindley said, 'Yes, I know who you are. As a group we are getting bigger and we are attracting more attention, so we have to be more careful about who we let in these days. After anyone registers to attend we do basic research on everyone who comes to the meetings.'

'Why?'

'Because we don't need negative energy in our meetings and sadly there are those who don't wish us well. It's to be expected when you are holding a microscope up to society.' He motioned towards the chairs and they both sat down. There was a table next to them but there was nothing on it, in fact there was nothing else in the room. It reminded

McQueen of the police interviews he'd attended a few times, sometimes as an observer and other times a wrongly accused suspect. It crossed his mind perhaps he should have asked for his lawyer to be present.

'And what did you discover about me?' asked McQueen.

'Well, you've got quite a CV, Doctor McQueen, but I see you are private detective these days? No doubt you've been sent along by someone who is concerned about our group?' McQueen didn't answer. 'I could easily have excluded you but I didn't because we have nothing to hide.'

'I'm a psychologist, I've watched your videos and your meeting interested me, that's why I'm here,' lied McQueen.

'Ah, the psychology angle, well that's why I was happy for you to come along. I am not interested in your gumshoe activities, your hiding behind bedroom doors, your sneaky photos, but I am interested in who you are, the man inside the detective's raincoat.'

McQueen didn't bite at the jibes.

'Really?'

'Yes, I've read you are a criminologist but, you see, I am a psychologist too, perhaps the greatest psychologist you've ever met.' He paused to let this resonate. McQueen couldn't tell if he was joking. 'It's true I don't have any official qualifications, I'm not a Doctor of Psychology like you but I am an expert in people. I am a professor of what makes them do the things they do.' And then he added ominously, 'And how to make them do it.'

McQueen wasn't sure why Zach was telling him all this, it sounded like school-ground bragging and it was at odds with the carefully scripted presentation he had just watched. He seemed to want to impress McQueen.

'I'm sure you are,' replied McQueen. 'The people out there certainly liked what you had to say.'

Zach shrugged.

'Do you know how I got interested in the psychology of people, McQueen? It was my mother. She had compulsive-obsessive disorder when I was growing up and it made life very difficult. That's why I hate it when I hear someone say they are a *little bit OCD* when they want all their pens lined up on their desk or they have to make sure all their shirts are straight in the wardrobe. They have no idea, none. My mother couldn't leave the house because she couldn't trust the door was locked. Some nights she couldn't go to bed because she wasn't sure that everything electrical had been turned off and unplugged. She would circle the house all night until she collapsed exhausted in a chair.'

McQueen had seen OCD patients himself when he was studying and he shared Zach's distaste for its trivialisation by tidy people. 'That's when I saw how powerful the mind could be and that's when I started to think psychology was the key. There are things that are frightening to people McQueen and I don't need to tell you that they aren't the same things for everyone. But fear is the primary motivator for all humans. You can't escape it, it's in thousands if not millions of years of our programming. Shakespeare knew it, he based whole plays on fear. *Macbeth* is full of it.'

McQueen didn't want to get side-tracked into a discussion on Shakespeare, he realised he might not get this chance again to speak directly to Zach, so he tried to cut through the chit-chat.

'So you try to cover all the bases in your speeches? Make sure you hit all the fears? But why? What are you trying to do other than frighten people?'

For the first time Zach smiled.

'And what do you fear, McQueen?' he asked. 'Or would you prefer I tell you what frightens you?'

'Go ahead, please do, but I can tell you I fear many things. I've met some dangerous people in my job, Mister Lindley, people who have tried to kill me, so I know all about fear.' Now it was McQueen who was doing the bragging, and it made him wince a little inside to hear himself.

Zach was shaking his head, the half-smile still on his face.

'I don't mean that kind of fear, I mean bigger, much bigger. I mean deep inside your own mind, when there's no one threatening you and the only voice is your own. Do you question yourself, Doctor McQueen? Have you found the mistakes you make in your life are becoming more frequent these days? What you fear is that you will be made useless by your age. You won't be able to help anyone anymore, least of all yourself. You fear that everything you've done will all mean nothing. And you fear one day you'll go running back to the bottle again, you'll start drinking again and this time you won't be able to stop.'

McQueen blinked, he wasn't used to being analysed himself, but it was all out there on the internet. His sobriety had been part of more than one magazine profile, he wasn't ashamed of it so it wouldn't have been hard to find.

'You asked me why I do this?' continued Lindley. 'What am I trying to achieve? I'll tell you. I want to change the world for the better. I want life to be better for the people who get shat on every day. I want to make an impact. I want the world to be a different place after I'm gone, because of me.'

'A legacy?'

'Call it a legacy if you want but understand I don't want money, doubters won't believe that but I really don't. I know there have been leaders who have spoken about the dignity of poverty while they drive a Rolls Royce paid for by their followers, but that's not me. I have no interest in all that. I'm not after their money,' he was pointing at the door to the hall that had been full of his followers. 'I want to make their lives better because they are good people and they deserve better lives.'

'That's noble,' said McQueen, 'but how do you propose to do that?'

Zach shook his head again, the smile had gone.

'It's too early for me to tell you the details. We are not ready, but what I can tell you is that I think you can be a big part of it.'

This last twist took McQueen by surprise, in fact he was knocked back a little.

'Me?'

'Yes, that's why I asked to speak to you tonight. I think you could be a very valuable and useful member of our group. Your expertise would be precious to us. No one could want you more. We are an organisation that runs on motivation and psychology, and we could offer you the chance to make a real and lasting difference to the whole world. It would be your legacy if you like? I'm inviting you to join us, Doctor McQueen.'

On the drive back from the meeting in the rainy blur of traffic lights, McQueen found himself once again thinking about magic. Not the supernatural, mystical, fantasy variety that was so popular in books about schoolboy wizards but the down-to-earth, stage-conjuring, disappearing-woman, your-card-is-the-queen-of-hearts, sawing-a-person-in-half style of visual trickery. Like a lot of young kids, McQueen had been fascinated by magic tricks as a child and after being given a book by his uncle one Christmas had learned some basic sleight of hand tricks. He'd pored over the diagrams and instructions but he'd never been dexterous or confident enough to successfully pull off the tricks in front of his friends. He also didn't have the patience to put in the thousands of hours of practise in front of a mirror required to perfect his act. He'd soon lost interest in the book but by that time he could make a coin vanish in his hand but that was about it.

McQueen may not have had the talent or dedication to become a magician, but his early studies of conjuring had given him something far more valuable than a few party tricks. The theories of stage magic had been his first introduction to the world of mass deception and therefore opened the door to human psychology. It had been the starting point of a lifelong fascination with the mind that had led him to his eventual career.

Misdirection was the basic tool used by all magicians.

The McQueen Legacy

The ability to make you look at one thing while the action was happening elsewhere was the key to it. He'd also learned that immensely elaborate illusions could be constructed around the simplest of tricks. As he'd grown up he'd noticed these weren't techniques that were confined to people in top hats and capes. Criminals, whether they were crooked politicians or street conmen, all leveraged a victim's natural desire to see what they wanted to see, rather than what was really right there in front of them.

McQueen was aware that what he had been subjected to by Zach Lindley was a form of cold reading, a method used by fake psychics the world over. By incorporating high probability guesses along with broad statements under the guise of supreme confidence they create the illusion of knowing something about you that you haven't told them.

Lindley had looked at McQueen's CV and his background, and reasonably assumed a man of McQueen's age and life experience might well be questioning himself, that he might have made mistakes (who hasn't?), and that he might be worrying he was losing his effectiveness. Lindley had already read that McQueen had previously changed careers which pointed to a person who might have certain dissatisfactions. He'd also guessed McQueen might be wondering about mortality and his legacy, common enough threads for anyone who has ever tried to achieve anything. And the drinking? There had been newspaper articles in the past in which McQueen had talked openly about his sobriety, he made no secret of it, and it was an easy step to think that the fear of relapse was ever present. None of Lindley's statements about what frightened McQueen were particularly insightful, they just happened to be right. It was simply a version of, *the card you are thinking of is the ace of spades*. In every good lie there is a grain of truth, the convincer, the tiny sparkle that makes you think the rock might be gold.

When he pulled up outside his flat McQueen didn't get out of the car, he sat for a few minutes in the darkness, he wasn't ready to break his train of thought. He couldn't allow himself to be distracted but he still had nothing concrete to tell Tania. It was true Richard had fallen for the seductively comforting messages of Lindley's group, he was a trusted member, but was that dangerous? Maybe Zach Lindley really did wish good for the world, maybe Richard would benefit from the nurturing and come out as a more focused and purposeful member of society? McQueen seriously doubted that outcome, but he wasn't yet in a position to refute it. As much as there had been a general theme of how things were so wrong in the world there had been no hate speech, there had been no call to arms. McQueen had heard nothing about the spilling of blood being the way to fix things.

McQueen looked up at the window of his flat through the rain drops that chased their way down the car window. His flat, another small empty space for him to ruminate in. From car to flat, from flat to office, a life of swapping one box for another until you reach the final box. Maybe Zach was right, maybe what he needed was a place where his experience and skills could be valued? Zach had said there was nowhere in the world where he would be more wanted. Zach Lindley had been offering a lasting legacy, something

The McQueen Legacy

to live on after he was dead, and what could be wrong with that?

For now, though, McQueen had no choice, he'd have to go along with it and he had told Lindley he would think about joining his group. He was under no illusions, he knew exactly what they wanted, they wanted his name. They wanted the credibility he could add. He wasn't a celebrity but he was as close as they had come to so far so they wanted to welcome him in. It was a dangerous game. Have you got the tiger by the tail, or has he got you?

Sixteen

Detective Tracey Bingham's caseload didn't leave much time for worrying about anything else let alone McQueen, but that didn't stop her from doing it anyway. They had history. Professionally, they had worked together brilliantly on many occasions but, more than that, he was a friend. It bugged her she'd had to rush away from their meeting in Roundhay Park, especially as it was just as he started to open up about his close brush with falling off the wagon, but duty had been calling. Contrary to the appearance she'd given she had not taken his concerns about Judy Greene lightly, even though she had played down the implied threats. The hard fact was that as a police officer there really wasn't much she could do at this stage but it didn't mean she had forgotten about it.

Tracey had been snowed under for a week but, eventually, in her lunch break, she ran some checks through the database and pulled up the old case files of baby Mason. Even for a seasoned detective like her they made ugly reading. Interestingly, McQueen wasn't mentioned in any of the related documents and his name hadn't come up in the

The McQueen Legacy

statements Judy had made at the time. The case was rightly focused on the perpetrator, Paul Mason, Judy's husband and the father of the child. Tracey raised an eyebrow when she read that Judy had been right, Mason was now out on parole and living in a half-way house outside Leeds. Skimming through the notes, Tracey could see initially Judy hadn't tried to point any blame towards McQueen, not publicly anyway, so what had changed? She reasoned with the passage of the years rather than abating, her pain must have festered and grown inside like a spiritual cancer. They say time heals all wounds, but maybe not. Tracey had never faced a personal trauma on the scale of Judy's and she could only imagine how something like that could change you forever. The release of Mason along with the unrealised twenty-first birthday of her child must have been a trigger that stirred up so many awful memories for Judy. But was it enough to turn a peaceful woman into a violent person? Someone who might use a knife? Judy Greene's personal record was clean, she'd never had so much as a speeding ticket. That didn't mean she couldn't lose it in a moment of rage, but it would be completely out of character if she did.

Tracey pulled up the mugshot of Paul Mason taken not long after his arrest, it was a depressing image. In the modern world of carefully-crafted, filtered, and enhanced online profiles, mugshots stood out as an unvarnished visual truth and they were never flattering, not even for good-looking celebrities. Paul Mason's picture looked particularly rough. One of his eyes was half closed, the other staring wildly at the camera. His wispy hair was in disarray and he looked every inch the public perception of what a child murderer should look like. Tracey was about to close down the image when Sarah, one of her colleagues, passed by, a coffee in hand. She glanced at Tracey's screen as she squeezed past but then stopped.

'Oh, are you working on the Paul Mason thing now? I thought that was Chambers' job?'

'Detective Chambers? I don't know what you mean? This is an old, closed case, more than twenty years old in fact.'

'Yeah, okay, but I mean the stabbing?'

Tracey swivelled in her seat to face her colleague. She liked Sarah and, as one of the only other female detectives in the station, they shared a certain unspoken bond.

'Sorry, what are you talking about? I was just checking out this historical case for a bit of background. Someone came to me with a minor complaint concerning one of the people who was involved.'

'I'm talking about that guy, Paul Mason,' she said gesturing towards Tracey's screen. 'I thought you knew, he was stabbed to death in an ex-offenders' half-way house.'

Tracey was stunned and looked again at her screen as she scrolled down through the entries for Mason.

'Well, that information doesn't seem to have made it through to the database yet. When did it happen?'

'Night before last, I think?'

Tracey blinked, not sure she had heard it right.

'Have they got a suspect?'

'Not yet, but you mark my words, it'll be something to do with drugs. You know what scum like that are like, they get out and they go right back to it. Good riddance to bad rubbish if you ask me.'

It was the kind of knee-jerk remark Tracey had got used to hearing amongst her colleagues but it never sat well with her.

'C'mon, Sarah, this was a human being you're talking about.'

But Sarah was unabashed.

'You've read the file, he killed his own child while he was under the influence for Christ's sake. His lawyer tried some bullshit defence about intrusive thoughts. I know they said he'd had mental health problems for years but his lifestyle choices were his problem. He was a violent, junkie creep.'

Something about this man's crime had obviously touched a nerve with Sarah, she was a mother to a little girl herself perhaps that was it, but Tracey was only half listening to her diatribe.

'I need to speak to Chambers,' she said.

It's always satisfying to be the first one with a piece of juicy news, but now that she had dropped her bombshell Sarah had lost interest in the conversation. She shrugged and pushed on past Tracey's desk.

'I think he's gone to the crime scene today,' she said moving away, 'but I imagine he'll be back soon.'.

Tracey kept her eye on the door and when Detective Steve Chambers finally weaved his way through the crowded office and arrived at his desk Tracey was waiting for him.

'Chambers, I only just heard about this Mason stabbing you're working on, I need to talk to you about it,' she said, before he'd even had time to sit down. He dropped his canvas bag onto his desk and took off his jacket before draping it over the back of his seat. He looked slightly puzzled, stabbings were not exactly a rare occurrence so he was a little surprised at Tracey's interest.

'Any idea who did it yet? Any suspects?' she asked.

'What's it to you?'

'Listen, Steve, I might be able to help you.'

Chambers sighed.

'The guy was living in a house with eight other ex-offenders. At least three of them have form for violence. All of them have a history of substance abuse. The murder weapon is missing. The forensics team are still assessing the physical evidence, but right now, yes, I've got plenty of suspects.'

'Okay, well I'm afraid I might have one more to add to your list. You know about the ex-wife? The mother of the child?'

'*Duh, yeah.*' Tracey ignored the nasty sarcasm and let him carry on. 'Of course I do, Judy Mason now Greene again. I know you think I swan about making it all up as I go along but I do read this shit you know.' He pointed at the pile of paperwork on his desk. 'What about her?'

'Judy Greene turned up at a friend's office recently and she seemed quite upset. She said she might want to get back together with Mason, and she made a big deal of having bought a knife.'

'Did she make any threats?'

'I don't think so, not directly anyway.'

Chambers narrowed his eyes as he mulled over this new

information. It smelled a lot like an unwanted complication to him and balanced against a houseful of old lags it was an unlikely lead. Sure, she had an obvious motive but to bear a grudge for more than twenty years took some doing. However, now she had been brought to his attention she was someone he'd have to spend precious time following up. Chambers hadn't sat down, it would have meant Tracey standing over him and he didn't like that power balance. He folded his arms.

'This friend of yours? The one Judy Greene went to see? Is this McQueen again, by any chance?' Tracey knew Chambers had never liked McQueen and he wasn't going to be open to suggestions or tipoffs coming from that direction.

'That shouldn't make any difference,' said Tracey.

'So it *was* McQueen?'

'I'm just trying to help a colleague, Detective Chambers. You know, no stone unturned?'

'Look, right now I'm focusing on the highest probabilities. I see it like this, Mason gets out, tries to get his hands on some drugs, he's got no money so maybe he ends up owing someone, whatever, they stab him. That's going to be the main thrust of my enquiries until I've exhausted that angle. I'll wait until the forensics come back but, until then of course, I'm going to keep an open mind.'

Tracey was sure an open mind was precisely the thing Chambers did not have and she had helped to close it by introducing McQueen into the conversation. Chambers was right, though, statistically the chance of the murderer being one of his housemates or one of their associates was very high, but Tracey still thought it prudent to warn McQueen to watch his back. She held up her hand in surrender.

'Detective Chambers, you seem to have it all under control,' she said with her sweetest smile, and walked away.

Seventeen

Carl had not long arrived home, he was still changing out of his suit and Lia was standing in the bedroom doorway, arms folded impatiently watching him. She'd only been home a short time herself, but since then she'd been prowling around the small flat waiting to unload some of her stress.

'I'm just saying, the sweet old woman could be playing me,' she said.

'Yep, could be,' answered Carl as threw his shirt in the general direction of the laundry basket.

'The intruder, the one who was apparently searching for her evidence in her house? The one who supposedly tried to strangle her? I didn't see his face but it could have been her son.' Carl didn't respond to this bombshell so Lia pushed on. 'The one who pushed past me and knocked my head against the wall? They could have set it up to look as if she'd been attacked but maybe it was all for my benefit?'

'Why?' mumbled Carl.

'So I could corroborate her story that some mystery people, possibly from Summertown Industries, are the ones who stole the money and now they are trying to silence her.'

'Uh huh, I see,' he said.

'I mean, they knew exactly when I was arriving and they could have timed it so she wasn't actually hurt but it looked like she had been.' Carl nodded. He was sitting on the edge of the bed now in a sweatshirt and jeans. There were a few moments of silence as they looked at each other. Lia was not getting the response that she had expected or hoped for.

'Are you taking this seriously?' she eventually asked, sounding a little hurt.

'Look, Lia, I did what I could, I looked at the spreadsheets for you and I told you what I saw. Meanwhile, I have a job of my own, remember? A job that pays my salary, by the way.'

'I know but—'

'I have a huge presentation to the board tomorrow and I need to spend some time prepping for it tonight. Remember, I'm not the detective, you are. You've chosen a very strange career, Lia, and I support you and I always have. Sometimes it's more dangerous than I would like, but hey, that's how it is. But the point is, you chose it not me. If you have work questions then you need to take them to your boss, but you won't do that, will you? Because you want to prove you don't need his help and can do it all by yourself.'

Lia slumped a little against the door frame, she seemed slightly deflated. In a funny way against her expectations she had actually been feeling more pressure since they had hired Dan, the new office administrator, who had taken over her mundane office tasks. Dan was great, very efficient, and he hadn't required much handholding but now she didn't have the daily burden of the admin, it highlighted that Lia needed to justify the expense of an extra person by excelling at her new role.

'Thing is, McQueen didn't want to take this case in the first place,' she said quietly. 'It was me who pushed it through. Right from the start I believed Mary Bolton and, well...'

'And you don't want to be wrong?'

'No one likes being wrong, do they? Besides, McQueen seems kind of distracted at the moment, not like his usual self. He used to be rock solid, but I'm not sure now. To be fair, he hasn't been telling me much about what he's working on, either. I know he's been contacted by some woman about a child that died years ago, trying to put some guilt on him. It's all very tragic and her blaming him sounds like bullshit to me, but I'm sure it's getting to him and I don't think I can go to him now and tell him I'm struggling with this. Especially when he said we shouldn't get involved in the first place.'

Carl got up from the bed and crossed to the door. He put his arms around her and gave her a hug.

'You're doin' great,' he said into her ear. 'And maybe you're not wrong about Mary Bolton, anyway? Maybe you're jumping to conclusions but I still think it would be good to share it with McQueen. I know you want to present him with a perfectly solved case you've done all by yourself but you're supposed to be a team, aren't you?'

Lia's phone began to ring and she reluctantly pulled away from the hug so she could pick it up from the dressing table. She checked the name, frowned, and declined the call without answering it.

'See?' she said. 'That's Mary Bolton again. She keeps ringing me to suggest things I should be doing, to push me in certain directions, to pester me about what I've done so far. I keep telling her I'll update her when I've got something to say but it doesn't satisfy her. Plus, she's told her lawyers I have important evidence for them so they've been badgering me, too.'

'Okay,' said Carl holding up his hands. 'Like I said, I've got a presentation to do tonight, so I'm going to see what we have in the freezer for dinner and then when I've grabbed something I need to concentrate on *my* work.' As he passed Lia who was still brooding in the doorway, he gave her a kiss on the cheek.

'One word,' he said. 'McQueen.'

Eighteen

Tania's phone had been on her desk, next to her computer keyboard, blankly staring up and silently taunting her for almost an hour before she finally gave in and checked it for the hundredth time. Her disappointment surged when she saw there still wasn't anything new from McQueen. In his previous update, he'd said he was going to one of Lindley's meetings, but he hadn't told her yet what he'd learned.

She had stored his number on her phone under the name *Claire* in case Richard saw it flash up on her screen. Even this tiny protective deception left her with a pang of guilt, hiding a name was the sort of thing people having affairs did, wasn't it? Once again she found herself wondering if the problem was her, was she just over-reacting to the whole thing? It was possible Richard's interest in Zach Lindley was actually a good thing. She had to admit, since he had been going to the regular meetings he had become a more focused and purposeful human being, happier, perhaps? And then one of the nights a few weeks before he'd come home and burst through the door in a state of high excitement. He was very animated and she hadn't seen him smile as much in a long time. It turned out there had been a new development; he'd been entrusted with a job within Zach Lindley's organisation, although he'd been vague about whether this was a paid position or not. His answer when she'd asked him directly had been "it's in the mix" and she knew better than to push him further. What she did know was that their joint account was still paying all the bills although it only had her input.

There had also been changes to Tania, some of them physiological. Her pregnancy, which had seemed very unreal to begin with, was now starting to announce itself to her consciousness. Her body was changing and with that had come an increased desire to seek security. The thought of moving to join a community in rural Senby was about as insecure as she could imagine. In fact, it sounded crazy and she was sure very few women in her position would put up with such a scenario especially at this crucial time in her life. However, there was one massive problem at the heart of her situation and it was overriding all logic and sense: she loved Richard and couldn't bear the thought he might leave her to go on his own. Boom, that was it, it was like an immovable rock in the middle of a road and she couldn't get past it. That's why she needed to know what the Lindley group was up to, not so she could leave Richard, but so she could prove to him the group was a bad idea with bad intentions and that he had to leave.

Tania stared at her computer screen, the figures were there, bold, bright, and uncompromising but they meant nothing to her today. In truth, she had done very little productive work for weeks and it was sure to catch up with her sooner or later. She had plenty of colleagues at work but no real friends, no one she could confide in. It was her choice. She didn't want anyone she worked with to know anything about her personal life because she didn't want them to have anything they could use against her. As brutal as it sounded that's how she thought about her work, it was a competitive tank of sharks and she had seen the disastrous results of over-sharing before. Any signs of weakness could be seized on by smiling rivals as everyone scrambled to climb the greasy pole. And it wasn't unreasonable paranoia either, Tania had seen it in action. "Don't give that juicy project to Frank, his wife left him, he might mess it up." "Don't invite Bob to the meeting, his son got arrested and his mind's all over the place." Tania was already fighting the woman-in-a-man's-job fight, she didn't need to add, "partner has joined a cult" as a complication. As far as her workmates were concerned, Tania was efficient, reliable, and steady, and that's the way she wanted to keep it. Little did they know, inside she felt like she had been drinking acid.

At some point she would have to tell HR about the pregnancy, but before she did she wanted to feel a little more in control. She wasn't under any illusions, HR worked for the good of the company not the individual, so she wanted to be ready to present a complete water-tight plan before she approached them which included knowing where she'd be living. She wanted to have her ducks in a row, as her boss would describe it. He was a man who loved a cliché. "Less is more", "your starter for ten", and, "oh that's a bit last minute dot com," were some of his favourites, but until she heard from McQueen less certainly felt like less.

She checked her phone again. Nothing.

Nineteen

McQueen snapped awake from another troubled dream, his heart pounding, his pillow damp with sweat. It seemed to be happening a lot lately. Unfortunately, whenever his subconscious chose to torture him, it had no shortage of images to choose from his catalogue of gruesome memories. It took a few minutes for the kaleidoscope of mental pictures to fade and a few more for the morbid dread to dissipate. He wasn't sure why he was resisting going back to his therapist after she'd been so helpful in the past, but actually he did know, he just didn't want to admit to himself that it was a warped and self-destructive sense of pride which was telling him he was strong enough to get through this. After all, he was a psychologist wasn't he, was there anything he didn't know?

He looked at the clock: 4:32 a.m. and he knew he wouldn't sleep any more so he rolled out of bed and headed for the shower. At five-thirty he was showered and dressed. It was too early for breakfast, his stomach couldn't handle anything stronger than tea until at least eight, so he picked up his laptop and set off for the office.

At his desk he started to feel better, the work environment had a calming effect on him, even though he was still alone. Dan and Lia wouldn't be in for a couple of hours, so he busied himself with the list of emails Dan had flagged as important as he waited for the other two to arrive. He wanted to have a general catch-up with his staff on all outstanding issues but forcing itself to the top of the agenda was a text he'd received in the night that he wanted to share with them urgently and in person. Given the relaxed nature of the office he sometimes forgot he was an employer and he had certain legal obligations, the primary one being not to expose his employees to danger. Frankly, he didn't need any legal reminders not to risk the safety of anyone, employee or not, but still it was worth remembering.

McQueen opened his drawer and took out his old Montblanc fountain pen. It was hardly used these days but from time to time he liked to scrawl something in wet, black ink on a clear piece of paper as a point of focus. Somehow, the slowness of the action helped him to think.

There were certain words that had entered the modern lexicon which set McQueen's teeth on edge, and one of them was monetise. He unscrewed the cap of the pen and wrote the word and then looked at the eight letters stretching out in his uneven scruffy handwriting. He thought of it as a nasty little group of symbols with an evil sneering face. It wasn't so much the American mish-mash construction that offended him so much as it's insidious influence on just about every level of society. Largely driven by social media it had come to mean: a thing happened, so let's make money out of it. Sometimes the event was achingly trivial and sometimes chillingly evil, it didn't seem to matter one way or another; money was money. My dog has a funny way of eating, film it, monetise it. A woman gets attacked on a late-night bus or a youth is set upon by a machete wielding gang. Don't put down your phone and help, monetise.

For all Zach Lindley's claims he wasn't trying to make money from his growing following, McQueen didn't believe him. In block capitals he carefully wrote ZACH? next to *Monetise*. He hadn't figured out what the scam was yet, but he was certain there was one lurking under the blame-everyone-else rhetoric. It wasn't ticket sales. Yes, you had to pay to go to the scheduled meetings but it was a nominal amount, the tickets weren't expensive at all and the proceeds surely only just covered the cost of hiring the hall. But, of course, whenever money changes hands online there is background data gathering, maybe there was something in that? As yet McQueen hadn't witnessed any blatant fund-raising activities either on the videos or in the hall. Perhaps for the chosen ones the price of moving to the utopian farm in Senby was going to be a commitment to sign over all their worldly assets? That was a cult tactic which had certainly been used before. McQueen hadn't given a direct answer to Lindley about the offer to join them, as much as the notion repulsed him he didn't want to reject it out of hand. Cynically he was hoping he might get access to more information if he strung them along, but Lindley wasn't a fool, far from it, and surely he'd have his suspicions about McQueen?

He turned to his computer and clicked on YouTube to see what Zach's latest post was. He was confronted by the usual close-up of Zach's face.

'They made you have an untested vaccine for a disease they had made up. They locked you down and they stripped you of your rights. Do you know why? Because they are scared of you and your independent thoughts.'

McQueen shook his head and closed down his screen with a heavy sigh. Whatever he thought about Lindley, he had to admit the man was leaving no theory untouched in his trawl for followers through the depths of the internet.

On his desk McQueen's phone buzzed with a message and he saw it was from Tania.

Latest update???

He closed his eyes and grimaced, unfortunately he didn't have anything useful to tell her yet, but he knew she must be getting frustrated at his lack of feedback. He had been researching Lindley but it was proving to be a fruitless task. The guy seemed to have appeared from nowhere less than a year before. Suddenly, he had propelled himself into the spotlight and McQueen hadn't been able to establish a backstory even though he had access to specialist databases and official records. Lindley seemed to have been born or invented from nothing, which in itself was telling in this day and age. Everyone has some kind of digital profile so the lack of a footprint told McQueen things were being deliberately hidden from curious eyes.

He read Tania's text again and then feeling guilty he texted back.

I need more time. I'll get back to you when I have something concrete

He didn't want to mention he thought the whole case could be mushrooming and leading him away from her initial request. What had begun as a fairly straight-forward job of checking on a partner's behaviour, bread and butter to the private eye game, was taking a more sinister direction. Tania's relationship problems were feeling like the tip of the iceberg. She had been the one to bring his attention to Zach Lindley but it could be that whether her partner was in danger or not there was a much bigger story developing.

Dan and Lia arrived within minutes of each other in a bustle of bags and the clatter of keys dumped on desks. McQueen listened and then shouted through to them, 'Hey, you two, grab yourselves a coffee and when you're ready can you come in for a second?'

Once everyone was in McQueen's office he got right to it.

'Okay, last night I had a text from a friend, it was unofficial so I won't name names but she has good connections to the police force.' He might as well have said it was Tracey Bingham, as they both knew who he was talking about.

'Dan, a few days ago you might remember we had a visit from a woman called Judy Greene?' Dan nodded.

'She'll be in the log, do you want me to check?'

'No, that's fine. Lia, this is the Judy who is the Ms Intrusive Thoughts I told you about?' He paused for a second and then took a deep breath.

'I could make this more complicated than it is, and I don't want to over-dramatise it, but basically when she came here she showed me a knife she had just bought that she had in her bag. She didn't threaten me, but now I've been told that her ex-husband has been found stabbed to death.'

'The husband who killed the baby?' asked Lia. Dan, who had been unaware of the details of the historic case, opened his eyes wide, an almost cartoon reaction to shock.

'Yes,' said McQueen, 'but as yet they don't know who stabbed the ex, Judy is actually very low on their list of suspects due to the fact he was living in a half-way house with some ex-cons.'

'Did I screw up? Should I have not let her in?' asked Dan.

'No, no, remember? I told you to let her in after she buzzed on the security entry and gave the password, 'intrusive'? All I'm saying is that, even though I don't see this as much of a problem, you need to know about it and we should all be aware and maybe a little more vigilant than normal, just in case.'

'In case she comes back with the knife for you?' said Lia with her usual bluntness.

'Or one of us?' asked Dan. McQueen could see the realities of working for a private detective agency were finally hitting home for the young man.

'Oh, wait, don't get the wrong idea, you two are safe,'

said McQueen, as reassuringly as possible. 'I can almost certainly guarantee that. Dan, this whole thing relates to an incident from many years ago, before you were even born. It concerns a person who has some very specific grievances against me and her ex-husband—'

'Her ex-husband who is now dead,' broke in Lia, but McQueen chose to ignore the heckle.

'—And it's really nothing for you to worry about.'

He checked their faces to make sure the message was getting through. Lia was untroubled but Dan clearly was not. It wasn't the kind of morning briefing he'd had in any job he'd ever done before.

'Dan, really, there's nothing to be concerned about, I'm only mentioning it because it would have been negligent of me not to. If she turns up again, which she won't, and I'm not here, don't let her in. Now, back to business, can I just have some time with Lia, we've got some things to discuss?'

Dan gave a weak smile and then got up to return to his desk. McQueen turned to Lia.

'So, anyway, tell me about Mrs Bolton and the missing millions,' he said, deliberately changing the subject.

Lia didn't need a second prompt, she'd been desperate to share her own burden and she quickly ran through the developments on the Bolton case.

'Now I know you didn't want to take this case,' she said.

'That's irrelevant, Lia, we're a team and we both made the decision to take the case, so just tell me where we are.'

Lia ran through her main doubts which centred around her fear Mary Bolton may well have stolen the money and she was using the McQueen agency to help to get her off.

'I know lawyers defend guilty people all the time, but that's not why I got into this,' she said. 'If she did take the money and her son is helping to concoct a story that will cast doubt in court, I don't want to be part of it. But I am already part of it because I gave a sworn statement to the police about Mary's supposed attack, and now I'm thinking there's a good chance it was all staged.'

McQueen was about to calm Lia's fears when there was an enormous crash from the other room and the sound of breaking glass. They both jumped up and ran through to see that Dan had fallen from his chair. The front window was smashed and a brick was lying in the centre of Dan's desk. McQueen rushed to what was left of the window in time to see the taillights of a motor scooter as it screamed out of the carpark, a black-clad male figure steering the weaving bike out onto the road.

'You okay?' Lia shouted at Dan as she ran over to help him up. She brushed some shards of glass from his hair. He didn't seem to be injured but was too shocked to answer. McQueen grabbed the desk phone and called the police, knowing it was a futile gesture but needing to make the report.

Lia had crossed to the brick, she leaned over it, being careful not to touch it. It was wrapped in white masking tape and there was a message scrawled on it in black. Lia read out what she could see.

'It says, "*Back Off*", and...' something else, smaller, she put her face even closer taking care not to put her hands on any glass so she could read aloud the words, '"*Petrol next time*".'

Twenty

'So tell me that again,' said Zach. 'I'm not sure I heard you properly.' He was holding his weekly strategy meeting with his inner team of three trusted followers, one of whom was Tania's partner, Richard. They were sitting amongst the plush, low couches and heavy coffee tables of the Belvedere hotel. It was a sombre, classy setting and felt a little like the kind of place where the aristocracy hang out after a day of shooting. There was even an open hearth with its pile of unlit logs. It wasn't cold enough for a fire but the display was there to tell you that should there be a sudden arctic snap, the hotel had you covered. It was all part of the atmosphere the Belvedere was striving to promote, comfortable Yorkshire country living. Zach had chosen the venue for its hushed gravitas and the sense the only people who would have meetings here were serious people.

Although he'd said these informal business meetings were a platform to share future strategy, these weren't open discussions about the direction the group was taking, they were essentially Zach telling the others what was happening next. Typically, arrangements for upcoming live meetings were laid out along with the associated roles and responsibilities for the team. It wasn't a forum for questions other than clarification of specific practical details, anything more searching or involved was quickly 'parked for now' and then never returned to. The three-man team had quickly learned not to bother asking those kinds of questions.

The weekly get-togethers were a chance for Zach to give extremely vague progress reports on when the move to the farm in Senby was going to happen. Richard had been waiting for his moment and when Zach finally mentioned Senby, Richard had politely interrupted to share the wonderful news that he would not only be bringing his partner along to the farm, but also an unborn child, or a new-born baby, depending on when the move actually happened.

On hearing this Zach had stopped moving, his froth-filled coffee cup was halfway to his lips and he asked Richard to repeat himself. Joey and Brice, the other two team members said absolutely nothing, but they turned their attention to Richard like automated security cameras.

Richard had been excited to have something fresh to tell Zach. He thought he'd be impressed that he was thinking so far ahead, that he had put the group at the forefront of his future life plans, but now sensing a change in the atmosphere Richard stumbled a little.

'Well, Zach, I know your vision, we all know your vision, or at least I know the outline of the vision you

The McQueen Legacy

have shared with us so far and I know our mission to is to make a new template for the future. To set an example through our actions and surely—'

'Let me stop you there,' said Zach, and an icy blast no roaring fire could have helped with seemed to swirl around the table. 'Were you under the mistaken impression we are setting up some kind of baby-factory hippy commune?' It was said with no apparent bitterness or sarcasm and Zach's face was completely blank so there was no way for Richard to read the reaction. He hoped it was Zach's attempt at a joke and so tried to laugh it off.

'No, I don't look good in a kaftan and I don't eat lentils,' he chuckled but he was the only one laughing. Becoming serious he added, 'But what is this better future we're building if it's not for the children we bring into it?'

Zach put down his cup and leaned forward, his elbows on his knees, his hands clasped together.

'Richard, have you gone mad?' Zach was staring straight at him along with Joey and Brice whose expressionless faces hardly masked the fact they were curious to see how this interaction was going to pan out.

'Have you not listened to anything I've said?'

'Yes, but—'

'This is not a game of happy families, Richard. We have serious work to do, probably the most serious work you have ever done in your whole life and it will take everything we have. There will be painful sacrifices. Your partner, Tania?'

'Yes?'

'Since that first time, she doesn't even come to the meetings anymore does she?'

'Er, no but—'

'But that's okay, that's what I saw in you, Richard. Even though you got no support from her you kept on coming. But she didn't return because she is not committed. And do you know why she isn't committed? It's because she is one of those people who has had it all handed to her on a plate. She does not know your pain. She doesn't know what it's like to struggle like you have, she hasn't faced the barriers you have and so it's easy for her to think life can go on as it is.'

'Women are like that,' said Brice with a shrug, 'sneaky.' Richard flashed a glance at Zach but the statement went unchallenged. Richard didn't know much about Brice except that he lived on his own. Next to him on the over-stuffed sofa, Joey was nodding in agreement. It was then that Richard allowed himself to acknowledge something he had noticed but had chosen to ignore, the audience at the most recent popular meeting had been ninety nine percent men. There had been women at the early meetings but just like Tania they had slowly dropped away, it must have been something about the atmosphere, something which was undetectable to Richard. Numerically it didn't matter, their seats were easily filled by eager young men.

Richard had so many conflicting emotions but there was no escaping he'd felt Zach's disapproval like a physical slap across his face. This was a club he'd found that seemed to understand and encourage him, and the idea they might no longer want him was too much to bear. Maybe Zach was right? Life had not been easy recently and maybe it was down to Tania? She did have that superior attitude, always criticising. She was money obsessed and never slow to point out her salary was what paid the rent.

Richard looked at the stone-cold faces in front of him. He could see it now, he'd made a misjudgement but it might not be too late, the door might still be open. At that point all thoughts of Tania and their child were no longer relevant, the only thing Richard wanted was to be back in favour with Zach.

Zach's dark eyes took it all in, the distress in Richard's face, the hunching of the shoulders and the desperation displayed in the light covering of sweat on his brow. Zach saw himself as a scientist observing an experiment, he liked to change the variables just to see the effect, to learn and use again.

'This may be my fault,' he said, softening his tone. 'I may not have been clear with you and if that was my mistake then I apologise, but I will be clear now. There will be no children, no wives, girlfriends or partners coming along for the ride. Every single person who joins us at Senby will be there to dedicate themselves to our purpose.'

There was a moment of silence between the four of them, no one daring to ask what the purpose might be.

'So, are you still up for this, Richard?' asked Zach.

'Absolutely.'

Zach now had a broad grin, which looked oddly out

of place but the others followed suit, the visual signal had been given they were all friends again now.

'I'm so pleased to hear that because you should know we have to kill anyone who wants to leave, especially anyone with your level of inside knowledge,' Zach said, grinning. Joey grinned, Brice grinned, and even Richard managed to grin because this was clearly a joke, wasn't it? It was like the standard old cliché: *I could tell you a secret, but I'd have to kill you afterwards.*

'Now, Richard, I have a personal question for you,' Zach continued with the grin toned down to a joyless smile. 'Who controls the finances in your house, you or her?' Richard swallowed hard and blinked. This was an area that left him feeling extremely uncomfortable. 'Don't be shy,' coaxed Zach, 'we've all got each other's backs here. No secrets. So is it you or Tania?'

This line of questioning had caught Richard completely off-guard and he found himself floundering.

'Well, er, I mean, it's only money. It's all shared but Tania works in banking.'

'I know.'

'And so I leave a lot of the complicated finance stuff to her.'

Zach nodded. The smile had completely dissolved away.

Like many great performers the blankness in Zach's face worked as an unreadable canvas where his audience was able to project their own interpretation of what he might be thinking. At that moment Richard was seeing implied criticism and it was causing him pain.

The McQueen Legacy

'You might want to think about that,' said Zach. He sat back on his sofa and finally got around to sipping his coffee. 'Going forward, I have some excellent advisors, legal, financial, who could help you by the way, if you need them.' And then like the turning of a page on a wind-blown book he addressed all three of them again,

'Okay, let's make sure we have everything set up for Saturday's meeting. Have you background checked all the registered names, Brice?'

'Yes, only one rejected, a local journalist.'

'Good work. We don't need nosey tattletales lurking around. We have nothing to hide but when they find nothing, they make things up, and it's always negative, because that's how the establishment works. Am I right?' They all murmured their agreement. 'And did you see a Doctor McQueen on the list?' Brice frowned and then scrabbled with the sheet of paper he'd been holding.

'No? I don't think there was a McQueen? Wait, isn't that the guy who came to the last meeting? I wanted to reject him because he's a private detective, but you said to let him come and then you met with him afterwards?'

'Yes, because you didn't look deeply enough. Sure he's a private eye but it's just a side-hustle, he's also a very well-respected forensic psychologist. He has quite a profile, he's been on TV numerous times, he could be very valuable to our image.'

'But maybe he's investigating us?' ventured Brice.

'True, maybe that's what enticed him in to visit us but once he saw our vision he couldn't help but be seduced.' Zach was smiling again, a sign to the others everything was going to be alright. 'And the great news is that Doctor McQueen has actually asked to join our group. I'm considering his request because I think he could add some weight to our public profile. I also think he could be valuable to us, give us some professional guidance on making our messages even more persuasive.' There were no questions asked, but the faces Zach was studying didn't look convinced. 'You do know that Disney, the biggest mind manipulators in history, employ psychologists? Every film, every song, every cute little cartoon creature has to pass through the approval of a team of psychologists? Did you know that?'

Brice was shaking his head, 'Really?'

'Why do you think grown men cry when they see some of those films. People come out of the cinema feeling uplifted, happy, and ready to spend money. Do you think that's an accident?'

Zach's intuitive sensors were telling him one of the team was not fully engaged and he needed to nip that in the bud as soon as possible.

'Richard?' He said it sharply, Richard had been staring into space but quickly snapped back into the room.

'Yes?'

'Saturday. The meeting. Are you okay to take care of front of stage again? Just in case we get any troublesome hecklers?'

'Sure. Absolutely. One hundred percent.'

'Good, good. Because as I've said before, any time someone like me steps forward with new and radical ideas for change that are seen as a threat to the establishment, there will be dissenters. There will be people who will try to raise doubts. You guys have faced it all your lives. Every time you came up with a better way of doing something, there was some moron waiting to shout you down. Am I right?'

The three men once again nodded in agreement.

'And if we get a trouble maker,' said Joey reciting from memory the procedure, 'me and Brice come off the door and we quietly and politely, so as not to disturb the meeting, escort them off the premises.' He smiled, proud to have got the wording right.

'That's right,' confirmed Zach, 'you get them away from the hall, off to the carpark, *and* if you should happen to kick the living shit out of them on that journey to their car then it will only serve to remind them to stay away next time.'

'Got it,' said Brice and Joey in unison. It was a second later and almost imperceivably more quietly that Richard also added, 'Got it.'.

It was such a subtle difference but nothing ever went unnoticed by Zach, every flinch and twitch was always noted and mentally catalogued. He was a spider noticing the change in air current caused by the beating wing of a doomed moth seconds before it hits the web.

Twenty-One

On the carpark's CCTV footage, McQueen and Lia watched the grainy moving image of the motor scooter weaving as it approached their building. The rider got off, took a brick from inside his jacket, lobbed it, and then jumped back on his bike. They'd scrutinised the video at least fifty times but there wasn't much to see. The thrower was dressed in black and was wearing a full-face helmet and the bike's registration plates had been covered.

'I can't believe how old school that is,' said Lia. 'I mean in these days of anonymous online trolls and digital threats, the old brick through the window is almost retro.'

'Yeah, quaint and if we had decent double glazing it would have probably bounced off. Mind you he knew which window to hit, there might be something in that?'

The police had arrived later in the day, they'd taken the brick away in an evidence bag, snapped some photos and McQueen had sent them a link to the CCTV video. They'd said they didn't hold out much hope of finding the culprit but they dutifully went through the official checklist. No one had actually been hurt so McQueen could see the incident was already being considered as low priority.

The insurance company's emergency repair team had replaced the glass and Lia and McQueen had swept up all the debris. It had not been a good morning for Dan, a brick bouncing across your desk followed by a shower of glass was an upsetting office experience but McQueen refrained from letting him know if he stuck with the McQueen Agency he was likely to see a lot worse. Instead, he had sent Dan home to change his clothes and recuperate. As a responsible boss he'd also asked Lia if she needed to take some time. She hadn't answered, simply arched her brow and given him the withering look you give anyone who insults you.

'Okay, fair enough,' he mumbled. 'So, the question is who wants us to back off? Would have been nice if they'd signed it.'

'Well, obviously, could be Summertown Industries? Maybe they've heard we've taken on the case and they don't want us to help defend Mary Bolton? They want the trial to go through smoothly and they don't want us to dig up dirt on them?'

'Yep. Could be.'

'Or it could be Mary Bolton herself, or her son, because they want to add to their victimisation story and give the false impression that Summertown are evil?'

'Yep.'

Lia pointed towards the filing cabinet in the corner of the room that held the old case notes.

'Or could be any of those people or their families? Revenge from someone we've convicted?'

McQueen shook his head, 'Nah, unlikely, "*back off*" sounds current. If it had been "*I'll get you back*", then maybe.'

'Okay,' said Lia, 'what about on your side? Could it be this cult you're dabbling with?'

The idea he was dabbling made him smile.

'Again, unlikely at the moment, they are trying to recruit me not push me away, unless it's someone within the group who doesn't want me to join?'

Lia cocked her head to one side and McQueen remembered he hadn't updated her on the way the case had been going. He quickly ran through the outline and how he'd attended the live meeting and finished by saying he wasn't sure where it was going, but that the client was getting impatient.

'And don't forget,' said Lia holding up a finger to make the point, 'there's still Tracey's message about the stabbing.'

'You mean as in, *don't investigate the killing of my ex, back off*? Could be, I suppose, nothing should be dismissed but that's certainly not her on the bike.' He nodded in the direction of the screen which had a frozen image of the motor scooter disappearing out of the carpark. Lia shrugged.

'It's not that hard to find a kid who will throw a brick for twenty quid. The rider doesn't have to be involved with the underlying reason.'

'You're right about that. It's the wild west out there on some of those estates and there's always a brick-for-hire.' They both smiled.

'So what's our tactics? What do we do?' she asked.

'We just carry on doing what we're doing. We stay on

The McQueen Legacy

our guard but we ignore the threats.'

'Including the petrol threat?'

'What else can we do other than put a guard outside twenty-four hours a day? It's a nice idea but something we don't have the budget for. Anyway, I'm not going to let a little old-fashioned intimidation spoil my day, Lia, so I'm choosing to ignore it. However, I can't insist on the same level of blind pig-headedness from you. If you want to spend more time out of the office and work from home then I'll understand. In fact, it might be a good idea until we get some idea of what's going on.'

'Thanks, but my guess is if they come with a petrol bomb it will be at night,' she answered. 'They probably want to scare us not murder us, and I'll be sure to be away from here before it gets dark. Anyway, that's just a precaution because I think it's an empty threat.'

'I hope you're right because our insurance premium just took a nasty leap up for next year.' They looked at each other and silently agreed the subject was closed, they were both already bored of it.

'Anyway, what's your next step with Mary Bolton?'

'Not sure. She's been getting quite demanding actually, keeps ringing me to tell me what I should be doing next. '

'Nice. I love a bit of micro-management by a client.'

'Yeah, and there was that other stuff she'd been finding out about me, she knew Carl's name and about his job and neither of us had mentioned it. But it was almost like it was the softest of threats but a threat none the less, like, *I know all about you and I know where you live so don't cross me* type thing.'

'I agree, it was strange.'

'Yes, and meanwhile Carl's gone as far as he can with the financial records He saw possible evidence of money laundering, but nothing he could swear to in court. He'd get ripped apart by a real forensic accountant, but there are faint clues. So what do you think?'

'My advice? Have you thought about sitting down with Mary and having a real heart-to-heart? Just lay it all out on the table, all your suspicions, what's the worst that can happen, she fires you?'

'Well that's exactly what I did. I went back and even had a biscuit and a cup of tea but it was all a bit soft from me, she ran rings round me, so maybe you're right, maybe it's time to give her a bit of a grilling. I just wanted to get your opinion in case I was missing something obvious.'

'Of course, we could still walk away. Charge her nothing and tell her we've decided the case isn't for us?'

Lia was shaking her head.

'Not my style,' she said. 'Besides I'm not saying she's guilty and if she is completely innocent, I would be abandoning her and that's exactly what Summertown Industries would want. No, I want to know for sure before I let it go.'

'Okay, it's your call,' said McQueen. 'Do you want me to come along with you to speak to her?'

Lia bristled at the suggestion.

'To keep an eye on me, you mean?' she asked.

'Not at all. I thought it might help to good-cop bad-cop her. You could be the friendly face who's keen to help her and I could be the grumpy agency boss asking all the tricky questions?'

'Thanks,' she said, 'but I'd like to see this through myself. Mary and I have built a relationship and I don't want to ruin the dynamic.'

In truth Lia knew what he was suggesting was probably a good idea but her pride would not allow her to let him bail her out. She'd handle it, she was sure about that.

'And what about you, what's your next step?' she asked.

'With the cult? What I need to do is really drill-down on Zach Lindley. There's no way he can have appeared from nowhere, there must be a trail somewhere. My main focus is trying to find out what the scam is. That has to be the key to it. How is he going to make money from his devoted followers? Once I know that, I'll be able to give a clearer picture to Tania.'

'Yeah, I guess if he was in America he'd have registered as a religion so he didn't have to pay tax.'

'I think Zach keeps it all purposely vague and non-specific so he can't be pinned down. He keeps pushing all the right buttons as far as his followers are concerned but there has to be a way to break through that.'

'And what about Intrusive? Are you going to do anything about her?'

'No, not unless she comes back or sends me any more messages. I've told the police everything I know, the knife and what she said, it's up to them now. Far be it from me to interfere in a police investigation.'

They both laughed at this, almost everything they'd done in the past had been seen as interference by the police, right up until the criminals were put in prison.

They both stood up and crossed over to the new window still dirty with the fitter's finger marks to look down on the carpark.

'Do you think Dan will be back?' asked Lia.

'I hope so, he's been pretty good. As you know, the last office manager I had was so bad I had to promote her to investigator.' He turned to see her face. 'I hope she's not regretting it?'

'I'm not,' she answered quietly, 'but I'm not so sure about my boyfriend. In fact, I might not tell him about today's window action, so y'know, if you happen to speak to him maybe don't mention it?' McQueen stayed quiet. He was in no position to give relationship advice. His ex-wife had never come to terms with what she saw as the ridiculous career he'd chosen for himself so he knew the kind of questions Lia was probably facing. Sensing the downward drift of the conversation, McQueen clapped his hands loudly and turned away from the tarmac view.

'Finding people, that's what private investigators are supposed to be good at, so I need to find Zach Lindley before he was Zach Lindley.' He was just crossing to his office when his phone buzzed in his pocket. He took it out, saw the name and this time without hesitation answered it. Lia couldn't help hearing the one-sided conversation.

'Hi, Tania, I was going to— Okay. What do you mean he didn't come home? Two nights ago? Have you contacted the police?' The call went on a little while longer and then eventually it finished with McQueen promising to pay a visit.

Lia had got the gist of it, but when he'd ended the call

he said, 'Looks like we've got a missing person case now. Tania's partner, Richard, went to meet his colleagues in the group two nights ago and he hasn't been seen since.'

'I heard you mention the police?'

'Yes, they wanted to leave it for forty-eight hours of course, he's a grown man but now they've spoken to Lindley. Apparently he admits he saw Richard in The Belvedere Hotel for a business meeting along with two of his other associates. Loads of witnesses so he couldn't really deny it but then Richard left and that was the last time anyone saw him. Meanwhile the joint bank account has been emptied.'

'Sounds like he's done a runner. What does Tania think? Has he done this kind of thing before?'

'Tania? As you'd expect she's very emotional and she's probably not thinking very clearly at the moment.'

'And?' repeated Lia. 'What's her instinct? She knows this guy better than anyone, where does she think he's gone? What's her take on it?'

'Her take on it? Oh, she's fairly sure she knows exactly what's happened. She thinks Zach Lindley's evil cult has taken her partner and killed him. That's her take.'

The office door swung open and both Lia and McQueen gasped and jumped in surprise, betraying how on-edge they were both feeling. It wasn't a petrol bomber. Dan walked in, smiling in clean clothes and hair looking like it had been recently washed.

'Dan, mate, I thought you'd take the rest of the day at least,' said McQueen. Lia had already given him a hug.

'Oh no, way too much to do. Nice window,' he said

pointing at the new glass.

'Listen, it was a difficult morning and—'

'Nonsense,' answered Dan. 'You must be joking, it's the most exciting thing that's ever happened in any office I've ever been in. I don't want to lose this job,' he added, 'so I wanted to get back before you hired a temp.' He'd already sat back at his computer and was tapping away.

Lia looked at McQueen and shrugged with a smile.

'I think he might have passed the induction test,' she said.

Twenty-Two

McQueen and Tracey Bingham were sitting on their favourite bench as her dog, Charlie, once again failed to bring the tennis ball back to them. He was never keen on the dirty old ball that had become hairy with use and McQueen often wondered why Tracey even bothered with it. He wasn't interested in chasing sticks either. Food, however, was a different matter and the rustle of the treats bag would bring him galloping back in seconds.

'Do you ever get nostalgic for those relaxing days of academia before you ever became a private eye?' It wasn't the kind of question Tracey normally came up with, she was usually all business with barely a wasted word for deeper thoughts. He was a little taken aback.

'No, why do you ask?'

'I just wondered if you might get sentimental from time to time and hanker for the times when people weren't trying to threaten, intimidate, or kill you?'

He sniggered.

'I never get sentimental, Tracey, nostalgia can be

dangerous, you know?'

'How's that?'

'I don't want to be the boring psychologist but did you know many years ago nostalgia was actually considered to be a mental disease?'

'Really?'

'Yeah, and not only that, it was thought it could be fatal. They believed you could actually die from nostalgia.'

'Amazing.'

'And now it's been watered down and sanitised and it's just another way to sell records and T-shirts. Nostalgia has been given a face-lift and monetised.'

'You're boring me,' she said good naturedly.

'In answer to your real question, no, I wouldn't have my life any other way. You're not making an impact and you're not saying anything in this world unless someone somewhere wants you to shut up. But seeing as you brought it up, what about you, Detective Bingham? Is this what this is about? Do you ever wish you'd taken a different direction than joining the police?'

'No, no, never. Like yours, the job has its challenges but I love it.'

Charlie had wandered off to stalk a couple who were walking past hand in hand, probably in the hope they had snacks, so Tracey called him back. Slowly he returned and McQueen leaned down and patted his huge solid Labrador flank and rubbed his ears.

'Obviously, you must know about the brick through the window?' he said.

'Of course I do and I spoke to the lab last night so I can

tell you they haven't even looked at that famous brick yet. There's a backlog of serious crime evidence to work through and I think yours is fairly low down the list.' She saw his expression. 'A window got smashed but no one died.'

'I get it,' he said.

'Meanwhile, a few of us have had a look at the video footage but no one recognised the person on the bike. So, in short, nothing to report.'

'I didn't think there would be.'

'And as for Judy Greene and the stabbing of her ex, I only sent you that warning text because I thought you should know.'

'Yes, thanks.'

'I'm not working that case, but from what I hear from my colleagues they aren't even going to interview Judy.'

'Really? Did you tell them about the knife in the bag and she mentioned possibly visiting him?'

'Of course, but as I said before lots of people buy kitchen knives. Anyway, they've got a hot suspect, someone from the half-way house who had a nasty argument with Paul Mason in front of five witnesses. This guy's got a history of drug abuse and violence and frankly they don't want to muddy the water with other less obvious options.'

'You mean they don't want to waste their time?'

'I'm afraid that's how police work goes sometimes, pick the most likely path and stick to it.'

'Okay, well to be honest, even though it's because they can't be bothered, they are probably right. I never really saw Judy as a stabber. She's a bit messed up and she wanted to shake me up and let me know she hasn't forgotten me or how she thinks I ruined her life, but it's a huge leap to see her as a murderer.'

Tracey checked her watch, as usual she had somewhere more important to be, so she snapped the lead onto Charlie's collar and pointed to her car visible in the carpark.

'Gotta go.'

As they walked back McQueen said, 'The name Zach Lindley, ring any bells?'

She shook her head. 'Should it?'

'He's some kind of YouTube guru a lot of people are interested in but what I want to know is where was he and what was he doing before he was offering easy answers to lost souls on the internet.'

'And as far as the law is concerned, because as you know that's my only focus, what's he done wrong?'

'Nothing. Yet. But he was the last to see a man who has now gone missing and that man is the partner of a client.' Tracey was fussing with Charlie and clearly wasn't interested.

'What about you?' she asked completely changing the subject as she bundled Charlie into the car. 'Staying away from the booze?'

'So far.'

'Even when the brick arrived by special delivery?'

'Especially when that happened. Mind you, it was pretty early in the morning.'

Tracey placed a hand on his shoulder, patted it as if he was Charlie and then gave it a long squeeze. It was a touch that said everything she couldn't articulate about how much she wanted him to stay safe. McQueen nodded to let her know the message had been received.

'You too,' he said.

On her drive back to get changed for work something was nagging away at Tracey about the name McQueen had asked her about, Zach Lindley. She'd said she didn't recognise it but on reflection it had stirred something familiar in her memory. She was good with names, at any social gathering she only needed to be introduced once to the guests and she could generally remember everyone's names the next day. If anyone told her about their siblings who weren't even there, she'd remember them too. Sophie, Tracey's partner saw it as a superpower due to the fact she could never remember what anyone was called thirty seconds after being told the name.

With McQueen, she'd dismissed Lindley out of hand because she was distracted, but now in the quiet of the car it suddenly came back to her. It was Detective Chambers, her colleague, who'd said the name. A few days before he'd been at his desk with a small group of three other male officers crowded around his screen. They were watching something and laughing, and she'd definitely heard Chambers say, 'Mr Zach Lindley, telling it like it is as usual.' There was some whooping and agreement from the others. When she'd shouted over to ask what they were doing the group mumbled and dispersed and Chambers had said, 'Oh, nothing.'

She was used to not being included in the boys' club and thought it might have been something pornographic they'd been watching, in which case she wasn't bothered by the snub. It had crossed her mind at the time to search the name to see what it was all about, but then she'd decided it wasn't worth the effort. It was a decision she felt she might have to revise now McQueen had mentioned something about a missing person.

Twenty-Three

Maggie was an old friend of McQueen's. They'd met at university but professionally she was also the therapist who had helped him to navigate his darkest moments. He'd suffered flashbacks and waking nightmares after almost being killed by a psychopath. Asking for help had been a big deal for him, after all he was a psychologist and it felt like a small defeat, but when the adage 'physician heal thyself' hadn't cut it, he had finally turned to Maggie.

Before Maggie, he'd gone to his GP about the flashbacks, long before covid, back when you could actually get an appointment with a live human.

'Have you had any suicidal thoughts?' The doctor's eyes had been focused on the computer screen rather than him, her fingers impatiently curved, ready to clatter down onto her keyboard. She'd probably glanced at his medical notes but she hadn't bothered to ask him what he did for a living. He hadn't told her he'd been on the other side of this conversation himself a few times. He was very tempted to joke with her and say of course he'd had those thoughts, everyone had them, didn't they? The noose? Everybody imagined the noose, didn't they? Everyone knew where all the pills were hoarded, where the nearest tall building or silent river was? But he could see she had no sense of humour so instead he simply said *no*.

Her fingers dropped as she click-clacked his two-letter response and there it was, he was officially not at risk. 'But I was in a terrifying life and death situation and I keep getting these flashbacks and nightmares.' In the end, she had prescribed him a drug called Doxazosin for the nightmares, he knew what this was and that it was usually prescribed for high blood pressure or prostate problems and he'd never bothered to collect it from the pharmacy.

Maggie didn't like to use the label PTSD, she saw it as an unhelpful way to lump a group of disparate symptoms into one hugely daunting disease which then had to be overcome. *A mental health mountain*, as she liked to call it. Her approach was much more about breaking down the problems into individual manageable chunks. Her talking therapy was centred around facing the awful memories that were causing the issues with honesty, and then letting them go. Easier said than done, but it had helped McQueen and after a while the terrifying dreams had subsided. He'd stopped attending the sessions when he felt he'd made enough progress, but now the dreams were back.

The therapist was a busy woman, demand for mental healing was high these days, so sitting in the intimate gloom of the living room of his flat, McQueen rang her number at the pre-arranged time. After the initial welcomes and niceties McQueen pushed on, not wanting to waste a single second.

'Listen, I'm thinking I might need some sessions again, but as I mentioned in the text there's something specific I want to ask you about first.'

'Okay.'

'Erm, as usual, I've got a few things playing on my mind, Maggie, it's the nature of the job I suppose. One of the issues has resurfaced as a result of something that happened twenty-odd years ago. I don't want to get into it now because I've had time to come to terms with it, but I also have this more recent thing that's been eating away at me. I think it might be what's fuelling the dreams. It's even pushed me close to taking a drink, and you know how much I want to avoid that.'

Maggie left a silence until he continued.

'There was this guy, a psychopathic serial killer called Patrick Sutton. You may remember the case? It was in the news a lot about eight months ago?'

'I remember it,' said Maggie.

'Anyway, I won't go into the details but the point is I could have stopped him sooner. If I had acted faster with the information I had at the time, I could have prevented him from killing his last victim.' Again there was a crackling silence on the line. 'That's what really gets to me,' he continued, 'because I know he had a wife and kids and right now they are in a living nightmare with no husband or father all because I dithered.'

'And how does that make you feel?'

'Not great. In fact, terrible. I've been replaying it over and over in my dreams. It's always the same thing, I'm in my office, I make the call, I present my evidence and the police grab him. I feel huge relief and then it all comes crashing down. I wake up and that's not what happened.'

'But I thought you did help to catch him?'

'But it was too late by then.'

'And what do you want to do about it now?'

'The only positive thing I can think to do is to meet his widow and apologise and ask for her forgiveness.'

McQueen had expected Maggie to agree that owning up to his failing, facing it head on and apologising in an honest way was the right way to go, but he was wrong.

'How will that help her?'

'Her? Well, she'll know the truth.'

'And how will it help this grieving woman? Are you bringing her justice? She already has justice, Patrick Sutton is in prison. Have you thought that perhaps you might make things worse for her?'

'How? How could it be worse, her husband is dead?'

'Think of the things that torture you, McQueen. We've talked about this before. Isn't it the thoughts of the things that could have been prevented, that didn't need to happen which cause you the most pain? Isn't it ruminations on what might have been that are the hardest to take? Right now this poor woman knows a maniac killed her husband, that's hard enough to accept let alone some private investigator thinks he could have saved him.'

Maggie couldn't see it but McQueen was nodding into the phone.

'So you're saying I'm being selfish?' he asked.

'I didn't say that.'

'No, but you're saying that by baring my soul and trying

to make myself feel better I could open up a new avenue of hurt for this bereaved woman and her family? You're saying ignorance is bliss, or at least in this case ignorance is slightly less painful.'

'Take a step back. You're crystal balling, McQueen. The truth is no one knows what might or might not have happened in some other chain of events. Who's to say that by accusing Sutton you might have sparked a panic reaction where he went on a rampage and killed several people? Perhaps by taking your time you saved lives? And think of the lives that were saved when you did stop him.'

McQueen snorted into the phone.

'You can laugh,' she said, 'but my point is that it is impossible to know what might have happened. All we can work with is what *actually* happened, and far less of it was within your control than you think. Thinking it was in your control is just arrogance on your part.'

'Arrogance? Is this your tough love? So where does that leave me, arrogantly struggling with guilt for the rest of my life?'

'Earlier on you said you wanted to ask his wife for her forgiveness but don't you think that's placing an unfair burden on her?'

McQueen hesitated. 'Yes, I see that now. I've been self-obsessed and you're right I hadn't thought through the impact it might have on the family.'

'Meanwhile, McQueen, I think it's time for you to be a little kinder to yourself. You need to work on forgiving yourself for not being able to save them all.'

Twenty-Four

Dan was alone in the office, he enjoyed the quiet when the other two weren't there yelling into their phones or smashing away at their keyboards. He liked both his colleagues, especially Lia, but he was a man who preferred complete silence to concentrate on his work. There was no distracting background music playing so when the security entry system buzzed it was almost deafening. Dan checked the screen and his breath caught in his throat. It was the woman, the woman who had visited McQueen before, the one who according to McQueen had brought a knife.

'Hello?' she said, squinting into the door camera.

'Hello, how can I help you?'

'Can you let me in? I'm here to see Doctor McQueen.'

'I'm sorry, he's not in the office at the moment.'

'Oh, right. How long will he be?'

'All day,' he lied. 'I don't expect him back today at all.'

'Ah, right. Can I leave a note for him?'

'Yes, of course, put it into the letterbox on the right and—'

'No, I mean can I come up and write a note for him? I

The McQueen Legacy

don't have a pen, or paper.' She was smiling in a very friendly way and Dan couldn't help thinking that she looked harmless. Something about her hair and the shape of her face reminded him of his mother.

'Hello?' she said again. 'Are you still there?'

'Yes, it's just it's against corporate procedure to allow clients into the office area when the principals are not in attendance.' He was panicking a little and knew how ridiculous this sounded even as he said it.

'Principals? What are you talking about? All I want is to write a short note, it's good news, something your boss will want to see. What's the problem?'

'There's no problem. It's just we had a certain security breach situation earlier in the week. A glazing thing and we have certain protocols to adhere to.'

'Whatever, listen, one short note and I'll be out of your hair. I mean I don't really want to wait out here all day.'

He could have stonewalled and played the "only following orders" card, but for some reason he didn't. She was just a middle-aged woman who wanted to leave a message, how bad could it be? He pressed the door entry and a minute later Judy Greene was at his desk. Seeing her in the flesh he remembered the same coat and bag over her shoulder from her previous visit. With a jolt, he realised this was the bag that might contain a knife. Up close she looked a lot less like his mother.

She took the pen he offered her and the blank piece of printer paper and leaning over in front of him started writing. As she did, without looking up she said, 'Do you know who you work for?'

'McQueen? Yes, of course.'

'Clever man, isn't he? Do you admire him?'

'I suppose so. I'm new here and I'm only the admin guy, I deal with the paperwork, I don't really get involved with any of the cases.' She looked up from her writing and as she did the bag swung round in front of her.

'Did he tell you what he did to me?' This was said quite aggressively and Dan was already regretting letting her in.

'No.'

'I went to him as a frightened young mother and he gave me some of his *expert psychology advice*. Did he tell you that?'

'No.'

'My husband had been saying he was scared he might kill our baby but McQueen told me I had absolutely nothing to worry about. Can you imagine?'

'No, I can't.'

'And I admired McQueen, he was my lecturer, I thought he was a god, that he was so clever he knew everything and so, of course, I believed him. And then my husband did it. Yes, he killed Katie.'

Dan was frozen. The woman wasn't crying or shouting, she was almost serene, which was somehow worse.

'That's terrible,' he managed to say. 'I'm so sorry.' There were things he wanted to say in McQueen's defence but he didn't want to antagonise her. 'That must have been awful for you. I don't know how you've managed.'

Sometimes people soften when shown sympathy, but Judy Greene remained unmoved. She'd heard enough pitying declarations of sorrow from people who couldn't possibly know her pain to last her a lifetime. She folded the note she'd written and placed it in front of Dan and carefully put the pen next to it.

'One piece of good news is that my ex-husband, the murdering bastard, is dead. It doesn't bring Katie back, but it makes me feel better. If we lived in a country with the death penalty he would have been dead years ago, but we're too civilised for that, aren't we? Too forgiving.'

Dan didn't know what to say, but he watched closely as Judy's hand slipped into her bag.

'You know what they say in Texas?' she asked. 'They say a dead child murderer doesn't reoffend. I like that. Do you want to see something?' She didn't wait for him to reply she quickly pulled something from her bag and Dan couldn't help flinching, when he saw a flash of metal. He eased back in his seat ready to run but then realised it wasn't a knife she was holding, it was silver a framed photograph. 'That's Katie,' she said, showing him the picture. 'Three weeks old.'

'She looks lovely,' said Dan, not knowing if that was the right response.

'She was. And your boss, your *precious* Doctor McQueen, promised me she would be safe.'

Dan couldn't help himself, 'I'm sure he thought she would be?' he ventured. 'I'm sure he didn't want any harm to come to her?'

'You're sure, are you?' she spat. 'And what good does that do me?'

She put the photo back in the bag. 'I wanted you to know that's who you work for. That's the kind of man he is. A fraud and a liar. Why would you want to work for a man like that? Maybe now you know, it's time to look for another job.'

She was staring at Dan and he wasn't sure if this was some kind of masked threat. Was it *get another job or else?*

He stared back at her but said nothing. It was like a minefield anything he said might be the thing she didn't want to hear.

At last she broke the gaze and turned away for the door.

'Make sure he gets that note,' she said over her shoulder.

Once she'd left Dan quickly got up from his desk to make sure the security door had closed properly behind her. He followed her on the CCTV as she crossed the carpark, got into a car and drove away. He looked at the note on his desk and even though it had McQueen's name written on it his curiosity was too powerful. He saw most of McQueen's business emails anyway so how was this different? He opened the folded paper.

Congratulations, McQueen. You are the only one left with Katie's blood on your hands.

Twenty-Five

No matter how innocent Mary's motivation might be, Sekalyia felt as if the older woman had been giving her the run around from the very start. From the moment she'd disturbed the house intruder, Lia had been on the back foot, reacting and trying to catch up and Mary had kept the boat rocking with constant calls and texts. Now it was time for Lia to get ahead of the game and try to take some control. The first part of her plan was to turn up at Mary's house unannounced to catch her off-guard and not give her any chance to prepare her story.

Lia rang the doorbell and thirty seconds later Mary opened it, her look of surprise was exactly what Lia had been aiming for.

'Oh. I didn't know you were coming around? I wasn't expecting you today, Lia.'

'No, sorry, but I was in the area and I thought I'd drop by. Can I come in?'

Mary hesitated slightly and then stepped back into the hall leaving the door open behind her for Lia. She followed her into the living room and the older woman seemed a little flustered.

'Can I get you something—' but Lia politely cut her off.

'Don't worry, Mary, no tea, coffee, or biscuits required today, thanks,' she said making it sound as if she was doing Mary a favour. Mary took the over-stuffed winged armchair and Lia sank into the sofa which faced the TV across the room.

'Is this about the text I sent you this morning?'

Lia couldn't even remember what the text had said, she'd become so weary of Mary's messages she could hardly bring herself to read them.

'No, this is about some of the questions I have.'

'Okay.'

'Mary, do you understand that for this relationship to work, there has to be trust?'

Mary laughed.

'Are we getting married?' Lia saw this was how Mary was going to try to retake control of the conversation, by laughing off anything that might be challenging, so she had to close that down quickly.

'You can laugh if you want to, Mary, but it's your backside that could end up parked on a prison bench not mine. A woman of your age, let's be honest, it could be a death sentence.' Mary couldn't miss the tone and stopped smiling. 'You want us to do the best job we can and to help you. For us to do that, we need to know everything.'

'You do know everything, I've told you it all. And you saw for yourself how low Summertown will go to make sure I take the blame.'

Lia was ready to play good-cop bad-cop without bad-cop McQueen even being there.

'Frankly, Mary, my boss—'

'McQueen?'

'Yes, my boss has never been convinced about this case and he's really putting me under pressure. Understandably, he doesn't want the agency's reputation to be jeopardised if it turns out you did steal the money.' Lia had expected Mary to be outraged by this suggestion but she didn't bat an eyelid, so Lia pressed on. 'He thinks the scene I witnessed with the intruder might have been staged. McQueen even said perhaps it could have been set-up by you and your son to implicate Summertown. You know, paint them in as bad a light as possible and muddy the water, as you call it?'

'Does he?' was all Mary said.

'Yes, he also has suspicions about the financial records, cash coming in, cash going out, and cash that seems to disappear.'

'And what about you, Sekalyia, what do you think?'

'I'm on your side, Mary, I'm with you, but I need something reassuring to tell him.'

'Do you think I wanted to be choked? You came in when I was being strangled. Well that's what you said in your statement to the police, anyway. Are you now saying you were lying to them?'

Lia was no expert but from what she could remember the cardigan had been quite loosely wrapped around Mary's throat. It didn't mean it hadn't been tighter moments before, but it wasn't life threatening when she'd seen it.

'Look, what does it matter to you, anyway?' said Mary. 'If I get off, you'll get paid. I thought McQueen was running a business?'

'Mary, I'm putting my neck on the line for you so I'm going to ask you directly, is there anything I should know?'

'No.'

'Did you have anything at all to do with missing money?'

'No.'

'Did you have anything to do with staging that home invasion?'

'No.'

All of Mary's negative answers had been delivered with a steady, clear voice, she had never broken eye contact with Lia and she hadn't shuffled in her seat or hesitated once. Either she was telling the truth or she was a confident liar committed to her story.

'Do you believe me, Lia?'

Lia's eyes flicked down for a second to the pad on her lap and the notes she'd made. She looked back up again at Mary's expectant face.

'Yes, Mary, I do, like I said, I'm on your side.'

The sound of the front door opening echoed along the hallway and both women's heads swivelled to face the open living room doorway. Lia felt an irrational pang of fear and her heart began racing. A moment later they were facing a young man in a dark hoody.

'Chris, this is Sekalyia, she's from the private detective agency who are helping my lawyers,' said Mary then she turned to Lia. 'This is my son, Chris.'

Managing to swallow down her initial nerves Lia stood up, moved towards him and extended her hand. They briefly shook hands, his hand cold from outside felt rough but Lia wasn't as interested in the welcome as much as she was in trying to assess if she had met this man before on the doorstep. He was the right height, he was solidly built, and he was wearing a hoody, but it wasn't enough to make a definite connection.

He looked slightly uncomfortable and he was scowling at his mother.

'You didn't tell me you were having a visitor, Mother. I like to be warned about stuff like that.'

'Oh, that's my fault,' said Lia. 'I dropped in as I was passing by.'

'Really. That was thoughtful of you. And how's it going? When are you going to get these ridiculous charges dropped?'

Lia smiled sweetly. 'We're working on it.'

'My mum has never stolen anything in her life.' He seemed to be getting quite angry and he was pointing a finger inches from Lia's face. 'What you've got here is a big, corrupt company looking for a scapegoat. They chose the oldest employee 'cuz they thought she'd be the easiest to frame. It's sick. It's absolutely sick is what it is. They are a bunch of crooks.'

'Oh, Chris,' said Mary gently, 'it's not Lia's fault.' But Lia had not been phased by his onslaught, her mind was still on her job.

'What do you know about them?' she asked. 'Summertown Industries? What makes you think they're crooks?'

'Well you're supposed to be the private investigator but

it's pretty bloody obvious, isn't it? Two mill goes missing so they try to pin it on an innocent old woman. Then they send someone round to strangle her, and the police still haven't found the guy. That wasn't just a burglary, it was an attempted murder. The police ain't done nothing. Useless.'

He had taken his finger away from Lia's face but he was still swaying angrily from foot to foot. If it was an act then he was doing a good job of coming across as the concerned son. He appeared to be highly agitated and he was struggling to contain the energy. Lia could imagine that in the right circumstances he could easily be a violent person. However, it was true the police had not been able to track down Mary's attacker. They hadn't had much to go on but it was easy to see why Chris might think they were dragging their heels.

'Yeah, you're right, they can be slow. Where were you that morning?' Lia asked as casually as possible.

'What?'

'I mean if you'd turned up instead of me, big lad like you it might have been a different story?'

'You're damn right about that. I'd have killed them.'

'So, where were you?' Lia gently pressed. 'Your mum told me you're looking for work at the moment?' For a few seconds Chris didn't answer and then Mary spoke for him.

'He was at the gym,' said Mary. 'He goes every morning.'

Chris nodded, 'Yep, gym.'

'Oh, that's amazing, good for you. I've been going to the gym recently as well,' she said with her friendliest smile, 'but I'm thinking of changing mine, it's getting very crowded. Can't get on the machines. Which one do you go to?'

Chris looked at her and narrowed his eyes, she could almost see the cogs turning as various scenarios ran through his mind. This time Mary didn't offer an answer. Eventually he said, 'Big Guns, Rocastle Street.' Lia wrote it on her pad.

'Thanks, might give them a try,' she said. Gyms usually had signing in procedures. Guessing her possible motive he added, 'It's good there because they know me through my old contacts so I don't need to sign in or anything, I come and go as I please.'

Lia could see she wasn't going to get anything useful out of either of them now so she turned to pick up her bag.

'How's the head?' asked Chris, the hint of a smirk on his lips.

'Pardon?'

'Mum said you took a whack on the head when you were at the door and the guy ran out?' Unconsciously, Lia's hand flew to her wound, which was now completely healed but still tingled at her touch.

'It's fine,' she replied.

'Glad to hear it. You were lucky, really. Could've been a lot worse. People can die from a single blow to the head.'

Lia tucked her pad into her bag then draped it over her shoulder. She was about to say he sounded like her boyfriend, but the thought of bringing any mention of Carl into this particular conversation repulsed her. Instead, with a smile she said, 'I'll remember that.' She nodded goodbye to Mary who had become strangely passive ever since her son had arrived, and then left.

Twenty-Six

McQueen had turned off the main road and was now bouncing along a pothole-infested private track that took a dog-leg left behind an overgrown hedge and then headed up an incline into a field. With every violent dip the car took he winced at the thought of his poor old suspension. He didn't know a lot about cars but he knew the springs weren't designed for this kind of punishment. This was a route meant for country-born tractors not city-bred saloon cars.

He edged forward but started to think he'd got the wrong road because all he could see in front of him was the narrow track with an expanse of scrubby grass on either side. Weaving to dodge the worst of the craters he ventured on until, after about two hundred metres, the horizon dropped away revealing a large valley and the roofs of several farm buildings at the bottom. He stopped the car to try to take it all in and then, knowing he didn't have the kind of mind that could retain landscapes or views, he took a picture with his phone.

Feeling slightly relieved he had found it, he drove on down to the concrete courtyard of the main farmhouse and stopped next to a heavily dented four-wheel drive vehicle. Standing outside the house, arms folded waiting for him, was Zach Lindley.

The conversation he'd had with Tania had not been easy. Richard had been missing for a week and a half with not a clue as to where he might be. The police had taken note of the missing money and seemed to have decided he was an adult who didn't want to be found. When Tania had tearfully explained it was especially difficult for her because she had recently discovered she was pregnant, the two male officers had exchanged a *well-there-you-go* look.

The police had the power to demand to see the CCTV footage from the Belvedere and any other cameras on the route away from the hotel but they hadn't done it. McQueen rang Tracey Bingham to ask her off the record why it hadn't been followed up.

'I'm not on that case, McQueen, but I would guess it's a resource issue,' she had said. 'It takes a lot of time and effort to obtain videos in the first place, there are a lot of privacy issues to address, especially for a hotel. Then it takes hours to review the recordings. Frankly there's only one way this guy Richard is going to warrant that kind of work.'

'You mean if his body turns up somewhere and it looks like murder?'

'Exactly.'

Although McQueen didn't have the same reach as the police, he had gone through all the usual steps he took when searching for a missing person but had also drawn a blank. What he could say was that it didn't look as if Richard had left the country, at least not using his own name. He also hadn't shown up in any hospital yet. The best lead was still his last meeting with Zach.

After his initial lack of useful feedback on Zach's group and now his inability to magically produce Richard from behind a glittering curtain, Tania had lost faith in McQueen. She didn't go as far as to say he was fired, what she actually said was given the output she would find it very hard to justify paying him. It sounded to McQueen like the kind of line used by someone who works in finance. If he'd wanted to be an arse about it, McQueen could have pointed out that as stated in the original contract the McQueen Agency was not a "no win no fee" operation, private investigators are paid for the hours they put in not their results, but he didn't say that, he let it go. She was very upset and he didn't really care about the money because this had turned into an investigation which had intrigued him more than anything he'd worked on in ages.

Like a journalist chasing a local human-interest story that has the potential to be a huge national event, McQueen wanted to get to the bottom of the Zach Lindley phenomenon. The man seemed to have tapped into something fundamental, although McQueen couldn't see exactly what is was. It was an illusion with no substance, a tantalising mirage in the desert that draws you towards it and then disappears when you finally get there. Or perhaps it sucks you down into deadly quicksand. The disappearance of Richard could mark a new phase, though.

If it was connected to Lindley's group then it might be the first indication of something more sinister than mere online hate-baiting.

There was only one way to find out more about what was going on which was to get closer to Zach Lindley and the best way to do that was to join the group. McQueen had left a message for Lindley through his website and then a few hours later the guru had rung him back.

'Zach, I've been thinking about your offer to join you?'

'Yes?'

'I've watched a lot of your videos now and it's all starting to make sense.'

'Good.'

'But before I make any kind of commitment there's something I'd like to know.'

'Okay.'

'There's a lot of talk about the whole group moving to a farm near Senby?'

'That's right.'

'I need to know if that's real or is just a carrot being dangled to make people think there is more to this than the odd meeting?' It was a provocative question aimed at opening him up but it also had the potential to put him on the defensive.

'It's real,' answered Zach without hesitation.

'Obviously, I have a certain professional reputation as a respected psychologist.' He didn't mention his reputation as a private investigator, Zach surely knew about that but McQueen didn't want to highlight it, he also didn't want to give the slightest hint he was interested in the whereabouts of Richard. 'And I wouldn't want my name associated with something that turned out to be a pipedream and—'

'Come and see it.'

This took McQueen by surprise.

'Pardon?'

'I'm inviting you to come and visit the site and see for yourself how real it is. Very few people have seen it yet, I wanted it to be fully ready before I made it public, but this is how much I value your participation, McQueen. I'm willing to give you a sneak preview, to show you what you can be part of.'

It was more than McQueen could have hoped for. Trying not to sound too eager he accepted the invitation; the arrangements were made, the directions were sent, and two days later he was bumping along the track.

'That track is pretty challenging,' McQueen said climbing out of his car.

'Yes, I'm not aiming for easy access,' said Zach. 'I'll give you a quick tour, you can touch the walls and see how real they are.'

McQueen had been on working farms before but this one clearly hadn't been doing much work for a few years. There were a number of brick-built out buildings including an old milking shed with its concrete flooring and cow sized cubicles as well as a partially caved in roof. There were big empty barns that had probably housed winter feed and other buildings one of which held a rusty old tractor. The farm certainly existed but McQueen couldn't imagine what it was going to become. They finished the tour with a walk

The McQueen Legacy

through an old orchard and out onto one of the fields.

'That's the boundary,' said Zach pointing to a line of trees in the distance. 'And on this side,' he said turning around, 'is a river. So we're pretty secluded and it's going to be easy to manage who comes and goes.'

'And are you going to farm here?' It seemed like a perfectly reasonable question given what he had been shown.

'God no,' answered Zach, 'this is about cultivating minds not crops.'

They walked back to the main courtyard but Zach didn't invite him into the house, instead they stood out by the cars.

'So what's the plan, Zach, I see a disused farm but what would I be joining exactly?'

'The living quarters aren't ready yet,' he swung his arm to indicate the dilapidated buildings. 'So initially we will have a tented village.'

'Like an army camp?'

'And then as the refurbishment is completed we will move in.'

'Who's doing the work, have you lined up some builders?'

'We have experts among our number.'

'And what about everyone else, what will the rest of the group be doing?'

'Learning, growing, and preparing.'

'Preparing for what?'

For the first time Zach smiled.

'You haven't joined us yet. All will be revealed.'

It wasn't an answer at all but McQueen could see he

wasn't going to get any more than that.

'Psychology is everything to me,' said Zach, standing now as he did when he was on stage but this time his only audience was McQueen. 'Because the greatest miracle in this world of miracles is the human mind. It elevated us above every other animal on the planet and so being able to understand and harness its power is the most important thing imaginable. You, Doctor McQueen, have studied the criminal mind and your insights and teachings can be invaluable to our group. I cannot tell you more than that for now, because it could jeopardise our purpose, but what I am saying is we need you.'

McQueen was leaning against his car trying to judge whether there was any opportunity to steer the conversation towards Richard's disappearance, but it was no good, it would be too obvious and clumsy.

'All this refurbishment and setting up the tents is going to cost a lot of money, how are we funding it?' He had deliberately used *we* to try to mark his inclusion. Again, Zach smiled.

'Okay, there are things I can't tell you yet, but as a gesture of trust there are some things I will share with you,' he said. 'I've told you before there is no one who reads people better than me, so I will tell you about you.'

'Go ahead.'

Zach was pacing again. 'You first looked at us in your capacity as a private detective because someone asked you to check up on us. Then, when you had seen the videos, you started to see there was something there. There was truth and sense in what I was saying. Then you came to the meeting, you saw how invested our followers were and you were impressed. That's when I showed we are a serious group because we'd done our research, and we knew who you were. More than that, I asked you to join us and it planted a seed. It's been growing inside you, the feeling you could be part of something much bigger, more meaningful something that could make your whole life and career worthwhile. It could be your legacy. Chasing adulterers in the dead of night is beneath you, McQueen, and you know it. We are building something here that will make a change, it will be monumental and you can be part of it.'

McQueen didn't know what to say. He wasn't going to ask his only real question again, *what the hell are you up to?* because he knew he wasn't going to get an answer.

'All this refurbishment, all the tents, all the food, the practicalities, this is all going to cost money, right? And who owns this farm anyway?' For a second, McQueen imagined a befuddled old farmer locked in the farm house behind Zach that he hadn't been allowed inside. Zach was studying him, head cocked to the side.

'I know what you want to know,' he said. 'You want to know when I'm going to ask you for money. When I'm going to rip off the people who come to the meetings.'

McQueen caught out fumbled.

'No, I... I just wonder how this is going to be funded?'

'I'm going to tell you this and I hope it goes no further. Think about it, McQueen, the people who come to my meetings have no money, that's partly *why* they come. They are the disenfranchised, the losers who have been fighting the system all their lives and getting beaten down by it. I don't want their money, I don't want your money. I am a very wealthy man, McQueen. In another life I made enough money that it became meaningless. I still make money without even trying. In answer to your question, I own this farm. I was the one who donated it. I will be paying for the refurbishment. I am doing this because I believe I have found a way to turn society on its head. What I am offering you is the chance to be part of a movement that changes the world for the better. In one hundred years, when everyone you know is dead, you will still be remembered for your contribution. *That* will be your legacy, McQueen.'

Twenty-Seven

This time McQueen had invited Dan to the Italian for lunch along with Lia. It meant they'd had to pull another small table over to their usual table for two but the waiter was happy to do it for such regular customers. McQueen felt it was important to keep a team vibe between the three of them and he didn't want Dan to think he was being left out or was considered to be less important to the agency. Office resentments are easy to ignite and difficult to douse, so he felt it was better to try to head them off before they started. However, at Dan's insistence on the table in front of them was the office mobile phone where any incoming calls would be diverted.

For a change, McQueen had ordered pasta, he hadn't been bothering with food much at home so he thought this lunch might see him through for the day. Dan had copied his order, but Lia had stayed with her usual salad.

'Tell us about this Zach Lindley thing,' said Lia after the plates had been served.

'Yeah, a lot of my mates have been watching those videos,' added Dan. 'He's got some interesting things to say.

One of them had even signed up to go to a meeting.'

McQueen stared for a few seconds at his steaming pasta before answering.

'How can I explain this?' he started. 'Let me see. I suppose I'd start with Zach's interest in psychology. Now, some people believe the only purpose of psychology is manipulation. For instance, we all know the big supermarket chains use all kinds of manipulative tricks to make us buy more. They entice us towards impulse buys, from the sweets near the tills to the way they price their goods to make them look like bargains. You know? Such as meal deals where you end up with a packet of crisps you didn't want. In fact, almost every sales message you ever see anywhere has some element of buyers' psychology in it. And it works, punters can be manipulated. Zach is one of those, he thinks if he gets the persuasion right he can influence anyone.'

'So, what's he selling?' asked Lia, but McQueen hadn't finished his explanation.

'I don't want to put you off your lunch but have you ever heard of zombie ants?' Both Lia and Dan shook their heads.

'Okay, here comes a short boring nature lesson, my apologies to David Attenborough. In the tropical rainforests there's a fungus called Ophiocordyceps but people usually just call it Cordyceps. Like all living things it wants to reproduce in the most suitable place possible, and for the fungus that's the damp forest floor. But the problem is it doesn't have legs, so it chooses something that does as a mode of transport. It infects an ant. It doesn't just ride on the ant, because the ant might not go where it wants to go, so it gets into its brain and takes the ant over and makes it do what it wants it to do.'

'Hence zombie ants?' asked Dan, who had stopped eating, his fork poised over his food.

'Exactly. It changes the ant's behaviour. Left to its own devices the ant wants to stay nice and cosy in its nest with its mates and maybe sometimes go out to forage for food. The fungus says no, you're going to leave the nest, go down to the forest floor, find a leaf and use your jaws to attach yourself to it, where I will send out my spores.'

'So, are you saying that Lindley sees himself as cordyceps? He wants a bunch of zombie ants?' asked Lia.

'Kind of. I do think he sees psychology as merely a tool to control people. I think it's a game to him, to see how far he can push it. At first I didn't really understand why he was interested in recruiting me, I thought perhaps it was to use my name and reputation, but now I'm starting to think he sees me as the ultimate challenge. I know that sounds a bit big-headed but if he can manipulate a person who is supposed to be an expert in the field of criminal psychology, then surely he can control anyone?'

'What about the guy who's gone missing?' asked Lia.

'Richard? Yes, as you know that's how I got into this in the first place. I was asked by his partner to find out if this was a dangerous cult and maybe it is. Perhaps Richard found the danger before I could see it and warn him.'

'What's your plan?' asked Lia.

'I'm going to let Zach believe I'm going along with his ideas, that I'm enthralled and then once I get closer to the group I can find out if there is any connection to Richard's disappearance. He met with them on the day he went missing but they say he left in a happy, motivated mood. That's what they told the police, anyway.'

Dan was picking at his spaghetti, the mental image of fugus-infested ants still too clear in his mind.

'And what do the police think?'

'They think he's done a runner from his pregnant wife.'

'Right, and so far you haven't got any other clues?' he asked.

'No, but I have found something out. Something that blows one of my previous theories out of the water. I was sure that like ninety-nine percent of these things — this whole thing — was a scam to fleece his followers for money so I'd been trying to trace Zach Lindley's back story, where he'd come from, what he'd been doing before he burst onto the scene. I was searching for a low-level con man with a criminal history but it turns out I was looking in the wrong places. It transpires he was a highly successful hedge fund manager who went by the name of Gavin Cooper. He is very, very wealthy and then about a year ago, he took on this new Zach Lindley persona and started flooding the internet with his videos.'

'Why,' asked Dan. 'If you've got all that money, why would you bother?'

Lia grunted dismissively

'What else do very rich people do when they've exhausted all other options? When they've done all the cars, boats, houses, and private islands?' she said. 'I guess they find ways to amuse themselves by messing with other people's lives?'

'It's a good point,' said McQueen. 'Have you heard of anhedonia?' Dan shook his head. 'Sorry if this is turning into a lesson but anhedonia can sometimes be part of depression, it's the inability to feel pleasure in anything at all. They feel nothing. It can sometimes lead sufferers to seek out increasingly more dangerous thrills to try to feel more alive.'

'And would starting a cult fit that category?'

'It might do. Anyway, that's where it is,' said McQueen. 'I'm going to keep developing my ties with Zach Lindley and his group, or cult, or army, or whatever it is until I can get to the bottom of what he's up to. I'm also going to try to find out anything I can about the missing man. I'm doing it for me and it's not going to be a paying job, but that's what I'm doing.' The other two nodded agreement. That was the beauty of being the boss, no matter how uncommercial or ill-advised a decision he made, there was no one to tell him not to.

'Now, enough about me, Dan,' he said. 'Any more contact with Judy?'

'No, nothing.'

When McQueen had returned to work later on the day Judy Greene had been to the office, Dan had hurriedly told him what had happened and handed him the note she'd left. McQueen read the words that congratulated him on being the only one left with blood on his hands, sighed, and folded the note again.

'Did you read it?' he asked Dan who nodded sheepishly.

'I thought it might have been something urgent and I might need to call the police or something and—'

McQueen held up his hand to stop him.

'It's okay, Dan, I would have read it too in your position especially after she'd been there. And you're right, for all you knew it might have said there was a bomb outside.' Then, knowing Dan must have questions he might not be entirely comfortable asking, McQueen told him the full Judy Greene story from the very start; the advice he'd given Judy, her unstable husband, and the tragic outcome. Dan started to say he thought the fault clearly lay with the deranged husband but McQueen held up his hand again.

'Thank you, I appreciate your support but I only told you all this so you could know the facts and make your own mind up about the blood on my hands.'

The restaurant was busy now so they were all conscious to keep their voices down. It probably wasn't the smartest idea to discuss their business in a room of strangers but the informal setting was something McQueen valued.

'Lia? How about your case, what's the latest?'

'I tried to throw the old woman a curveball by turning up unexpectedly at her house. I didn't hold back, I confronted her head on with some blunt questions and told her how sceptical and suspicious my horrible boss is about her story. At the same time I showed her how much I was behind her and how she could trust and confide in me.'

'And?'

'She remained rock solid. Her answers were the same and she never wavered. Also, I met her son. He came in when I was there. As you'd expect, he came across as angry and pissed off we haven't cleared his mother yet.'

'And could he have been the guy who pushed you over?'

Lia shrugged.

'Could be. Right height, right size, but that's not narrowing it down much.'

The couple on the next table seemed to have slowed down their meal, they weren't talking much and McQueen could tell they were probably listening in to the entertainment that his table was providing.

'Okay,' he said. 'Let's save this for later and just eat our food and talk about our hobbies for a while.' Dan and Lia both frowned not understanding why the conversation was taking this turn but they got it when McQueen motioned his head towards the next table. 'Not sure how data protection legislation feels about chatting in restaurants, but I'm sure it's probably a no-no.'

'Yeah,' said Dan. 'I did some online learning courses in my last place about the GDPR Act 2018. There are some scary fines in there, that's for sure, but I don't remember there being a module on talking about clients in Italian restaurants.'

After they had finished their lunch and they were leaving, McQueen whispered to Lia.

'I had a thought. You said the son has been living in Spain? Might be worth trying to find out what he was doing out there?'

'I had the same thought,' she said. 'Maybe he came back with a money problem?'

'Back to Bank of Mum for a cash injection?'

'I'll look into it.'

They were walking now back towards the office.

'But you still believe her?'

'I think so,' said Lia. 'At least I want to, anyway. And by the way, she tried to give me a big bundle of cash. I didn't take it but she said you'd want it. So believe her or not after what you just told us, this is the only paying job we've got at the moment, and Mary Bolton has certainly got the money.'

'That's what worries me,' he answered quietly.

Twenty-Eight

Sitting in the impressive waiting area of the head office of Summertown Industries, Lia couldn't help feeling slightly intimidated. It was partly the surroundings and partly knowing what she was about to face. There were several expensive low-level leather couches arranged around a black marble coffee table casually displaying an artfully spread selection of glossy company magazines. Summertown Industries presented as the industrial equivalent of a rock star. There were also a couple of laser-engraved industry awards made from solid lumps of crystal glass sparkling away. On the seats opposite her a couple of men in smart suits were nervously talking through their pitch in hushed tones. She heard the older one talking.

'You keep your mouth shut unless they challenge the numbers, that's when you step in.' It made Lia wish she had Carl with her. He had briefed her on some of the anomalies he'd spotted in the Summertown spreadsheets, but if any of that came up she knew she would be way out of her depth and she really didn't want to look like a fool.

She had never expected them to agree to meet her when

she'd made the speculative call, so when they had invited her to come to their office, she'd been surprised, but not so shocked that she didn't agree immediately.

A young woman came out and ushered the two salesmen through the inner doors and Lia found herself muttering "good luck" under her breath. It was as much for her as the two guys. Eventually the same young woman came back.

'Sekalyia Campbell?' as if there was a chance the only person left waiting might not be her.

'Yep,' said Lia standing up and straightening her jacket. As a last action she turned her phone off before dropping it into her bag.

She was taken along a corridor until they reached a door labelled 'Boardroom' and she was shown in. On the other side of the huge oval table were three men. The first introduced himself.

'Hello, Sekalyia, my name is David Hutchinson, I'm the HR Director here at Summertown Industries. This is Phil James, he's our company lawyer, and Mr Shelley here is one of our security staff.'

If she had been feeling intimidated before this was a show of power designed to move that feeling up a notch.

'Well thank you for meeting with me, Mr Hutchinson. As I said on the phone, I'm Sekalyia Campbell and I work for the McQueen Agency—'

'We know exactly who you are,' said Hutchinson, 'you see we have private investigators of our own, Ms Campbell. They work under the guidance of Mr Shelley.' He nodded towards the man on his right who had the obligatory

The McQueen Legacy

security officer's shaved head and thick neck. 'So you'll be surprised how much we do know.' The trick when faced with a difficult audience was supposed to be to bring them down to size by imagining them in their underwear. It had never worked for Lia, so she had her own technique of diminishing them. There was baldy on the left with no imagination and the need to look tough. On the other side was the lawyer who must have been forty but was still clinging to the same spiky hair do he'd probably had as a teenager, even though it was now mostly grey and thinning at the top. And in the middle there was Mr HR who looked like a frog. Not his fault he was ugly, but he'd probably been over compensating for it all his working life.

'Right,' said Lia, deciding right there and then not to be intimidated by these corporate stooges. There was something about situations like this which brought out the best in her. Very early in her school days she had learned not to give an inch to bullies. It was all about attitude, bullies look for weakness, they are drawn to it like flies to jam, if the jam turns out to have chilli powder in it, they don't come back.

'I'm flattered by your attention,' she said, 'but it does make me wonder why you would go to that effort and expense?'

'It's our job to do everything in our power to protect the company's interests. Your client, Mary Bolton, stole a considerable amount of money from us—'

'Allegedly,' butted in Lia, 'you haven't proven that yet.'

'Oh, but we will and we have to set an example to any other would-be thieves that no crime will be tolerated in this company. Mrs Bolton has hired a legal representative well known to us, and I might add notorious in the criminal fraternity, along with you and your boss to fight the case. So be it, but we will match fire with fire.'

The aging teenage lawyer took over with a slightly softer tone.

'What we are hoping to get from this meeting today, Sekalyia, is to impress upon you how hopeless Mrs Bolton's case is. If you are a professional with integrity you will then feed this back to Mrs Bolton and advise her the best option is to plead guilty. Then, if we get our money back we will not push for a custodial sentence. That's the best we can do.'

'That's interesting,' said Lia, 'because Mary has already passed on to us extensive financial records—'

'She should not have taken those from the building, and we demand their return immediately.' This was the lawyer again, and Lia got the impression he was showing off his stern voice for the benefit of other two. Lia ignored his demand and carried on.

'Those records seem to show unusually large amounts of unaccounted cash coming into the business and then mysteriously leaving again. Mary says, and is willing to testify, she made a personal note of cash transactions she had been asked to keep off the official books. Any thoughts on that?'

The three men stared at her without answering.

'And I know you'd like the memory stick back, but how far would you go to get it? Far enough to send someone round to her house to steal it? And I'm sure you'd like her to shut up, but how much? Enough to have someone try to strangle her?' She was looking now at Shelley, the shiny-headed security guy who was looking at her from beneath his Neanderthal brow.

'Are you accusing us of something, Ms Campbell?' asked the lawyer. 'Because you should be very careful about slanderous accusations.'

'No, of course not, but while we're on the subject and as you said you know exactly who I am and where I work, were you aware that a brick telling us to back off came through our window and landed on my desk recently? I was just wondering if any of this sounded familiar to you?'

She studied the bullet-headed security grunt, if anyone knew about brick throwing it would be him. His face remained impassive.

'Now,' she continued, 'you told me what you hoped to get from this meeting and I'll tell you what *I'd* like to get out of it. I'd like you to see this case is going to make a bigger stink than Summertown Industries can afford to have. We are *not* going to back off. If *you* are professionals with integrity, I'd like you to feed that back to the people who make the decisions, because it certainly isn't you three, and advise them it would be in their best interests to drop all the charges and move on. And that's the best *I* can do.' The men exchanged a look. She'd taken a couple of shots so it was time for them to hit back, so Lia braced herself

'I'm sure you know about her son?' asked Shelley in a London accent so thick it was hard to understand. 'The right charmer of a drug dealer? Recently been released from a Spanish jail? Ow's that going to look in court? Are you sure the doting mother wants all that dragged up?'

'And it will come out,' added the lawyer. 'He is part of her motive and her need for money so he will have to be put under the spotlight.'

Lia tried not to show any surprise but she was kicking herself she hadn't done her research on Chris yet. If what they were saying was true she should have known it going in.

'Okay,' said Hutchinson, 'that's it. You asked for a meeting and we gave you one. Let the record show we have been fully cooperative and open. As we've said, go back to your client and advise her the least messy and damaging route for her will be to plead guilty and we will do what we can to minimise the punishment.'

Lia had already stood up and gathered her bag.

'Thank you so much for finding the time to meet with me,' she said. 'And as *I* said, go back to your bosses and tell them the least messy and damaging route for their precious corporate image and brand is to drop all charges.' She turned to leave but then stopped and turned back.

'You think you are the big dogs in this fight,' she added. 'You think you are powerful enough to crush a single old woman to cover your losses and then sweep it under the carpet. Shall I tell you who the real big dogs are? These dogs are slow moving but their jaws are strong enough to bite through the steel and concrete of any business.'

There was silence in the room and Lia let it hang for a couple of seconds.

'Is that supposed to be you and McQueen?' smirked Hutchinson.

'No. HMRC,' she said. 'Yep, His Majesty's ol' taxman

loves the smell of dodgy books and cash that might indicate money laundering. They love that stuff, and once they get their teeth in, they never let go.'

Once she was outside and walking across the carpark, Lia let out a huge breath. It was a confrontation that had taken her right back to the playground. Of course, it wasn't the same schoolyard content, the school battles had been centred on such trivial things she couldn't even remember them now, but there had been the same hateful emotional force directed at her. Fortunately, this time she hadn't ended up with her hair pulled or her knees grazed. She wasn't sure where she'd got the HMRC stuff from, she'd been winging it, perhaps it was something Carl had mentioned but wherever she'd dredged it up from it seemed to have touched a nerve. All three of the men's faces had frozen at the mention. She'd also been stretching the truth a little when she'd said Mary was willing to testify about the off-the book cash payments. Mary had only mentioned them in passing and hadn't wanted to get into detail, but it wasn't really a lie because Lia felt she could be convinced to speak up in court once the risk of jail became real.

As she approached her car she saw next to hers was a black Audi and in it were the two salesmen she'd seen in the waiting area. She couldn't hear what they were saying but they didn't look happy. The older one was aggressively tapping his finger on the steering wheel and he seemed to be berating the younger guy. She wondered what McQueen would be saying now if he'd been in her meeting. She hadn't really gained much and she'd maybe shown too much of her own hand. She'd allowed her pride and anger to drag her into a verbal boxing match when she should have remained cool and calculating. However, she had learned they intended to use Mary's son, Chris, and his dark past if it ever got to trial so she knew she needed to get up to speed on that as soon as she could.

As she pulled out of her space, the two in the Audi were still picking apart their own presumably disastrous meeting. Probably a sale lost and a bonus missed. Not for the first time she thanked the lord she didn't work in sales, the private eye game might have its challenges, but the need to make people buy things they don't want wasn't one of them.

Twenty-Nine

Dan rolled into the carpark good and early, parked in his usual spot and then took his phone from the cradle to answer a message from his mother. She was always texting him first thing in the morning but he knew even when the message came at eight, his mother had probably been up since five waiting to send it. Generally, it was about one of her impending medical appointments but sometimes it was simply to tell him about an offer not to be missed in the local supermarket. With his head bowed over his mobile, he didn't notice the figure approaching his passenger side but he looked up as the door suddenly opened. Before he could speak a figure swung into the seat beside him. He couldn't quite compute what was happening but Judy Greene, wearing the same coat she'd had on when she'd visited the office and with the same bag on her lap, got into his car.

Dan had been told by McQueen the police were still investigating the murder of Judy's ex-husband and the only development had been two of the half-way house suspects had been eliminated from the inquiry, but there were still three left to grill. Judy was so far down the list that she still hadn't been spoken to by the police yet.

Dan's eyes were inevitably fixed on Judy's bag and the way her right hand was out of sight inside.

'Judy,' he said. 'What are you doing?'

'I realise you won't be letting me in there, anymore.' She glanced towards the office front door, and its prominently positioned security camera. 'I can't believe you still work there,' she said, staring forward out of the windscreen at the row of trees that lined the carpark. 'After what I told you, you still work for him.' She didn't sound angry or deranged, it was more disappointment he could hear in her voice. 'Did you give him my note?'

'Yes, I did.'

'What did he say?' Dan wasn't sure what she wanted to hear, what the right answer to this was. That McQueen had fallen to his knees crying and begging for her forgiveness? The truth was the note had prompted McQueen to explain the whole tragic story from the beginning, and that Dan had concluded McQueen had nothing to answer for.

'He didn't say anything,' he said choosing the most neutral response he could. She snorted in disgust.

'Sounds about right.' He looked at her sitting there after all these years of suffering and what he saw was a defeated and grief-stricken woman, about the same age as his own mother. He could see the pain that pulsed around her like an aura. Suddenly, he was no longer afraid of her. He knew that even if she had a knife in her bag she would never use it on him. He was an innocent, she would recognise that, he was certain.

'Who do you think stabbed your ex to death?' he asked.

The McQueen Legacy

It had leapt from his mouth before he'd had time to screen it, but she didn't seem shocked.

'A hero,' she said, and then she reached for the door handle.

'Wait.' She paused and looked at him. 'My name is Dan and any time you want to talk,' he added holding up his phone. She looked puzzled. He handed her the mobile. 'Please, put your number in, we don't have to meet in a carpark, we could go for a coffee?'

'Why?' she asked. 'So you can keep track of me for your boss?'

'No,' he replied. 'Because your story has touched me, and because I think you might need an ear.' She didn't look convinced but she did tap a number into his phone.

'Are you going to keep working for him?' she asked.

'Right now, I need the job,' he answered truthfully. Staring into the distance again she gave a little mirthless half smile.

'That's how they get you,' she said more to herself than him. 'It always comes down to money.' Her hand moved as she twisted in the seat towards the door and Dan saw the flash of the metal frame and realised it was the photograph of her daughter she'd been clutching. She pulled the catch but before she could get out Dan spoke.

'My mother lost a child.' Judy stopped still and looked at him, trying to judge if this was bullshit. 'My brother,' he added. 'Terrible accident. A homemade crib my father had built. David got his head stuck in the bars and choked. My mother never forgave my father. She tried, she tried really hard, but she never could. I know it's not the same as what you went through, but...'

Judy mumbled. 'I'm sorry, but it's not the same. That wasn't a deliberate murder,' and then she got out of the car. Before she shut the door she added, 'But thank you, Dan, for the number. You are too kind a person to be working here.'

He watched her walk down the carpark and get into her own car. She must have been sitting in it waiting for him to arrive and he hadn't noticed her when he'd driven in. He wondered for a second if she was going to sit there and wait to ambush McQueen, but after a minute her car started up and drove out.

His phone pinged with a message and his chest felt the tingle of anticipation — had he made a connection? But it was only his mother again. He checked it and smiled, apparently mangos were on offer for one day only.

Thirty

McQueen padded through to the kitchen in his bare feet, squinted at the clock that said five-thirty, and put the kettle on. He was out of pods for the fancy coffee machine but once he'd made himself a nasty cup of instant he headed back to bed. He stopped in the doorway for a second as something shuddered through his memory leaving a mild trace like a gust of wind crossing a corn field. It had been a while since he'd had to bring two cups back to the bedroom with him. Not since the loss of his previous partner, Emma Cullen, to the bullet of a psychopath's gun. With his free hand he touched his side which still bore the scar of the shot that had been intended to kill him, too. Everything changes but one silly thing he missed was sitting propped up on the pillows and discussing the day ahead with Emma.

Even though he always woke early, since he'd resumed his therapy sessions with Maggie, albeit only over the phone, McQueen had been sleeping much better and the disturbing dreams had mostly abated. Mostly. It was as if there was a pressure valve and by sharing his thoughts with her, the dreams escaped in a hiss of steam rather than having to force themselves to bubble up in his sleep.

And, of course, she had been right, there was nothing to be gained by bleating to Sutton's widow about how guilty he felt about the death of her husband. A killing he *might* have prevented although, in his mind, it would always be a killing he most certainly could have stopped.

He'd also not experienced any more cravings for alcohol, although like a shark circling its prey in dark waters, he knew it was out there waiting, endlessly patient, dead-eyed and hungry for his flesh. Some of the credit for his clarity was owed to his therapist but some of it was surely due to Zach Lindley. Since Tania had introduced him to this case, McQueen had thought of little else. It was like an ear-worm tune that drives you to distraction as you hum it for the millionth time. It was a puzzle with almost unlimited potential for harm. The man was a puzzle, the followers were puzzling and the purpose of the venture was a mystery. Was it all just a rich man's folly, an amusement for someone who had exhausted all other distractions? Would it all turn out to be a ridiculous waste of everyone's time once Zach had found something else and moved on? The farm had been interesting in that it existed, but it was still only a run-down farm. For all Zach's stated plans, it was a long way from being ready to house his supporters.

And now there was a missing person added into the mix, but why would Zach have disappeared one of his own loyal followers? It was much more likely Richard had decided to go away for a while and McQueen could see why the police had taken a similar view. Perhaps he'd found out that Tania had hired McQueen to investigate his relationship to the group and he'd felt it undermined him? After all, Zach's philosophy, whatever it turned out to be, was something he obviously felt very strongly about. McQueen had seen it before in other cases. A spouse confronted by irrefutable evidence of infidelity and lies would often try to turn the blame around. *You hired a private investigator? To follow me? How could you?*

McQueen was making his way to the shower when he heard his phone ring, so he quickly went back to the bedside table where it was charging. It was Tracey Bingham and as it was so early he knew it had to be important.

'First of all, McQueen, I am doing this as a favour but it will be the last. I can't be your personal police force. Understood?'

'Of course.'

'I know you have an interest in Farnham?'

McQueen had to think for a second before it clicked. 'Oh, wait, Richard Farnham?'

'Yes, the missing person. His partner is a client of yours, I believe?'

'Yes, yes, got it now. Any news? Has he been found?'

'I'm sorry to say a body has been found. Under some leaves in Stanmore Woods.'

'Let me guess, found by a dog walker?'

'Always the dog walkers. The body hasn't been formally identified yet, but off the record, based on the age, build, and clothes, we believe it to be Richard Farnham.'

McQueen had been hoping that for Tania's sake he was going to turn up chastened and apologetic but there had always been the chance the next time she saw him it would be on a mortuary table.

'Oh, damn. Has Tania been told?'

'Yes. She's being picked up to make the identification.'

'Any obvious signs of cause of death?'

'Too early to say.'

'But no knife sticking out of his chest or bullet hole through his head?'

'Too early to say.'

'And covered in leaves, unlikely to be suicide.'

'Too early to say.' This was Tracey telling him that, although she was prepared to let him know the main news, she wasn't about to give him all the details.

'So will you be going back for the CCTV now and pulling out all the stops? Hopefully the trail isn't too cold by now.'

'Look, McQueen, I'm only telling you about this because I know you were searching for him and now you can stop. Also, so you don't put your foot in it with his partner who is likely to be extremely distressed.'

'Me? Would I do that?' but Tracey had already hung up.

Thirty-One

When Lia got home and slammed the door behind her after meeting with the executives of Summertown Industries, she was bristling with anger. Driving back she'd gone over the encounter in her head hundreds of times and the replays resulted in the smooth edges of the civilised discussion being broken off leaving behind in her memory a sharp, spikey argument. As is always the way, her mind was full of the clever things she should have said and the ways she could have handled it better.

Once inside the flat, she took her immediate frustration out on Carl's breakfast things that were still on the kitchen island by throwing them into the dishwasher. 'Was that so hard?' she said to no one.

Carl wasn't home and she was glad about that, it wouldn't have been fair for him to take the brunt of her feelings for the bullies. Her doubts about Mary had evaporated in the face of her dislike of the three arseholes. It even crossed her mind that if Mary had stolen the money then good luck to her, but she quickly squashed that notion. A crime was a crime and she wasn't in the business of supporting criminals whoever they were.

It was the patronising dismissiveness which had annoyed her the most. They'd seen her as an easily-frightened woman who would run back to her client in tears and tell her to plead guilty. It was the way they'd assumed she was no more than a little girl who could be pushed to one side. She was aware she was possibly reading more into it than she should, it could simply have been three company execs doing their jobs, but Lia's interpretation had taken on a personal dimension. She'd never liked the "it's my job" get-out clause for professional cruelty. If someone is paying you to do something does that negate all moral responsibility?

She stood in the kitchen and forced herself to take some slow, deep breaths. She wasn't being professional, she knew that. She was allowing her emotions to influence her thinking which was not only childish, it could also be dangerous. Getting herself under control she opened her laptop and began doing what she should have done before going in, she started researching Chris Bolton.

Using the specialist database the McQueen Agency paid to access, it didn't take long to discover what Shelley the security guy had enjoyed telling her was true. Chris Bolton had recently been released from a Spanish prison after being convicted for drug offences. She looked at the stats, apparently there were about a hundred British nationals currently eating Spanish prison food and half of them were drug dealers. Chris Bolton had been living in Spain for three years before his lifestyle had eventually caught up with him. She looked at his mugshot, younger but the same sneer she'd seen when he'd been standing in the doorway complaining she hadn't had his mother's charges dropped yet.

The Summertown lawyer had been right, they would find a way to bring Chris into the trial to tarnish Mary's reputation and imply a motive — Mary Bolton, part of a criminal family, how could you trust her?

When Carl came home, Lia shut down the computer, waited until he'd got changed, and then handed him a glass of wine. She'd already started hers. She'd calmed down a lot by then and waited until he asked about the meeting before even mentioning it. He'd done a lot of really boring work on the spreadsheets so he was interested to know how that part of the discussion had gone.

As Lia took him through the details her anger began to rise again. The mental image of those faces was enough to do it. She ended up giving an impassioned blow-by-blow account that stressed how she'd given as good as she'd got. She thought Carl would be proud of the way she fought her corner and hadn't been dragged into a microscopic examination of the financials, but he didn't say anything other than the occasional raised eyebrow and sip of his wine. Seeing that something was amiss Lia stopped.

'What's wrong?' she asked.

'I forgot you were at that meeting today,' he said. 'So when your phone was turned off I rang the office. I worry, you know? Anyway, I spoke to the new guy, Dan?'

'Yeah?'

'He's a nice fella, we chatted a bit. Thinking I must already know about it he made some joke about a brick through a window. And then he told me what had happened.'

'Oh, that. It was nothing, Carl.'

'If it was nothing how come you didn't tell me about it?'

'*Because* it was nothing.'

'Has it occurred to you how dangerous this might be?'

'A brick?' She was being facetious, she knew full well what he was getting at. Fortunately, Dan didn't seem to have told Carl about Judy Greene turning up at the office with a knife in her bag.

'If Summertown Industries are a front for an international money laundering operation dealing in millions of pounds,' he saw Lia's eyes lift to the ceiling but carried on. 'I'm not saying they are, but *if* they are, it probably means links to organised crime and that means drugs. Which means there will be people involved who don't give a shit about other people's lives. Specifically, they won't care about your life, Lia. If you are getting in their way then it will make economic sense to remove you. If they have engineered this whole case against Mary Bolton to disguise a loss of a couple of million, and sent someone to choke her, then these are serious people.'

'Carl. I'm not stupid, don't you think I know that? But what am I supposed to do? Let her go to prison for something she didn't do? Besides, you worry too much.'

'And you don't worry enough.'

It had been a sore subject between them for a while. Carl had been clear in his desire for her to get a new job for a long time. It had come to a head after the incident in the carpark that had seen McQueen in hospital and Lia within inches of being shot herself. For her part, Lia had a clear idea of her career: do exciting things, don't get stuck in a job like Carl's where every day was the same round of bullshit meetings and pointless presentations. She'd never told Carl this, not even in their loudest arguments, but in a strange way he was her inspiration to stick at the McQueen Agency. Similarly, Lia was Carl's motivation to earn as much as possible without ever putting himself at risk of anything more dangerous than a missed promotion.

They both went into silent mode for a while as he prepared dinner. She knew what he was saying was out of love and concern for her but she couldn't let herself be stifled by someone else's worries. Eventually, as they ate the king prawn tacos, he broke the silence.

'So what does McQueen say?'

'McQueen's got his head buried in another case, some cult thing and I've told him I can handle this.'

'You can,' said Carl. 'Don't get the wrong idea, Lia. There's no doubt in my mind you are brilliant at what you do. That's not in question, but in future I want you to tell me everything, because it feels dishonest when I have to find stuff out. I know you're trying to protect me, but I just want you to be careful that's all.'

'Always,' she said with a smile. 'Super careful.'

Thirty-Two

Tania had wanted to meet but not at her house and not at McQueen's office, either. She wanted neutral ground so, between them, they had chosen the city of York again for their rendezvous. McQueen had suggested a few restaurants or some of the twee little tourist coffee shops but Tania had been clear she wanted to be outside away from people.

After walking in from the railway station and crossing the river, they went down some steps away from the bridge, past The Kings Arms pub that sat on the edge of the River Ouse and was famous for being flooded a couple of times every year. They walked in silence along the river and eventually plonked themselves on a bench over-looking the slow-moving water.

'Looks easy, doesn't it?' he said. He'd already told her how sorry he was for her loss when he'd met her at the station. It was the unimaginative and inadequate standard response to death, but what else can you say?

They both had cups of coffee in brown cardboard cups they'd picked up at the small cafe on the river bank.

'What does?' Her tone was flat.

The McQueen Legacy

'The river. It looks so calm as if you could easily swim across but several people drown every year trying. They're usually drunk, of course, but it's cold and deep and treacherous. They get cold-water shock or their feet snag on something below the surface. You'd never guess looking at it.'

'Bit like life,' she replied. 'Looks easy, but it isn't.'

He was sorry now he'd opened with a reference to drowning, it had been stupid but it was something he couldn't help thinking about when he was near deep water. It was one of his personal anxieties, the thought of swallowing water and not being able to breathe, of sinking and never being able to swim back up to the surface.

He wanted to know what the police had told Tania about Richard's murder, but he wanted to be sensitive in his approach, although sensitivities aside there was still a job to be done and things he needed to hear. But he didn't get a chance to ask, Tania had her own agenda.

'Do you even realise how badly you let me down?' she said anger flashing in her eyes. 'Do you have any idea? I asked you—*no*—I hired you and paid you to tell me if Richard was involved with a dangerous cult and you did nothing. That meant I had no chance to do anything. I didn't get a chance to get him out of there. You didn't answer my calls, you gave me no information. I asked you for feedback and you gave me none. Weeks went by and you sat on your backside cashing the cheques and doing nothing until finally they killed him.'

There was a lot in Tania's emotion filled rant which was incorrect but McQueen didn't want to get into that now. He didn't want to get defensive and for them to end up in a polarised argument. He'd seen grief and its effects before. She needed someone to blame, ironically it was like Zach Lindley said in one of his videos, "people in pain will always blame—you." McQueen let her get it off her chest.

'You were useless,' she continued. 'In fact, worse than useless because I was waiting on you. I did nothing because I was expecting a report or something from you.'

'I'm really sorry you feel like that, Tania,' he said. 'Have the police told you anything new? Have they looked at the CCTV from the hotel?'

'Yes,' she almost shouted and McQueen could see why she didn't want to be in a quiet coffee shop. 'It's too late. He's dead. Don't you get it?'

'Yes, I do, but if they did kill him maybe we can get justice for him and stop them killing anyone else?'

'What do you mean *if*? Of course they killed him.' She looked down at the coffee she hadn't touched. And then more quietly she said, 'He was there with three of them. They left after about two hours. The cameras in the car park show they all took separate cars. They all say they never saw him again but Richard's car has been found near the woods where...' Her voice faltered now and her anger cracked into tears. He gently put his hand on her arm and she didn't push it away. For some people there is something about grief that needs physical comfort.

'I'm so sorry,' he said. 'I had been working on it but I really had nothing to tell you and I didn't want to mislead you.' She was sobbing and rocking slowly back and forth on the bench.

'My child has no father,' she said. 'Do you understand that?'

He let her cry for a while and put his arm around her shoulders until they stopped shaking.

'I'm so sorry,' he said again. It sounded pathetic.

He desperately wanted to ask how Richard had died but wasn't sure how to phrase the question without being insensitive.

'I know this sounds stupid, Tania, but are they certain it was murder?' He felt her go rigid and took his arm away.

'You don't know?' she said looking at him, her face had hardened again, the tears had stopped. 'I thought you were a detective?'

'The police haven't released any information yet. I think they are trying to keep the press away from it.'

'He was hit from behind on the back of the head with a branch. *Blunt force trauma* they called it. Then when he fell down he was struck again and again and again. They aren't sure yet, it's too early to say but he probably didn't get a chance to bleed to death as he was already dead.' She had recited it like a boring shopping list but her fists were clenched and her hands were tucked in close to her stomach which, even under her black coat, was beginning to show the swelling of new life. 'So yes, they are sure it was murder.'

McQueen didn't say anything but he was already processing the information. Picking up a branch from the ground in a wooded area indicated an impromptu action rather than a premeditated plan. If someone had taken Richard there to murder him they'd probably have taken a weapon with them. Multiple blows long after the victim is unconscious and probably dead were usually the sign of extreme anger. He tried to piece the story together in his head. So, for some reason Richard went for a walk in the woods with Zach Lindley or one of his henchmen. Why? They'd just had a meeting in the hotel, why would they walk in the woods? So that Zach could pontificate on the glories of nature? Then what? Richard is walking ahead unsuspecting and he says something that enrages Zach? What did he say? Maybe he questioned Zach's purpose or threatened to go to the press? Maybe he even wanted to leave the group? There were so many possible scenarios but at the moment they were nothing more than wild guesswork.

'I wanted to tell you in person how I felt,' continued Tania. 'I foolishly thought it would make me feel better but it hasn't. I'm going,' she said standing up. 'And I don't expect to see a bill from you.' The truth was that McQueen hadn't been *cashing any cheques* as she'd put it, he hadn't taken a penny from her yet and he didn't intend to.

'You haven't and you won't,' he said. 'But so you know, I am still going to continue investigating Zach Lindley and his followers. I'm also going to try to find out who killed Richard. I might need to ask you some more questions later when it's a better time, I hope that's okay?'

'You mean when I'm not hysterically crying over the death of my partner?'

'I mean when it's not so raw. I realise it's painful but as I said before you may be able to help me bring some justice for Richard.' He anticipated her reply and added, 'I know it doesn't bring him back but people often say getting justice helps them, it gives them closure.'

'I don't want closure,' she said quietly. 'I want to turn back time.'

They walked together back along the river and then up onto the road to head to the station. On the narrow path across the bridge they had to dodge a large, loud, laughing group of young women in pink tutus and silver sashes each proudly announcing their personal link to the bride to be. McQueen stepped out of the way of the chief bridesmaid as she suddenly staggered to one side.

'You were nearly over the side there,' screamed the mother of the bride laughing madly.

When the group had passed, Tania stopped and turned to watch as they made their way towards the bars and clubs of the city. McQueen could imagine what had gone through her mind as she'd witnessed such a display of pure joy. She swung round and carried on walking.

'Do me a favour,' she said. 'Don't come to the funeral. I don't want to explain who you are to anyone.'

'Err, okay, if that's what you want,' he said.

It was a let-off really. McQueen hated funerals and he'd only intended going to see if Zach or any of the followers were there. He was sure they hadn't been invited but they might still show up.

They parted at the station. Tania was going back to Leeds but McQueen's car was in the station car park and he was going back to his office. He wasn't quite sure how to end the meeting, whether to give her a hug and tell her for the umpteenth time how sorry he was or to shake her hand

and tell her he'd be in touch. In the end he did neither because she simply said, 'Bye,' and walked quickly away.

It had all felt very odd. She had agreed to meet him solely to tell him that he had let her down? Or was she trying to gauge how much he knew? At least now he knew what had happened to Richard, but that too was odd. How had Zach convinced him to go for a walk in the woods? As yet, McQueen didn't know if Zach had an alibi and he didn't know who the other two men at the hotel had been. The one thing he was sure about was that there was another Zach Lindley village hall meeting coming up and he would make sure he was in attendance.

As McQueen got into his car his phone rang. He didn't recognise the number but he took the call anyway.

'Are you Doctor McQueen?' It was a woman's voice with a strong eastern European accent, he guessed Polish.

'Yes, how can I help?'

'I am Sonia Kowalska.' He closed his eyes for a second and leaned his head back on the headrest. 'Can you come see me? I have something to ask you?'

McQueen didn't hesitate.

'Yes, of course.'

'When?'

'How about this afternoon?'

'Yes, good.'

'Text me your postcode. I'm in York at the moment but I'll come as soon as I can.'

A few moments later and his phone buzzed with the address. He reached for his seatbelt. He'd recognised the name instantly. Sonia Kowalska was the wife of Tomasz, the man that Patrick Sutton had killed as his last evil act before being caught.

Maggie had advised McQueen to stay away from Sonia, but they hadn't discussed the possibility that she would ask to see him. He couldn't refuse. This was a woman who was a widow because he hadn't acted fast enough. It looked like this was going to be his day to get the metaphorical shit kicked out of him by bereaved women.

When McQueen arrived at the house he pulled up outside and composed himself. He'd spent the driving time formulating his defence. Yes, he'd had enough evidence to trap Sutton but he hadn't been sure he had enough and he didn't want a botched arrest to impact on the case. If the police ended up having to let Sutton go after McQueen had accused him, then he would have been forewarned and would have had time to cover his tracks and maybe destroy evidence. But the harsh fact remained, in the time McQueen had agonised over details Sutton had killed Tomasz Kowalska. He was sure Sonia had worked this out by now and she would have some punishing questions for him. There was no point avoiding it, though, neither his conscience nor his insomnia would allow that.

Even though there were three children living there with their mother, the house was spotlessly clean and tidy. Sonia opened the door to him and then took him through to a large open-plan kitchen at the back of the house and invited him to sit at the pine table which dominated the room. Sonia offered him tea, but he politely declined. They sat opposite each other. Sonia had her blonde hair pulled back into a tight bun, her face even without a trace of makeup was attractive, the sharp cheekbones a reminder of her heritage.

'I've been wanting to come and see you for a while,' he said. 'But I couldn't pluck up the courage.' She frowned and cocked her head to one side.

'Courage?'

'Yes. Ever since they caught Patrick I have known, what you probably know by now, that with the information I had at my fingertips I could have stopped him sooner. I could have stopped him before he killed Tomasz, and I carry a lot of guilt over that. I don't want to make this all about me but all I can say is I would understand your anger.'

She was still frowning but now she pointed a work-reddened finger at him.

'Anger? Are you police?'

'No, as you know I'm a private investigator. I was working for the sister of one of Sutton's previous victims. She wanted justice and she didn't feel the police were putting enough time and effort into finding her brother's murderer. I took a fresh look at all the known evidence and I worked on a suspect profile. I was able to pin-point Sutton. I had his job, I had his age, his size and even where he lived, but I didn't think it was strong enough, so I waited and then it was too late.'

'And then you went to police?'

'Yes.'

'And that's when they arrested him?'

'Yes.'

'So, without you he might have killed more?'

'Well, we'll never know. The police certainly had Sutton on a list of suspects, in fact they had interviewed him a number of times, but he didn't fit the profile they were working to, a profile they had come up with. I'm sure they would have got there in the end.'

Sonia got up and went to the kettle. She made two cups of tea and handed him one, even though he hadn't asked for it. She took the plastic container of milk from the fridge and put it down next to his cup along with a spoon.

'I don't know what you wanted to see me about,' he said, 'but before you ask me anything, I first wanted to apologise. I'm so sorry I didn't save your husband. I can't begin to imagine how hard it must have been for you.'

Sonia was shaking her head.

'No, it is not you,' she said. 'You are not police. They did not do proper job. You knew who was Sutton, why didn't they know? Why they not catch him? It is their job, not yours. That is why I ask you here. I have friend, he is lawyer, I am going to sue the police. Will you provide expert witness testimony?'

McQueen was taken aback. He'd expected to take a verbal beating the way he had with Tania earlier, but instead it was clear this was one grieving woman who did not blame him at all. They were stacking up, Judy Greene who partly blamed him for the death of her child and now Tania who, in her blind emotion of loss, felt he'd let her down, but this woman, Sonia, the one whom McQueen thought had every right to attack him wanted him on her side against the police? It was unexpected and he felt a surge of relief, Maggie had been wrong, the best therapy he could imagine was knowing that Sonia and her family bore him no malice.

'I have to tell you, Sonia, you won't stand much chance of success with a lawsuit like that. You'd have to show extreme negligence and it would be so hard to prove.'

'I don't care. I want to make a noise. I will make them see what they have done to me and my boys.'

'It was Sutton who did it, Sonia, not the police,' he said gently.

'But they are supposed to protect us. We trust them and they don't do it. So, will you be witness?'

McQueen had to think for a second. Sonia, a single mother now with three children to keep had probably had her head swayed by tales of a huge compensation pay-out by a lawyer who was chasing a cut. Meanwhile, McQueen's relationship with the police had never been good and Tracey Bingham already had to tread a careful path whenever she spoke to him. He wasn't sure how it would go down with her if he was part of a legal battle against the force but Tracey would always be his friend, he was fairly confident of that.

'I don't know how much weight it would carry,' he said, 'but if you included me as an expert witness, I'm happy with that.'

Thirty-Three

Every lunchtime Carl left his office to go to the sandwich shop around the corner. It would have been more economical to make his own sandwiches and Lia had even offered to make them for him while she was making hers, but he didn't take her up on the offer. It was a little daily indulgence, a sign of his corporate success, a bought sandwich from a fancy shop that had expensive bottles of olive oil and bunches of dried herbs hanging in the window. Toasted brie and mushroom was his current favourite.

Part of his reluctance about bringing in and eating his own lunch was based on the way he heard some of the other guys in the office laugh behind the backs of colleagues who did bring their own lunch in. They sniggered at the silver foil packages or plastic containers that appeared on some desks in the morning. Amongst a largely young, male, testosterone-rich working environment, it was seen as pathetic to be eating your own food. It was something the older guys did as they edged their way towards retirement. They were all working in a money-making industry, and if you weren't able to afford an expensive sandwich every now and then, it must mean you hadn't been hitting targets and therefore not been seeing any bonuses. It was stupid, but it was the way their minds worked. Carl didn't buy into it, but he also didn't want to be seen as an old duffer, promotions were lost on such perceptions. Going out for a sandwich was also a way to get away from his desk for half an hour, that's the way he justified it to himself anyway.

He thanked Luigi for the greaseproof paper wrapped pack, took a Diet Coke from the fridge, and bleeped his card across the counter. As he stepped back out onto the pavement Carl was greeted by a young man who strangely seemed to have been waiting for him.

'Hi, Carl,'

'Hi,' he replied tentatively. He often bumped into people from the office, but he didn't recognise this guy who wasn't dressed like an office dweller, unless he was on his way to a gym in his zipped-up tracksuit. Carl's company was not some laid-back internet start-up where dress-code was *be comfortable*, everyone wore collared shirts, usually white, suit jackets draped over the backs of chairs. You never knew when the CEO might drop in and he based his personal dress-code on eighties bond-dealer culture.

'How you doing, bud?' asked the guy falling into step beside him.

'Sorry, do I know you?' asked Carl stopping to look more closely at the face below the baseball cap. The man was grinning, from a distance he would have looked very friendly but from up close Carl could see that there was no warmth in the fake grin.

'No, but you don't need to because I know you, bud,' he

said. 'I know you and your nosey girlfriend. I know where you work and I know where you live. You need to tell her she needs to keep her big nose out of things. She was warned to back off.'

Carl dropped his sandwich and can and grabbed a handful of the guy's top to pull him closer. The man's grin didn't shift. 'Easy tiger,' he said, his hand dropping to his waistband to expose the handle of a knife. Instinctively, Carl let go but the man stepped forward even closer. He was a good five inches shorter than Carl but he looked up from under the peak of his cap with eyes like cold marbles. 'Just tell her to back off and there will be no more problems,' he said and then very slowly turned and walked away.

A bunch of people were coming towards them, men and women chatting excitedly on their lunchbreak and Carl contemplated shouting to them for help but the thought of an innocent by-stander being attacked in a violent street melee stopped him. He dug in his pocket to take some video of the man but by the time he'd got his phone out the guy had already disappeared. He started to call the police, but then thought better of it, what was the point? Instead he picked up his sandwich which had broken out of its wrapper and threw it into the bin outside the shop. He retrieved his dented can from the gutter knowing he'd have to leave it a while before opening it, the drink inside was probably feeling about as shaken as he was.

The approaching group, oblivious to what had just occurred right in front of them, had now formed a queue at the sandwich bar. He assessed the waiting time and decided it was a good day to start fasting. It was supposed to be good for your body, anyway.

On a lot of people, the pressure of intimidation works fine, turning them away from an unnecessary hassle towards a quiet life, but for others it has the opposite effect only forcing their heels deeper into the sand.

When he got back to his desk, Carl tapped out a text to Lia.

Tonight let's take some time to go over that case of yours again. You can tell me some details. Maybe I can help?

There were things Lia hadn't been sharing with him to protect him from worrying and now he was going to return the favour by not letting her know about the threats. There was someone he was going to inform, though. Lia had a boss and in Carl's opinion autonomy, trust, and delegation were all very well but it was time for McQueen to step up.

Thirty-Four

It was a different venue to the previous one. Zach had obviously outgrown the capacity of village halls, this was more like a small theatre and, looking around, McQueen could see every seat was taken. As before, ninety percent of the faces were male. The guy on the door checking names gave him a nod of recognition.

'Hi, I'm Brice,' he said. 'Can you come and find me when it's finished? Zach would like to talk to you.'

'Okay.'

McQueen could see there was a different person in Richard's old position keeping watch near the edge of the stage. When Zach came out there was respectful applause this time rather than the silence that there had been at the last meeting. McQueen could feel in the atmosphere this movement was growing and, despite himself, he couldn't help feeling a certain excitement. It was easy to see how the lure of inclusion had captivated so many. There is something deeply attractive about knowing you are part of an exclusive club, like being into a hot new band that no one else has heard about yet, but you know they soon will.

The lighting was much more professional now and Zach was standing in a bright beam.

'So, let me tell you about immigrants,' he said. McQueen felt a cold flush wash over him and his stomach tighten. Finally, Zach was getting to the dog whistle rallying cry McQueen had suspected and dreaded ever since he'd started watching the videos. Zach had pushed every button in the repertoire of anyone trying to stir up the marginalised masses, and at last he'd reached the big one. But what Zach said next was the biggest shock of all.

'It's not immigrants who have been pushing you down all your life. Thwarting you at every turn, treating you like dirt. That's what *they* want you to believe, so you don't challenge their power.'

This was not what McQueen had been expecting and he tried to gauge the mood of the audience, but all he saw around him was rapt attention.

'They deliberately bring in a few immigrants so you will be bamboozled and blinded to what they are doing. It's a cheap magic trick. It's a street three-card con. While we think the queen of hearts is under their left hand, it's not even on the table and your money is gone. While we are watching the shores for immigrants they are using your data to build their A.I. to take every single one of your jobs. Phase one is already complete, the vaccine is in the blood of the nation. Of every nation. They control it all and their plan for you is bleak.'

If McQueen could have shouted out a question it would have been, "Who are *they*?", but he didn't.

'And yes, it's international. Who do you really think

brought down the twin towers on nine eleven?' This question got a lot of heads in the crowd nodding. And then he did something McQueen had to admit was very clever. 'The people who believe the official version of what happened in New York in September 2011 probably also believe the earth is flat and that Tony Blair is a lizard.' This got a ripple of laughter. It was clever because it aimed to give one crazy theory credibility by distancing it from the crazier conspiracy theories, the ones that could easily be debunked. It might've alienated a few flat-earthers in the audience, but he probably didn't want them on team Lindley. And his stance on immigration showed he clearly didn't want the Nazis either probably because they brought the wrong kind of attention and were so easily pigeon-holed and dismissed.

Zach's presentation went on for about an hour as it zigzagged across his usual touch points. Climate change was addressed, but again shrewdly it wasn't denied outright, it was presented as something *they* had manufactured in order to supress and control businesses and citizens across the globe. If McQueen had to sum up the whole hour in a few words he'd have said: *You've all been exploited by them, and things are going to get worse, but we can stop it, watch this space.* Zach still wasn't explaining his solution to the issues he was highlighting but it didn't seem to matter to the men in the theatre. It was enough that they had been recognised, that someone had seen their plight and understood their lives. At the end there was a standing ovation as Zach Lindley left the stage.

McQueen went to the exit when it was over and found

Brice again. As they walked together towards the stage door the young man slowed down.

'You're a detective, aren't you? I mean, as well as a psychologist?'

'Yes, I am.'

'You must have heard about Richard Farnham? The guy who was found in the woods?'

McQueen was surprised Brice had brought this up especially as he'd wanted to ask him about Richard but didn't want to make it too obvious. It crossed his mind that Brice might have been tasked by Zach to sound him out.

'Yes, I saw that story, he worked with you guys, didn't he?'

'Sometimes. He was part of the group.'

'Did you get on with him?'

Brice left that question hanging.

'I was there, you know?'

'Where?'

'At the meeting we had in the hotel, the last time anyone saw him alive.'

'How did he seem?' McQueen was trying to be casual, as if he was only asking out of curiosity.

'He seemed fine. He was maybe a bit quiet after Zach had to straighten him out a little bit, but not upset or nothing.'

'What do you mean?'

'Well he'd been talking about bringing his girlfriend with him to Senby when we go there, but Zach told him he couldn't.'

'Was he upset?'

'No, I don't think so, he just accepted it. I mean it makes sense.'

'And you never saw him after you all drove off afterwards?'

'Nope, me and Joey went to pub afterwards. There were witnesses, so I have an alibi.'

This was clearly a rehearsed line and McQueen felt he'd pushed this as far as he could without it being obvious the only thing he was interested in was Ricard's death. He didn't want Brice to be reporting it back to Zach. He was still trying to maintain the lose cover story he was there because of his interest in the teachings of Lindley, not on a job.

They were walking down a corridor now towards the dressing rooms so McQueen tried to change the subject slightly.

'Great presentation tonight. He really hit his stride. Made some excellent points.'

'Yeah.'

'So tell me, Brice, what brought you to this group? What do you get from it?'

'What do I get? Zach is a friggin' genius, that's what. He sees things as they are and he says them as they are. I've never met anyone like him. There's no bullshit. All my life people have been holding me back and from the minute I saw that first YouTube I could see here was a man who just got it.'

'And where do you think he is he taking us? I don't mean Senby, I mean as a group?'

'Well, wherever he's taking us, I'm going,' said Brice as he opened the dressing room door and let McQueen inside.

Zach was sitting at a chair with his back to one of those big mirrors with lights around them that actors use to apply their makeup before a performance. Brice had closed the door and left them alone. Knowing his discussion with Brice would be passed on to Zach, McQueen chose to get it in first.

'We were just talking about the guy, Richard Farnham, who used to work for you.'

'Yes, tragic incident. He was a very valued member of this group and I had big plans for him. Do they know what happened yet?' McQueen had to be careful not to mention anything that wasn't already in the public domain.

'I don't know. He had his meeting with you guys and then went missing. A few weeks later a dog walker found him in the woods.'

'How did he die?'

McQueen only knew this from what Tania had told him.

'I don't know, but the vague police statements in the press like, 'suspicious circumstances' seem to imply foul play.'

'Tragic. He'd only just told us the exciting news that his partner was expecting a child. I really feel for her. Let's hope the police clear it all up soon.' He clapped his hands to signal that the subject was closed before McQueen could dig any deeper. 'And now to you, Doctor McQueen. You've seen what we're about and I've given you exclusive access to our new home in Senby. I think it's time for you to make a decision, are you with us? If not, it's time for you to walk away, no hard feelings.'

'First, I have a question, and I'm sure you would expect

me to have a few, but my main question is what is the long-term plan? What is your goal for this group? When everyone is assembled in Senby, what happens next?'

Lindley's face remained impassive and it was impossible to read what he was thinking.

'What I am putting together is so important to the future of all of us that I cannot risk it being derailed. If I make my plans public, the same forces that keep us in our boxes will be brought to bear on my plans. They will be destroyed before they can take root. So I have a test, and this is the test, you are living the test. Based on everything I have said, in the meetings and online, do you trust me? Do you have faith I can change things for the better?' He was staring at McQueen, waiting for the answer. There was only one answer that was going to work.

'Yes,' said McQueen.

'Good, because faith in me is the most important element I need and you can only prove your faith by joining this group knowing I have a plan, by trusting in me. When the time is right everyone at Senby will move together as one well-oiled machine and it will be too late for anyone to stop us. So I ask you again, and I ask you for the final time, are you with us?

'Yes,' said McQueen without hesitation.

'I'm so glad to hear it,' said Zach with what passed for a smile. 'I do have some legal documents for you to sign, non-disclosure agreements, that sort of thing to mark your official entry to the inner group. Then we'll put a little statement together for our social media accounts saying how honoured we are to have the great Doctor McQueen join our throng.'

'Okay.' McQueen wasn't feeling comfortable, but he was managing to hide it.

'But I'm so pleased you've made your decision, you are going to be a great asset to this movement. Besides, we have to kill anyone who wants to leave us when they have gained the knowledge that you have.' He was grinning to show that this was supposed to be a joke. McQueen grinned too as if it was the funniest thing he's ever heard and then couldn't help himself.

'Is that what happened to Richard Farnham?' he asked, still fake laughing.

Zach laughed out loud, the first time McQueen had heard that sound from him, and slapped his leg.

'Very good,' he said. 'Very funny.'

Thirty-Five

'The police have spoken to me,' said Judy. 'About the death of my ex-husband. They got the story from somewhere that I had turned up at McQueen's desk with a knife in my bag and I had threatened to visit him. I wonder who told them that?'

They were in a cafe and both had over-sized frothy cups of latte in front of them. Judy Greene had taken Dan at his word and phoned him to arrange to meet up. It was a Saturday morning, outside Dan's working hours, but he'd chosen the time to underline he was prepared to back up his offer of a friendly ear. He had arrived on time but she was already there having secured a table towards the back, away from the few people seated at the window.

'I live alone,' she added, 'so I don't have an alibi.' She didn't seem to be particularly perturbed by that.

'Are you a suspect?'

She shrugged. 'Of course. I told them I wanted him dead and that I was glad he'd been killed.' Dan took a slurp from his hot coffee. He wiped away the comical froth moustache he felt on his top lip before he replying.

'And did you? I mean, did you kill him?' Dan asked the question but he wasn't at all sure what he was going to do if she said yes. He knew what he *should* do, but that wasn't the same thing at all. He was trying to build a trusting relationship with a damaged woman and turning her in to the police wasn't going to do much for that. She smirked.

'They say you should have no regrets. That's one of those bullshit toxic positivity things I see all the time online. Live, laugh, love, have no regrets. Well do you know what I regret, amongst everything else I regret? I regret it wasn't me that killed him. I could happily go to prison for doing that. But someone else beat me to it.'

She could have been lying, why would she have confessed to him? But Dan believed her. 'Now if they end up arresting me for his murder and I do go prison, it will be Paul Mason's final victory over me. He destroyed my life and, along with your boss who told them about me in the first place, he finishes me off.'

'That won't happen,' said Dan although he had no basis for this bold claim. 'I won't let it.'

She looked at him through questioning eyes, her hand absently stirring her coffee with a spoon. She seemed to be lost for a few seconds in the spinning patterns in the cup.

'You've heard McQueen's version, can I tell you mine?'

'That's what I'm here for.'

'As I told you before, I was a young mother. I was exhausted and trying to go to college at the same time. The baby wouldn't stop crying, we had no money, and my husband was saying those crazy things about the intrusive thoughts he was having. I didn't know what to do. I didn't

The McQueen Legacy

know who to turn to, should I have gone to the police? How do you go to the police and say your husband weeps because he has thoughts? So as I said, I went to McQueen for reassurance, and he gave it to me. He told me what I wanted to hear, and off I went. Then one morning, I had to get to an early lecture so I left the baby with my husband. He hadn't been working, due to his fear of hammers. Sounds ridiculous, doesn't it, but it was true? He was laying around the house and I resented him so much, I wanted him to take some responsibility, I wanted to make him step up. I put Katie into his arms...' Judy began sobbing and Dan took her hand in his. He wasn't a psychologist but even he could see it wasn't McQueen she blamed, it was herself. McQueen was just the acceptable scapegoat, the person who allowed her to live with herself.

'You couldn't have known,' he almost whispered.

'I could have known. I did know. I knew he wasn't right in the head but I let a stupid lecture stop me from being the mother I should have been.'

'I don't see it like that at all,' said Dan. 'If you had thought for one second he was going to harm Katie, you would never have left her with him.'

'And why didn't I think he would harm her? Because McQueen had told me he would never follow up on his intrusive thoughts.'

Judy's tears had gained the attention of some of the other people in the coffee shop, who probably thought they were witnessing an emotional scene between mother and son. Judy was gripping Dan's hand very tightly and when she looked into his eyes he saw a pleading expression that touched his soul. It had been a lot of years since Judy had lost her daughter but Dan could tell that time had not dulled the pain. His actual mother had been the same, she'd never got over the loss of Dan's brother and, to this day, she carried the grief with her. It was such a waste of life to not be able to move on and live, to write yourself off like that. Most people somehow manage to get past a tragedy but not his mother, and not Judy.

The ends of Dan's finger were beginning to turn white as Judy squeezed even harder.

'Are you my friend, Dan?' she asked.

'Yes.'

'Really?'

'Yes.'

'Then will you help me, because after so long it's too much to bear?'

'If I can, I will help you, yes.'

'McQueen has gone on with his life, he's become successful and famous, while I've been stuck forever. Will you help me to punish him?'

'What do you mean?'

'Will you help me kill McQueen?'

Thirty-Six

McQueen had spent a restless night turning in his bed, no nightmares, he hadn't slipped deeply enough into dreamland for those, but there was so much on his mind prodding him awake every time he drifted off. Once again, he had lapsed on his sessions with Maggie, it was as if as soon as he started feeling a little bit better, he stopped doing the thing that made him feel better. In clinical psychology they saw this behaviour all the time. One of the most difficult things about treating patients with serious mental health issues like schizophrenia, was getting them to keep talking their meds. When a person feels cured they can't believe they were ever ill. It was also why so many addicts relapsed and why the treatment programmes emphasised acknowledging every day that the person is an addict whether they feel like one or not. McQueen was painfully aware of that one.

The small pile of Zach's legal documents on his bedside table remained untouched. He'd managed to avoid signing them at the theatre saying he never put his name to anything until he'd read it properly and let his solicitor look them over. It sounded like a reasonable, adult approach and Zach had accepted it without argument as a sign that McQueen was taking his commitment seriously. In truth, in the past, he had signed all kinds of official papers to do with the business with barely a glance. Who had the time to read all that boring jargon? To him it was like the terms and conditions that come up every time you download something from the internet everyone whizzes through without seeing a word, scrolling down as fast as possible to click the "I have read and agreed to" button. It was a bad habit to get into and his solicitor had warned him multiple times about the folly of such laziness, and perhaps the advice had finally got through to him because he wasn't about to sign Zach's papers until the lawyer had read them first. But even that was a lie to himself, he knew he had no intention of ever signing the documents and he was going to use the famous slowness of the legal profession as an excuse to dodge that bullet for as long as he could.

An hour earlier than usual he swung his legs from under the duvet and let his feet hit the carpet. He went through his usual morning ritual of coffee and shower. At one point, a few months before, he had tried to incorporate stretches into the regime but it hadn't lasted. He understood the benefits but was missing the motivation to achieve them. Besides, the stretch positions felt silly especially if he caught sight of himself in the mirror.

The one thing he did appreciate was how much easier it was to get up since he'd stopped drinking. Previously, even if he'd had a mild night of a couple of bottles of wine and a few beers, he might not have had a full hangover but the

The McQueen Legacy

jaded, sluggish feeling of a person moving through treacle had persisted until lunchtime. He'd thought it was just a symptom of being alive and no longer eighteen until his liver recovered and the daily heavy blanket of over indulgence disappeared.

He was almost ready to leave for the office when the door buzzer went. He didn't have a video entry system, but there was an intercom for the front door, the entry being shared with three other flats. He was surprised to hear Carl's voice, recognisable even through the distortion of the speaker and fearing something might have happened to Lia, he buzzed him up immediately.

Carl was dressed in his work suit looking as sharp as ever. The two men shook hands, they knew each other fairly well but neither would have called the other a real friend. McQueen had been to Lia's flat a few times for dinner and Carl had always been a charming and entertaining host. Knowing Lia he wouldn't have lasted as a boyfriend if he hadn't been something special.

'Hi, McQueen, sorry to disturb you so early.'

'It's fine, Carl, I was just about to go to work anyway.'

'And I was just on my way to my office and I wanted to have a quick word.'

McQueen invited Carl into the living room, but he declined saying he wasn't going to be long.

'Is Lia okay?'

Carl took a deep breath and his pause gave McQueen a few seconds of panic.

'She is at the moment, but that's what I wanted to talk to you about. This case she's working on.'

'The Bolton case, what about it?'

Carl got right to it and explained what had gone on at the sandwich shop the day before. He didn't over dramatise it but he didn't sugar coat it either. He said yes, he was fine, but he hadn't told Lia about the incident because he didn't want to worry her. McQueen reluctantly promised not to mention it, either. And then Carl got to his real point.

'I think you put too much on Lia, and I don't think you are paying attention to what's going on. I think you put her in danger.' McQueen hadn't realised how the Bolton case had been developing and he could see now his focus on Zach Lindley had meant he'd taken his eye off the ball. Carl was right, it was McQueen's responsibility to make sure anyone who worked for him wasn't alone in dangerous situations. If his own head was in the firing line then that was his choice, but for an employee to be facing threats was unacceptable, let alone an employee's partner. However, there was another element to this, and Carl knew it as well as McQueen did.

'You're right, Carl, I need to support her better, but let's not forget this is Lia we're talking about. She's her own person and she makes her own choices.'

McQueen stopped short of telling Carl he had been willing to let this case go but Lia had insisted on taking it on. It would have sounded like he was blaming her and, at the end of the day, as her boss he had sanctioned her choice.

Carl held up his hand in acknowledgement but he wasn't finished.

'We both know Lia will take on any job that comes her way and she will never ask for your help. She has too much

The McQueen Legacy

pride and too much to prove. To you. So that's your job, McQueen, you have to manage it right. I may not know much about the private detective game but I do know about workplace management. You have to find a way to give her the help she isn't asking for.'

'You're right, you're right, but I hope you understand, Carl, how much Lia means to me, how much I rely on her and how much I trust her judgement.'

But Carl was unrelenting.

'That's great, McQueen, but if this turns out to be a money laundering, drug selling criminal organisation and Mary Bolton is only a pawn in the game, then how much you say you care about Lia will count for nothing. And don't ever forget, whatever you think of Lia is only a fraction of what she is to me.'

'I'll speak to her,' said McQueen.

As Carl turned to leave he said, 'By the way, if she ever finds out I've been here to talk to you about this she would hate it. She'd find it undermining and humiliating and then it might be my murder you're investigating next.'

'I understand, don't worry, she won't hear it from me.'

Thirty-Seven

There was only one way for Dan to play this. He'd spent the weekend thinking about it. He thought he would be the first in Monday morning but McQueen was already at his desk, and it looked like he'd been there for a while. When Lia arrived he asked her to come into McQueen's office with him because he had something to tell them both.

'Okay, I may have over-stepped the mark here but I want you to know I've had a couple of conversations with Judy Greene. One was in my car out in the car park and one was in a coffee shop on Saturday.'

'Did you bump into her?' asked Lia.

'No, we arranged to meet.' Both McQueen and Lia looked surprised but they weren't angry, which was what Dan had been partly expecting. 'Look,' he gushed, 'she's a lonely woman who has had some tough breaks and I know it sounds silly but in some ways she reminds me of my mother.'

'Ah, the mother complex, but she might also be a murderer,' said Lia gently. 'It's possible she killed her ex-husband.'

'No, she didn't do it,' replied Dan firmly.

'How do you know?' This was McQueen who was now struggling with the thought that yet another one of his employees had been placed in a possible danger which originated with him.

'I know because I asked her, and she told me.'

'Oh, right, she told you,' said Lia, the sarcasm clear in her voice. McQueen stepped in.

'Dan, until the police have got the culprit in custody, I'm really not sure you should be meeting up with her. You might be right and she might have had nothing to do with it, but—'

'There's something else,' cut in Dan. 'She seems to hold a lot of resentment towards you, McQueen.'

'I know.'

'Especially as the police have spoken to her now and she knows it was you who told them about the knife in the bag.'

'Right, well I had to tell them that otherwise it could have been withholding evidence.'

'And, at the end of our meeting, she asked me…' he paused, hardly daring to say it, 'she asked me if I would help her to kill you.'

'Kill me?'

'Yes, now I don't think she was serious, I think she was just being dramatic to emphasise how she feels about you, it may even have been a warped joke, but that's what she said and I felt I should tell you.'

'And what did you say?' asked Lia, her eyes narrow and searching.

'I said "don't be ridiculous".'

The three of them were sitting at McQueen's desk thinking through what had just been said. Dan was feeling some relief from having got it off his chest but now he was anxious about where it would lead. Lia gave McQueen a look and they held the gaze for a few seconds.

'I'm sure you are right that she didn't mean it,' said McQueen. 'People make those kinds of threats all the time, but there is one way to find out for sure.'

'Yeah, because if she did want to murder him she might try to find another person to do it,' added Lia, 'or try to do something herself.'

'So, what are you saying? What is this one way to find out?' asked Dan even though he had a sneaking feeling he knew exactly what was coming. McQueen leaned forward in his chair.

'You might not be comfortable with this at all, Dan, and I would respect that and you don't have to do it, but if you were to contact Judy again and tell her that you've been thinking about it, and you've had second thoughts…'

'You really feel sorry for her, McQueen has been annoying you, and you can see her point,' added Lia.

'And you're willing to help her, then we could see how far she is really prepared to go.'

'And she'll probably back straight out and tell you it's you who's being ridiculous.'

Dan puffed out his cheeks.

'So, I'd be like an undercover agent?'

'Sort of,' said McQueen. 'No gun, no badge, but you would need to record the conversations.'

'A wire? Wow. And what happens if she does want to

kill you and she does have a plan? She goes to prison, right?'

'Not necessarily, but there would be consequences, the main one being she wouldn't get to murder me.'

'Can I think about this?'

'Of course, and if you don't want to do it then that's absolutely fine, we'll find some other way around this.'

'I need coffee,' said Dan scraping back his chair with the backs of his knees. He went into the small kitchen and stood for a minute staring at the kettle before filling it. He felt like he was facing the biggest dilemma of his young life. He had built the beginnings of a relationship of trust with Judy and leading her on and spying on her felt like a massive betrayal. How would he feel if someone did that to his own mother? He regretted having told them about Judy. At the same time he could see McQueen's life might actually be at risk, besides this was part of his job now. He might only be an administrator but he worked in detective agency for Christ's sake, and wasn't there a little part of him that had wanted some of the action? Hadn't that been part of the appeal?

Lia joined him in the kitchen and watched as he slowly made the three cups of coffee.

'I know what you're thinking,' she said. 'I've been there. I know it's a massive leap from dealing with the paperwork and appointments to getting involved in the field, but let me say something, Dan. As I told you when I hired you, I started in your job, and McQueen gave me an opportunity. I grabbed it with both hands and it was the best decision I've ever made. I have never looked back, I love every minute of it and I wouldn't swap it for anything.'

Dan was stirring the coffee now and milk distribution was taking his full concentration. McQueen took the smallest of splashes to the point that it was hardly worth the effort, while Lia liked hers so milky they were always running out of milk.

'She trusts me,' he said quietly without looking up.

'I get it,' said Lia picking up her mug. 'I really do, but if she kills McQueen imagine how that's going to feel.' She took two of the coffees and went back to McQueen's office. Dan stayed in the kitchen sipping from his mug and staring into space.

At the beginning of their working relationship, Lia and McQueen had agreed to make all their case notes and reports available to each other via a computer workflow system. Lia had found the best software, installed it, and then patiently tried to teach McQueen how to use it. It was a good system and it meant if one of them was put out of action the other could easily pick up the case. McQueen loved the concept. The hard part was being bothered to transfer his notes from his brain onto the system, and that's why he rarely did it. Lia, on the other hand, diligently kept her records up to date so McQueen had been able to spend the early morning alone-time in the office bringing himself up to speed with the Mary Bolton case. After reading her report of the meeting at Summertown Industries, he could see why Carl had concerns and why the confrontation outside the sandwich bar compounded that view.

Over the years, McQueen had come into contact with the tentacles of organised crime many times, usually at the gritty street level. The simple tearful request of, *'I think my husband is cheating on me, can you find out?'* could often be the doorway to a pretty dark world. Surveillance of straying husbands often led to sex workers who themselves were usually addicts trapped in an exploitative criminal whirlpool. Above them were the pimps and traffickers. If you followed the chain upwards there were always well-insulated serious players at the top but McQueen had never needed to climb that chain, he had always stopped at the first link. As he'd never been involved in the breaking up of the gangs, they'd always left him alone. What he did know was at the highest levels they all craved the invisibility of respectability. They wanted to be left alone to make money hand over fist and not face any heat about it. Who would dare question the likes of Summertown Industries, with their prestigious awards and charity donations?

'Lia, I got in early because I needed to update the system with the latest developments on the Lindley case, but then I was side-tracked into your notes. You've been doing some excellent work. Summertown Industries? It's starting to look serious.'

'Yep, they're quite a bunch.'

'Mary Bolton hired us to help build her defence case but inevitably that's going to cause some friction with the prosecution's side.'

'It's in my report, McQueen, they want us to tell her she has no chance and she should plead guilty.'

'And I also saw that you did some background on Chris Bolton?'

'Yes, and he's a low-life, but he's not his mother and

having a criminal son doesn't make her guilty.'

Lia was taking a defensive stance because she felt she was having her homework marked and she wasn't sure why.

'Okay, I think we need to go back and see Mary again, and ask if Chris can be there, too. We'll confront them both with what Summertown have lined up against them and see if anything spills out of that.'

Lia was sitting with her arms crossed.

'We?'

'Yes, I'd like to come along this time, if that's okay?'

'What, you don't trust me now?'

'That's not it at all, Lia, and you know it. We are a team and I feel like I've been neglecting you. I don't like the way this case is turning out so before we go hell for leather against Summertown, I want to know if Mary has any more skeletons in the closet. If we are going to fully put our necks on the line against a possible criminal organisation, or a legitimate company with enormous resources, I want to know for sure we're on the right side of the line.'

Lia was watching him closely and she could sense something was off. Something had sparked his sudden interest in her case but she wasn't sure what.

'Is there something you're not telling me?' she asked. 'Because everything we've achieved so far in this agency has been based on us being completely open with each other.'

It was a sneaky gut-punch, she was good and she knew him too well, but McQueen had made a promise to Carl and he didn't want a domestic dispute on his conscience.

'No. I simply couldn't sleep last night. Something was

on my mind keeping me awake and I realised it was because I haven't been supporting you properly. I've been so immersed in my own stuff that I was letting things slide. I know you can handle it and you've been in dangerous positions before, but I can't afford to get casual about that.'

Lia didn't say anything, she was watching and listening. Her mind was calculating at a million miles an hour and the same intuition that made her such a good investigator was working against McQueen now.

'Did Carl speak to you? Because I know he's been worrying about this case, did he call you?'

'No, Carl did not call me and I didn't call him.' It was like a child's lie and he got right behind it. 'You can check my phone if you like, Carl hasn't called me in six months.' He slid his phone across the desk but she didn't pick it up.

'It's okay, I believe you, sorry,' she said finally relenting. 'Okay, I'll go and ring Mary to see when we can go over there.'

McQueen had not felt good about the game he'd had to play and he hoped his untruths wouldn't come back to bite him, but right now it was done and he had to concentrate. He started to look again at Lia's notes on Chris Bolton which had been gleaned from official Spanish police records. Chris was a young man who had lived an extravagant lifestyle in Spain for several years funded by his drug dealing until the Spanish police had caught up with him. Eventually, his home had been raided and a large quantity of cocaine and cash had been recovered. By the time he got out of prison and been deported, the house and all the cash had long gone, but there were still people he owed money to. Could that be the reason his mother had been tempted to dip into the company till? That would certainly be the angle the prosecution would take in court.

Carl had done a great job with the financial information, but unfortunately, if anything, it supported the case against Mary rather than her defence. Money had certainly gone missing and she had access to it, plus she had known some of the cash transactions weren't being properly recorded. Again, it was what the prosecution would focus on, they would task their forensic accountants with producing enough compelling numbers that no lay-person would be able to dispute them. A respected international company against an aging woman with a drug-dealing, jail-bird son, it wasn't looking good.

Lia came bustling back into his office and she looked completely bemused.

'Has she agreed to meet us?' he asked.

'Mary? Yeah, yeah, in a few days' time ,' she answered batting the question away with a wave of her hand. 'But more importantly, is there something you aren't telling us, McQueen?'

'Like what?' Carl was still fresh in his mind and he wasn't about to own up to anything until he heard what she was referring to.

'Dan just showed me the latest video on the Zach Lindley YouTube channel. It's about you, apparently you are now a fully paid-up member of his crew?'

McQueen quickly fired up his browser to see what she was talking about. It was true, Zach had gone early, he hadn't waited for McQueen to sign the legals, he'd gone ahead and made the public announcement. McQueen fumbled with his phone and checked Zach's social media accounts, the news was everywhere. It was a clever move clearly designed to force McQueen's hand and to show there was no backing out now.

'Okay,' said McQueen. 'Can you ask Dan to come back in and I'll bring you both up to speed on what it's all about.'

As he said this, his phone pinged with a message and he looked and saw it was from Tania, who presumably had also seen the announcement. He felt like he might be getting quite a few such messages so he turned his phone off.

Thirty-Eight

Tracey Bingham had always believed in McQueen and defended his corner, even when the pressure from her colleagues had made that difficult. They saw him as an annoying meddler and, worse than that, he was a lucky one who, by chance, had managed to show them up a few times by solving cases they had given up on. But for Tracey it was different. They had formed an early bond when she had been new to the job and there had been numerous times when he had helped her just as much as she had helped him. A lot of her early success had relied on his insights. Plus, he was a friend. Unfortunately, it looked as if defending McQueen was about to get harder than ever.

Tracey had been called into her boss's office to be told 'her mate' McQueen had been named as the expert witness in a lawsuit that had been raised against the force. Sitting behind his desk in his full uniform (no jacket slung over the back of the chair for this senior officer), Detective Chief Superintendent Gibbons read aloud the official complaint.

It said Mrs Sonia Kowalska was suing the police for gross negligence over the death of her husband, Tomasz, in relation to the Patrick Sutton case. Her claim was the police had failed to investigate properly when all the relevant evidence was out there. They had not arrested Sutton when they had the chance and not only that, they had all but hired him. She claimed they had not done the proper background checks on the security guard and allowed him to infiltrate the investigation as a local adviser. Kowalska's lawyer was saying by giving him privileged information the police had actually aided Sutton and made it easier for him to kill her husband. She stated their negligence had resulted in the preventable murder of her husband, and this was proven by the private investigator, McQueen, who had then forced them to follow up on Sutton from information the police already had.

Tracey had listened dutifully to everything that Gibbons said but couldn't help thinking Mrs Kowalska was right. Tracey hadn't worked directly on the case but she had watched as mistakes had been made and glaring red flags had been ignored. They had allowed Sutton in to help them but he'd been the fox in the henhouse.

Tracey also knew how much McQueen still agonised over the case, he'd been unnecessarily hard on himself but it had taken Tomasz's widow to pinpoint where the real failings had been. She was right, McQueen hadn't given them anything they didn't already have except an accurate profile. After the Kowalska murder, he had insisted they interview Sutton again by threatening to take his evidence to the press.

Gibbons was stern-faced, but that didn't say much about his mood because it was his demeaner no matter what he was talking about. He was never one for chit-chat or idle banter and Tracey had barely exchanged more than a few words with him in the whole time she had been there.

'Our lawyers are working on this and it will never come to court,' he said. 'As you know, we do everything in our power to protect the public and Mr Kowalska was no exception. Our number one priority in any situation is eliminating the risk for citizens. The safety of the people is always paramount in our planning and execution of our roles. We left no stone unturned in our pursuit of the perpetrator of these heinous crimes.'

It sounded like Gibbons was quoting from the manual in a blame-evading press conference and in other circumstances with another person Tracey would have said, *except the one he was under*, but she held her tongue. He continued. 'However, if by some unfortunate turn of fate, this groundless accusation does end up before a judge you can be a big help to us, Detective Bingham. By us I mean the force that you have sworn to uphold and your colleagues.'

'How's that?' asked Tracey, dreading the answer she knew was coming.

'You've been in courts before. How do lawyers deal with difficult witnesses? They undermine and discredit them of course.'

'Yes, they do,' was all Tracey managed to say.

'I'm led to believe you have a lot of personal and professional experience of McQueen? Yes?' She couldn't deny it, Gibbons would have been well briefed by her fellow detectives. 'We can use that. I want you to start compiling a report highlighting his failings and weaknesses. He's a drunk, isn't he?'

Tracey finally found her voice.

'No, sir, he hasn't drunk alcohol for years.'

'No matter, an ex-drunk, whatever, I want people to come out of that court believing he is the most unreliable witness they've ever encountered.' Tracey was feeling the panic of being trapped. This was a test of her loyalty on both sides and something had to give.

'I have quite a workload at the moment,' she started to say, but Gibbons dismissed that with a slight wave of his hand,

'Concentrate on this,' he said. 'We cannot afford to allow this lawsuit to go anywhere, for god's sake it would open the floodgates. I want you to give this your full attention but let's keep it between us. We'll call it Operation Check Mate.'

The Detective Chief Superintendent was obviously very pleased with the title he'd come up with as his face was now beaming. 'As a starting point this might help,' he said handing across a printed screenshot of a computer image. 'I've sent you the link in an email.' It was a picture of Zach Lindley's YouTube page, with the heading, 'Our Newest Member' and a picture of McQueen that looked like it had been taken from his website. 'Lindley's some kind of internet conspiracy theorist nut-job who's got quite an online following. Looks like McQueen has jumped onboard.' Tracey didn't like to tell Gibbons the so-called nut-job had quite a following amongst his own detectives.

Sir, I—' but Tracey's protestations were cut short.

'Dismissed,' said Gibbons and pointed at the door behind her.

Once she got back to her desk, Tracey went online to check out the YouTube clip. On screen, Zach Lindley was making a big deal about the fact the highly respected criminal psychologist and private investigator, McQueen, had officially *joined the fold* as he described it. What that meant exactly wasn't explained, the presentation was less like a cheerful welcome and more like a car manufacturer announcing a new model. Lindley was certainly waxing lyrical about the massive endorsement of his beliefs he saw in his new recruit. He kept saying McQueen had taken a good hard look at everything that Zach and his group were doing and had decided to join the cause. Tracey had never watched one of these ZL videos as they were tagged, but when the McQueen announcement had finished, the next clip automatically loaded.

Again, Zach's face front and centre in close-up glared out from her computer. 'There are two cop-out phrases that I will not tolerate. One is: *everything happens for a reason*,' he almost spat it out. 'As if the events that shape your life, even when they are catastrophic have some deeper meaning. It's a cop-out, it's what *they* want you to think, because the real reason things keep happening to you is because they want them to. It is the matrix.' He paused and glowered. 'And the other deliberately manipulative saying I hear all the time tries to draw some credibility from an old German philosopher and it is this one: *That which doesn't kill us makes us stronger.* No, no, no. That myth is perpetuated by the ones who are draining your strength little by little. It benefits them to see you get weaker and weaker while you are

The McQueen Legacy

conned into thinking that the suffering *they* cause you is somehow benefiting you. It is time to push back against what they want for you, wake up from the matrix and take control of your life.'

Tracey clicked the X and closed down the site. She looked at the print-out Gibbons had given her and shook her head.

'What the hell have you got yourself into, McQueen?' she said under her breath. 'Have you lost your mind?'

Thirty-Nine

It was a cloudy day and the room was dark even with the curtains drawn. Dan had half-expected one of those hoarder's palaces stuffed to the ceiling with years' worth of treasured possessions, old newspapers and magazines piled high in every corner. He was really hoping it wouldn't be a full-on nightmare of empty food tins and cat shit, and was immensely relieved it wasn't. He couldn't have dealt with either the smell or what it would have said about her state of mind. Instead the place was neat, clean, and unremarkable to the point of being bland. It looked like rented accommodation, when someone is ready to move out, though Judy had said it was her house and she would be there until she died. There was one large picture on the wall above the fireplace, it was a larger version of the framed picture of her daughter she had shown him before.

When Dan had called Judy to arrange to meet, she had invited him to her home with the reasonable argument that she didn't see why either of them should be paying four quid for a cup of lukewarm milky coffee. He'd agreed to come to her but it had ramped up his guilt by a factor of ten.

The woman was trusting him enough to invite him into her personal space and he was going to be turning up with a hidden recorder. In the films, sometimes gangsters frisked you for a wire, but Dan was confident it wouldn't be an issue with Judy. McQueen had given him the device and shown him how to use it but he was not feeling good about it at all. The tiny recorder was taped to the small of his back and felt to him like a rucksack while the microphone wire seemed as thick as a rope across his chest. Not for the first time, Dan wondered if he really was cut out for the spying game. He sat carefully in the armchair she'd pointed at trying not to lean on the recorder.

Judy handed him a mug of coffee.

'Three pounds and eighty-five pence please,' and then, 'Joking. Obviously.'

'Nice house,' he said for something to say. She looked around the room as if seeing it for the first time herself.

'You think? I bought it when my parents died, they left me some money. It's just a house.'

'I love it,' he said wondering how his voice would sound on the recording and if it would pick up that he was lying. He squirmed a little in his seat, desperately wanting to scratch his back.

'My life stopped you know?' she said. 'When Katie died. I tried, I really did. There is no untouched shrine in this house. There is no room kept as it was for her because she never lived here. I wanted to move on as they like to say these days. I pushed it away for a few years but it all came back. Whenever I would see a newspaper article about McQueen's latest triumph, or see him on some TV show pontificating about some serial killer or other, it would all come crashing back. He was in the papers all the time when he was dating that TV presenter for a while, until she was killed. Everything he touches seems to rot, doesn't it?'

Dan could imagine them listening back to this later in the office and how awkward it might be.

'So what made you change your mind?' she asked. 'About getting rid of McQueen?'

This was the bit Dan had rehearsed in his mind but he'd already forgotten exactly how he'd intended it to go.

'Er, well, he was having a go in the office about some files I'd lost but the files were right there, he just hadn't seen them. And I saw his nasty streak. He thinks he knows everything but he doesn't. And I thought about everything you've been through, how much you trusted his judgement, and I could see you weren't going to get any peace until he was dead like your ex-husband. When you first said it, I thought it was ridiculous but the more I thought about it the more sense it made. The bottom line is, I want to help you like I wish someone had helped my mother.'

It all sounded like garbled bullshit but Dan could see by Judy's face she was buying it. She was hearing what she wanted to hear and there is no bigger convincer than that. She was ready to believe that a simple misunderstanding in the office could make a person consider murder because that's what she wanted to believe.

'You see?' she said, an almost joyful expression on her face. 'You see what I've been saying? You understand now? You see the kind of person you are working for?'

'Yes, I get it. But are you sure, Judy? Are you sure this

The McQueen Legacy

will actually help you? Your daughter is never coming back you know that, even with McQueen dead she is gone forever.'

He was trying to give her an escape route. Normally a policeman in this situation would be trying to trap the person, to get them to commit to their crime, but Dan wanted for all the world for Judy to say she was only joking all along.

'You can do it,' she said. 'You have access and you know his every move. But I don't want you to go to prison, Dan, so you must come up with a fool-proof plan.'

Dan had been instructed by McQueen on what they would need from the recording. They needed specifics, so reluctantly Dan edged towards them.

'So, you're not joking?'

'No, of course not?'

'You want me to kill McQueen for you?'

'Yes.'

'So, you are definitely saying you want to ask me to kill McQueen for you and you are not joking?' It was starting to sound clunky and false to Dan now, and he was sure she would pick up on his intentions. She looked at him.

'Do it,' she said.

Dan didn't know if he'd got enough on the recorder but he had a very strong urge to get out of there now.

'Okay, this is going to take a little while, I need to make my plans and then we'll discuss them and I'll come back to see you.'

'Okay, that sounds good,' said Judy. 'Do you have any ideas? For how you'll do it?'

'Yes, I've got a few but I need to see how viable they are.'

He had no ideas and hoped she didn't press him.

'I'm so happy,' she said leaning over and squeezing his hand. 'Your mother would be proud.'

Forty

They pulled up outside Mary Bolton's house and McQueen took in the modest exterior and the slightly shabby garden. He came to the same conclusion as Lia had; this wasn't where all the money had been spent.

Mary let them in and then took them through to the living room where Chris, standing with his arms folded, was waiting for them. The good biscuits weren't put out this time and when Mary asked them if they wanted a cup of tea her son immediately interjected.

'Woah, Mother, what are you doing? We're not running a cafe here, these people work for us. If anything they should be making us tea.' He was pointing at Lia and McQueen who were sitting next to each other on the sofa. Mary looked a little embarrassed but said nothing.

McQueen wasn't surprised by the aggression, he recognised it as the classic learned behaviour of someone who had survived in prison. Chris had spent years submerged in a culture of concede nothing and don't let anyone take advantage of you otherwise they will think you are weak.

'It's fine,' said Lia, directly to Mary. 'I had one before we got here.'

'I'd have been more than happy to make you both tea if you'd come over to our office, Chris,' said McQueen, 'but you wanted us to come here.'

The son grinned. 'We're not traipsing all over Leeds. Like I said, you work for us. We call, you come running.' He snapped his fingers. 'Like a dog.' McQueen could feel Lia bristling next to him and he placed a gentle hand on her arm to calm her. 'So, what have you actually done? To get my mother out of this stupid charge?' he demanded. While the three of them were sitting down, Chris was still standing in the centre of the room and McQueen guessed he'd probably read somewhere you should always be physically higher to dominate a negotiation. It was why a CEO he'd known had insisted on his chair being the tallest in the boardroom. McQueen glanced at Lia to let her take the answer, after all she was the one who had done all the work.

'As you know, we've had an in-depth trawl through the financial information you supplied and it threw up certain anomalies.'

'This trawl was by your boyfriend, Carl?' There it was again, the disturbing name-drop of Carl even though Lia was now certain neither she nor McQueen had ever mentioned his name to them. She let it go and carried on.

'On the back of that, I have recently been to meet the executives of Summertown Industries.'

Lia had noticed Mary had taken much more of a back seat in this meeting than she had in the others, she seemed subdued and quiet but at this she sat up in her seat and spoke up.

'Who'd you see?' she asked. Lia consulted her notes.

'Let me see, ah, David Hutchinson HR Director, a lawyer called Phil James, and a security officer called Shelley.' Mary snorted.

'Pah, crooks the lot of them. Shelley's just a thug in a suit.'

Chris became animated again.

'And what did they have to say, are they gonna drop the charges, then? Did you tell them what a stink we're gonna to make?' His overt aggression was making things uncomfortable for everyone but only because it was so stupid.

'I wouldn't be doing my job if I didn't pass on their message, Mrs Bolton.' Lia still had her eyes on the mother. 'They said you had no chance in court and if you pleaded guilty they would push for a lesser punishment.'

'They *what*?' said Chris, his surly attitude bursting into full-on anger.

'Let's try to be calm,' said McQueen. 'There are things we need to discuss with you and it won't help if you are too fired up to listen.'

'Let them speak, Chris,' pleaded Mary but her son turned on her.

'Shut up, Mum, I told you let me deal with this, you've been screwing this up from the start.'

Lia and McQueen exchanged a quizzical look and McQueen tried to take some of the heat out of the situation.

'The official representatives of Summertown are only saying exactly what we'd expect them to say, but it's like the opening offer in a trade. They were chancing their arm and Lia dealt with it robustly by telling them about the stink you mentioned, Chris. But there was something that came up which was a bit of a surprise. One of the things Summertown are going to leverage is your criminal past, Chris.' McQueen paused and watched as that thought worked its way across Chris's face. 'Unfortunately, you have a record you didn't tell us about and it would have been nice to know your side of it before Lia went in there.' Mary was looking down at her hands.

'What's my past got to do with anything? I did my time and I'm a free man now, I had nothing to do with the money, so what are you talking about?'

'They are going to paint a picture,' said McQueen in his same even tone, 'and they will paint your mother as a someone who had to steal a lot of money to help her criminal son out of a hole.'

'We are trying to help your mother, Chris,' said Lia, 'but to do that we need to know everything, and if there is anything you haven't told us about, then we need to know it now.'

Chris threw up his hands. 'I'm sick of this. We're paying you to do a job, you just do your job, find enough to get my mother off and that's all you need to do. You find dirt on Summertown, we hand it to our lawyer and he does the rest. You don't need to worry about me or my background, he's the expert he'll deal with that.'

McQueen had made a decision for the sake of his agency long ago. There had always been a lot of dodgy money to be made working for criminals but it wasn't a revenue stream that interested him. Lawyers could defend the guilty with impunity by falling back on the rightful argument that everyone is entitled to legal representation no matter how evil they are. Private investigators didn't have that shield, at what point in helping a crook through the blurred lines of the law do you become a criminal yourself? If McQueen could be sure Mary had stolen the money he would have walked away right there and then, but he couldn't be sure and the shady past and obnoxious behaviour of her son didn't make her guilty.

Lia was smiling, as she spoke.

'Well, if it turns out Summertown Industries are responsible for the intimidation and the attack on your mother, then you'll have all the dirt you need.'

Chris now turned his full attention to Lia.

'And how is Carl? After his little altercation?'

Lia's mouth dropped open.

'What? What are you talking about?' Chris had a nasty little smile on his face.

'I heard he got stopped in the street and threatened?'

'How do you know about that?' asked McQueen and Lia's head swivelled to him, a look of incredulity on her face.

'I'm still connected,' bragged Chris. 'I hear things from the streets, stuff gets back to me.' Lia recovered quickly, she wasn't about to let him get the upper hand even if she had no idea what had happened.

'Oh, that, it was nothing, he's fine, we've been laughing about it.'

'Glad to hear it,' said Chris with a wink. 'You have to be

careful, there's a lot of scum bags out there.'

When they got back out to the car, Lia kept her broad smile on until they had driven out of the street and away from watching eyes.

'You knew?' she exploded. 'Something happened with Carl and you knew?'

'He made me promise not to tell you, he didn't want to worry you.'

'What happened?'

'I'll let Carl tell you the details, but essentially it was a version of the brick through the window. A guy stopped him and told him you had to back off.'

Lia banged her fists on the dashboard.

'I knew something was going on. That's why you wanted to come to this meeting, because Carl asked you to. No one is telling me the truth. Not the Boltons, not Summertown, not Carl, and not you. I asked you directly if you had spoken to Carl and you said no.'

'You asked me if he had called me and he didn't. We spoke in person.'

'Oh, that is pathetic, McQueen, what are you, five years old?'

McQueen pulled over to the side of the road and turned the engine off so he could turn and face Lia.

'Carl does not inhabit this working world, Lia. He hasn't chosen to put himself in danger every day but what he sees is the person he loves most in the world doing exactly that. He's no mug with his head in the sand, he knows how bad things can get. Of course he's worried and he has every right to be.'

Lia sat glowering, she knew McQueen was right and the fact Carl being concerned was in his favour, that he cared about her, but what was stinging was the feeling of exclusion. Men had been making decisions about the things she should and shouldn't be told behind her back. It felt as if they hadn't been taking her seriously and it was not something she could put up with.

'Okay, McQueen, it might feel trivial to you but if you ever do that again, I *will* leave and get another job at another agency. I can't be ambushed and made to feel stupid by a scumbag in an interview because of something you haven't told me. Is that clear?'

'Look, I'm sorry, Lia. I should never have promised him I wouldn't tell you but I was in a difficult position. Carl is a great guy and he helped me, he made me aware of how big this thing could be and how it's going to need us both working as a team to handle it.'

'No more lies?' said Lia. 'Not even lies by omission?'

'Don't worry,' said McQueen starting the car up again. 'You'll get it all, no matter how ugly it is and I'll tell Carl anything he tells me he might as well tell you first.'

'And what about Chris Bolton? Do you think he just, *heard it from the streets*?'

'Like most things in this case, Lia, I have no idea.'

When they got back to the office McQueen sent a text to Carl.

Sorry but Lia found out about your incident in the street. It wasn't from me, but you better be ready for some explanations. Good luck.

Carl met Lia at the door when she got home and told her exactly what had happened outside the sandwich shop, every detail even the threat of the knife. He wasn't in any mood to apologise for having gone to see McQueen, or for trying to protect her from worrying.

'Your issues are becoming my issues and I have the right to expect McQueen to do his bit to protect you. You may not think you need to be protected, but that's not the point.'

'How could you go to my boss behind my back? I would never do that to you. Imagine it? If I went to see your CEO and told him I think he's putting you under too much pressure, that you aren't getting any downtime at weekends? How would you feel about that?'

'Yeah, but my work isn't going to end up with me being dead, Lia, that's the difference.'

'Is that right? Do you want to check the figures on men having heart attacks? Or the ones on over-worked young men committing suicide?'

They stood looking at each other, both breathing heavily for a few silent minutes.

'I don't want anything to happen to you,' said Carl eventually.

'Neither do I,' she answered. 'And I don't want anything to happen to you either, especially not because of *my* work.'

'Okay, we're okay then?' said Carl.

'Yep,' she answered before they hugged it out.

Forty-One

They sat on the bench and watched the dog as he sniffed around in the long grass.

'He's learned your police instincts,' said McQueen. 'He knows if he keeps sniffing something interesting might turn up.' He listened for a chuckle from Tracey but there wasn't one. It was early and there weren't many people about yet, only a few other dog walkers with their poo-bags at the ready and a couple of people cutting through the park on their way to work. McQueen had read that Roundhay was one of the largest urban parks in the world and he could believe it although he, Tracey, and Charlie only used a fraction of it. Same circular walk, same bench. From time-to-time Tracey's partner, Sophie, joined them but not on days when they would be talking shop. Sophie was a vet and not the military kind so she spent her days with sick animals, not criminals. She was all about caring and healing, and any conversation that strayed towards the consequences of violence left her cold.

The grey sky suggested rain was on its way although McQueen's phone app had said not. In the park there was a lot of heavy sky to look at and he trusted it more than he did the phone.

'So, you've decided to sue the police?'

McQueen sighed. 'I'm not suing the police, Mrs Kowalska is suing the police. She only asked me to be an impartial expert witness.'

'You know how this works, McQueen, they are going to shred you. They are going to try to destroy your *expert* status.'

'I know.'

'The gloves will be off and everything will be fair game, every mistake and failure, every little fault you've got or ever had.'

'I know.'

'And they'll do it, too, because they've put an expert on the job. A McQueen expert.'

'You?'

'Correct.'

'Makes sense. It's what I would have done if I were in charge. Who is in charge, anyway?'

'Detective Chief Superintendent Gibbons.'

'Good guy?'

'He's a dick but he's my boss.'

McQueen didn't blame Tracey for following orders, it was the career she'd chosen and there are always sacrifices in any role. It was how any large organisation worked. A chain of command led by orders from the top. They were all the same, police, army, drug smuggling, and people trafficking gangs. He knew Tracey would do a good job but he also knew she'd be honest, she wouldn't make stuff up, she wouldn't need to. He was more than aware he could be committing career suicide, at the very least making himself a few new enemies on the force, but no matter how hard he tried he couldn't get away from the belief that he owed Mrs Kowalska and her family a debt.

'And this Zach Lindley thing, McQueen? What the hell is going on there? What are you doing?'

'All I can tell you is that it's part of a job.'

'We interviewed the three of them who were in the Belvedere Hotel over the Richard Farnham murder, they were the last to see him but they all have rock-solid alibis. They are clean.'

'I understand that, but have you guys looked any closer than that, at his whole operation? What it is that he's up to?'

'No laws have been broken, McQueen.'

'Yet.'

'Well, when they are we'll get involved, but until then he's just another conspiracy theorist with a growing online following. And as far as the world is concerned, you are part of his group now.'

'Oh I didn't get a chance to thank you by the way for letting Judy Greene know it was me who told you about the knife she had in her bag. She took that well as you can imagine.'

Tracey shrugged.

'One of my colleagues interviewed her because you put her on the suspect list. He must have let it slip about the knife and the veiled threat to visit her ex. Anyway, it doesn't matter because they think they've pin-pointed the culprit now and his alibi has evaporated. He knows we've got him, he's not admitting anything but he's starting to claim some mystery person contacted him to murder Paul Mason and offered him money.'

McQueen chose not to tell Tracey about the overt threat Judy had made against his own life, he didn't have much to tell her. Unfortunately, in his nervousness when Dan had sat back in Judy's chair, it had disconnected the microphone lead and there was nothing damning on the audio file. It had captured the greetings and Dan's awkward chit-chat about her house, but then there was nothing but a white noise hiss. As they'd sat in the office and listened back to it Dan had been devastated. To try to make amends he'd written down everything he could remember Judy saying but it was obvious that, until it was recorded, it was fairly useless. Lia had tried to convince him to go back again as soon as possible, but he said he couldn't see how he could do it again without tipping her off. McQueen could see how uncomfortable he was with the whole thing and stepped in let him off the hook. He didn't want to scare Dan away completely and he could see that was a possibility the way it was going.

Tracey called Charlie over and clicked his lead onto his collar.

'We can't meet like this anymore,' she said. 'Not until this lawsuit is resolved, at least. We shouldn't have met today.'

'C'mon, we happened to bump into each other in the park Tracey and you know I love dogs.'

'Yeah, well, try explaining that to a paparazzi with a telephoto lens.'

Forty-Two

When they held their de-brief the next day, they both agreed it had been a difficult meeting, made way worse by Chris Bolton's attitude. McQueen asked if Lia wanted to drop the case altogether but she insisted she was still committed to helping Mary. Her feelings were clearly influenced by the fact she'd been the one who'd taken the flak from the suits at Summertown, she'd seen what they were up against and she hadn't liked what she saw. Besides, she still believed in Mary.

Lia had picked up on how different the dynamic had been with Chris in the room with the normally chatty, confident Mary deferring to her son and hardly daring to speak. It had been disturbing and the moment when he'd told his mother to shut up had sounded as loud as an alarm bell in their ears.

'And there was that thing he said about her screwing things up?' said Lia.

'He was bullying her, wasn't he, or as I might say, he was displaying bullying behaviour traits?'

'Oh, yeah, he was being a bully alright. Anyway, that's

another reason why I want to help Mary. I don't like bullies.'

McQueen said he supported her choice to stick with it and they discussed what their strategy should be. They decided to shift their emphasis away from the Boltons to exert some pressure on Summertown Industries. They wanted to see if feeling some heat might cause the higher-ups within the organisation to reconsider their threats and maybe force them into a wrong move.

There weren't many ways you could get to a company like Summertown but, luckily, McQueen had one powerful tool still left to use: the press. Like all big corporations, Summertown Industries were very protective of their public image and bad press was something to be avoided at all costs. McQueen had a long-standing loose professional relationship with a journalist called Anne Kirkpatrick. Anne was hardly a friend, she had looked to crucify McQueen's image more than once when his high-profile cases were going badly, but she was always ready to hear juicy stories. So far, reports of the upcoming trial had been very understated but McQueen was about to stir that up. He wanted to change the narrative from, single column page six, "RESPECTED COMPANY CRACKS DOWN ON THIEF", to front page, "SHADY MULTI-NATIONAL CORPORATION WITH FINANCIAL IRREGULARITIES POINTS FINGER AT AGEING SCAPEGOAT".

McQueen couldn't tell Anne what to write, of course, but when he ran her through the story with her on the phone she was mildly interested. When he added in the home invasion attempted murder which hadn't so far been reported anywhere else, and the brick through his window, she was hooked. As icing on the cake, McQueen offered an interview with a weeping Mary Bolton along with a photo opportunity of the broken-looking old woman.

It took about a week for the story to appear both in the press and online, where it quickly went viral. The internet is a strange place and they had managed to capture the lucrative sympathy market, within another day a Go Fund Me page had been set up to help with Mary's costs and the donations flooded in. The irony of someone accused of stealing two million pounds receiving donations from the public didn't escape McQueen, but it also showed how successful Anne Kirkpatrick had been at painting Mary as a victim.

McQueen and Lia both couldn't believe how well the plan had gone but were bracing themselves for the backlash. At some point, Summertime were bound to deploy their own PR machine to plant stories about Chris Bolton's past, but they were ready for that. *You can't judge a mother by her son*, and *look at what a hard life the poor woman's had* might resonate with lots of parents.

Forty-Three

'So let's hear your plan.'

Dan was back in Judy's living room and it had taken a monumental effort of willpower to get him there. Surely she would realise what was going on this time? How could she not if he repeated the same questions? McQueen had been adamant what they needed was for her to clearly state her intention to kill him. She wasn't about to just say it, so once again Dan would have to play cat and mouse to try to get her to agree it's what she wanted. But it also had to not sound like something she could later claim was a misunderstanding or joke. Easy.

'Plan?'

'Yes, your fool-proof plan of how to kill McQueen? You said you had one?'

'Oh, yes, the plan.'

In the office Dan had been completely blank on this but with a little help from McQueen he'd come up with something plausible, he just hoped he could remember it.

'Are you okay?' she asked. 'Have you got a bad back? You're sitting very stiffly?'

The McQueen Legacy

It was the thought of the recorder burning a hole in his back that was making him squirm.

'Er, yes, I went to the gym yesterday for the first time in ages. Overdid it a bit.'

'Oh, dear, that must be painful.' Her sympathy was touching and made him feel worse than ever. 'Shall I get you a hot water bottle? I have one.' The thought of her reaching around near his back was terrifying.

'No, no, I'm fine, really.'

'Okay. So, that plan?'

'Right, so we need to make this look like an accident. That's what you want, isn't it? You want me to murder him and make it look like an accident?'

She nodded. Dan waited for her to say something for the recording but she didn't add to her nod.

'So I'm thinking car accident. As you know, McQueen had a drinking problem in the past. It's well known alcoholics fall off the wagon all the time. So if I wait until late one night when we are alone in the office I can drug him in his coffee. Then when he's drowsy I can tip drink down his throat. Then I can get him into his car and stage an accident.'

Judy leaned back in her armchair, a look of disappointment on her face.

'That's crap,' she said. 'It won't work.' When they came up with the plan they had decided it only needed to be good enough to get her on the device agreeing to it.

'Oh, why not?'

'A million reasons. The autopsy would find the drug in his blood, it would also find there was no alcohol in his bloodstream. And how are you going to get him from his office to his car? You going to carry him? I don't think so, especially if you have a dodgy back. And how exactly would you stage the accident? How would you get the car to drive into a wall at speed? It makes no sense.'

Dan sat chastened wishing he was anywhere else but in that room. 'The thing is, Dan, I don't want you to get caught because you would inevitably bring me into it.'

'So what do you suggest?'

'I'll come up with something,' she said. This was going disastrously and the one thing Dan was sure of was that he was never going to be doing it ever again, so he had to take his best shot.

'So, you're saying that you're going to come up with a plan to kill McQueen?' She nodded. 'I'm confused, is this going to be a plan for me to carry out or for you to do?' She narrowed her eyes and for a dreadful second Dan thought it was all over.

'Yes, Dan,' she said quite loudly, 'I'm saying that I'm going to come up with the fool-proof plan for you to kill McQueen because you have the access. Have I made that clear enough for you?'

'I think you have,' he said. She got up and crossed to the chest of drawers that was against the far wall. She took out a pad and then hunted around until she found a pen. She came back and dumped it into Dan's lap.

'Now, write down all of McQueen's movements as you know them for the next couple of weeks. Everything. When he's in, when he's at home, when he's out at meetings. Give me as much detail as you can remember so I can work out the best time to do this.'

Dan began to write. This was one task that he could manage easily, he had intimate knowledge of McQueen's diary, he kept it up to date every day. He wrote neatly and quickly. It felt nice to be doing something right for a change.

Forty-Four

Everything had changed. The pot holes had been filled with crushed rubble but it was still a bumpy ride and, as McQueen turned left at the dog-leg and looked down at the valley, he stopped the car. There had been a transformation. The terracotta-coloured roof of the farm buildings were still there but they were surrounded by a sea of white blocks, which he could make out as the tops of the tents. Between the various buildings, McQueen could see people milling around. He took out his phone to take a picture and then scrolled back and forth to the first one he'd taken weeks before to assess the differences.

When he drove on down to the farm the old gate was closed and there was a young man standing at it, clipboard in hand. Unsmiling, he came forward to duck down to the open car window.

'My name's McQueen, Zach Lindley is expecting me.' It sounded oddly formal like something you would say at the door of a stately home, not at a rusty farm gate. The man checked his list, had a quick scan around the inside of the car and then went to open the gate.

The McQueen Legacy

McQueen trundled past the rows of large white tents with their sturdy aluminium frames and sloping roofs, like marquees waiting for some enormous village fete. McQueen could see inside one or two of the structures and he saw two rows of bunkbeds in one of them and what appeared to be a kitchen in another. The sounds of construction were reverberating everywhere, the saws and hammers echoing off the red-brick walls of the old farm buildings. Everywhere there were men moving around with purpose, not speaking to each other, too intent on whatever job they had been given.

McQueen rolled into the main court-yard area and parked as before, and Zach came out of the main house to greet him, however rather than being kept out by his car this time he was invited inside. The interior hallway was not plush, plaster was coming away at the bottom of the walls and it obviously hadn't been decorated since its previous occupants. There was no carpet or trendy wooden flooring, just pragmatic old chipped and cracked tiles underfoot that had probably seen many a muddy boot. McQueen had thought perhaps Zach would be living in a leader's palace but it was clearly the man-of-the-people vibe he was going for.

At the end of the corridor McQueen was led into a room that contrasted sharply with what he'd seen so far. This room had been refurbished, redecorated, and refurnished in muted pastel colours like a hospital's quiet mediation sanctuary for bereaved relatives. With the door closed and the thick carpet the sounds of construction from outside were muffled to a whisper.

'Lot of activity out there,' said McQueen. 'Are they hired workers?'

'No, all followers,' said Zach. 'Working towards a common goal.'

'Which is?'

'Saturday the first,' he answered serenely. 'A date for your diary. All will be revealed on Saturday the first of June. And you must be here for that.'

'Wouldn't miss it for the world.'

A half smile flashed across Zach's face for a millisecond.

'Have you brought the legal papers with you? The ones I asked you to sign?'

'About that,' said McQueen. He was sunk into a sofa while Zach was sitting above him in a straight-backed chair. 'Sorry. They are still with my lawyer, I'm afraid. He's really dragging his feet, I've asked him to get his finger out but you know what these legal guys are like, I mean have you ever bought or sold a house? Nightmare.'

McQueen had only had one message from his lawyer after sending over the documents and it said, "Don't sign these."

'It would be really great if you could bring them before the big reveal,' said Zach.

'I must say I was a bit shocked to see all the social media coverage of me joining this group, by the way.'

'Was there a problem?'

'No, not at all, it was just a surprise. It would have been nice to have had a little warning.'

'Warning? I thought you'd be pleased. You are very

important to us, Doctor McQueen so I wanted to get the news out there as soon as possible.'

'Of course, me too, but I'm not as slick with the internet world as you.'

'I have a gift for you,' said Zach in the same understated tone that he always used. If it was change of conversational direction designed to keep McQueen confused and off balance it worked.

'A gift, really?'

'Yes. You see the police have been questioning myself and some of my followers about the murder of Richard Farnham and it needs to be put to bed.'

After being initially kept under wraps by the authorities the official news of the murder enquiry had now hit the press and outrageous rumours and theories were swirling around the virtual world. As the last ones to see Richard alive Zach, Joey, and Brice had come under some scrutiny even though they had alibis. McQueen guessed it couldn't have been comfortable for someone who spent so much of his time cultivating an online following to be part of the rumour mill.

'The gift I am going to give you is that I am going to tell you exactly who killed Richard.'

So, the pressure had got to Zach. McQueen waited without saying anything. When a suspect is about to confess you don't ever interrupt. McQueen was waiting for Zach to throw one of his underlings under the bus, would it be Brice or Joey? 'Richard had a pregnant partner, her name is Tania,' he said. 'She killed him.'

McQueen was shocked and he didn't manage to hide it.

'What? What makes you think that?'

'I don't think, I know. Richard was about to tell Tania he was going to come to join us here at the farm and she was being left behind. It was his decision entirely. He was also going to make a very generous donation to our cause. He took her to those very woods to break the news, because that's where they used to walk when they were first dating. That was the last thing he told me before he left.'

'And did you tell the police all this?'

'Of course not. I'm not going to put myself forward as a witness. I don't want to appear in court. I don't want this group to be part of that mess. I want nothing to do with the police, I don't trust them and I don't want them spending any more time looking at us. As far as they are concerned we know nothing and that's the end of the story. For instance, if someone had followed them to the woods to make sure that Richard had been serious about telling her, then that person might have seen the incident, but that person will never come forward.'

'So why are you telling me?'

'Because with your considerable skills as a private investigator you will find a way to put this all to bed without implicating us in any of it. Because never forget, McQueen, you *are* one of us now.'

As McQueen's car bounced along the track away from the farm he mulled over the possibilities. It sounded far-fetched and Zach could be trying to deflect attention and cover his own guilt but there was a ring of truth to what he'd said which left McQueen feeling very uncomfortable. He hadn't

The McQueen Legacy

thought much about Tania, she had kept him at arm's length since the murder so it wouldn't hurt to take a closer look. First he needed a big favour from Tracey but he wasn't sure he'd be able to get it with the way things stood with the impending lawsuit.

Forty-Five

As McQueen pulled into the parking space outside his flat, he noticed a black limousine parked a few spaces away but didn't think much of it. He thought it was probably for someone from the flats going to a posh event, it did happen from time to time. He could make out a driver in front but he couldn't see if there was anyone else sitting in the back. When McQueen got out of his car so did the other driver who then came towards him and McQueen wondered if he should get back in his car. The man wasn't dressed as a typical chauffeur, more like a taxi driver, he was wearing a black T-shirt, black jeans, and a pair of blindingly white trainers but he didn't appear to be carrying any weapons. Still, McQueen was wary, he had obviously been waiting for him.

'Doctor McQueen?'

'Yes.'

'Mr Preston would like to have a word with you. He's in the car, if you would?'

'Who the hell is Mr Preston apart from being a guy in the back of that car?'

'He's my boss.'

'Well, he's not *my* boss, so what does he want?'

The back door of the limo opened and the cheerful, friendly face of a middle-aged man peered out.

'You have an admirable reluctance to get into strange cars with strange men, Doctor McQueen,' said the man. 'But I assure you, you are in no danger.'

'That's good to hear but who are you and what do you want?'

'Please, Doctor McQueen, get in, I don't want to hold this conversation on the street. Danny will be staying outside, we won't be driving anywhere.'

'Who are you?' repeated McQueen. 'I'm not getting in until I know who you are.'

'I own Summertown Industries, Doctor McQueen, now will you get in?'

The roomy seats were as comfortable as you'd expect in a car that cost more than most people's houses, lots of leg room. McQueen sat beside Mr Preston but they were both half-turned to face each other. He was a well-groomed handsome man in a well-cut beautiful dark blue suit and in comparison, McQueen felt very shabby in his creased trousers and scuffed shoes.

'The reason I like to hold meetings in this car is that it's a special car, it can't be bugged,' he said amiably. 'And if you were wearing any kind of recording device the fancy sensors in the door frame would have alerted me. Also, they would have told me if you had anything large and metal like a gun. The windows are tinted so that even with a long lens there can be no lip-reading from outside.'

'For the owner of a highly respectable company you take an unusually large amount of precautions,' said McQueen.

'Yes, I suppose I do, but that's why I'm still around.'

'What do you want from me?'

'Firstly, I must congratulate you, you've done a great job, Doctor McQueen, in turning a very simple, boring case of corporate stealing into a cause celebre. Just as you hoped it would, your spin on the case has attracted much attention of the kind that I and Summertown Industries do not want.'

'I can't take all the credit,' said McQueen. 'The internet has a life of its own.'

'But you planted the seed with your pet journo, Anne Kirkpatrick, didn't you?' McQueen could imagine the horror on Anne's face at hearing herself described as his pet journo, if she was a pet she was the XL Bully waiting to rip its owner's face off. 'Now, when I said I was the owner of Summertown Industries, that wasn't strictly true. My name doesn't appear anywhere on any official documentation. We have a capable CEO and all the official legal side of things is taken care of, but I call the shots. I work directly for the syndicate who do ultimately own Summertown. My job is crystal clear, I have to present Summertown Industries as a legitimate, rock-solid company, with no controversy and no drama. It has clean money. The sort of money that can buy influence and power.'

'So drop the charges and this all goes away, surely Summertown can find some other way to bury a trifling two mill?'

'Well, here's the problem,' said Preston. 'The syndicate that do own Summertown, the people calling the shots if you like, come from a side of the business where stealing is dealt with in a much less merciful way. In fact, it's dealt with in a frankly cruel and brutal way. A bloody and brutal example has to be made of thieves to discourage others. It's barbaric, I know, but there it is. Do you understand?'

'I think so, you mean the drug smuggling criminal side of your squeaky-clean corporation.'

'I never said that, but I think you understand. I have had a hard time convincing my bosses that, to maintain our image, we have to make sure we use the courts. They want this business to be legitimate so it can open the door to the highest circles. Unfortunately, it's against their every instinct to use the law, but I have made them see sense for their long-term future. But I won't be able to hold them off forever. Now, I have to apologise for the clumsy, amateurish scenes you've already witnessed. The brick and the threats against your assistant's boyfriend? That's what happens when you leave things to people who are too young and too enthusiastic, too keen to please. It won't happen again.'

'And what about the attack on Mary Bolton in her home?'

The older man laughed.

'Not us, I'm afraid. That was beyond stupid. My point is this, McQueen, to save my reputation someone has to go to jail for the missing money. I don't care if its the mother or the son, but the alternative is they will probably both end up dead and that *will* be out of my control.'

'But what if she didn't steal the money?'

'Mister McQueen, sorry, *Doctor* McQueen, please don't take me for an idiot.' For the first time McQueen saw the face behind the mask of amiability. 'What if I told you we know exactly where the money went and we know the people who it was paid to? The money itself is already back in our possession. It's not about the money, it's about the way it looks. No one can be seen to steal from us and walk away. We don't want any more publicity and we don't want a trial. We want a confession, otherwise there will be a funeral and you can count on that.'

Preston leaned across McQueen who flinched but he was only stretching to open McQueen's door. All pretence of friendliness was gone.

'Don't forget, a mother will do a lot to protect her son but when the son is nothing but a mangy dog that favour is not always returned. Meeting's over,' he said his craggy face now illuminated as he turned his attention to his phone.

McQueen watched the limousine drive away and then dug his own phone out of his pocket.

'Lia? Hi, yeah, listen you wanted to be kept in the loop, right? Well I'm about to loop the hell out of you.'

Forty-Six

They were in the office early because McQueen wanted Carl to be there, too, which meant he had to fit it in before going to his own office.

Dan had also come in and he was sitting quietly to one side of McQueen's crowded room. They had already listened to the recording he'd made of Judy and they'd given him lots of praise and pats on the back. Lia had said he had the makings of an excellent investigator, which he knew was patronising nonsense. What he hadn't told anyone was he'd already started applying for other jobs. All they were waiting for was for was Judy to deliver the actual McQueen murder plan and then at that stage they would involve the police. Dan was secretly praying her plan never materialised.

McQueen ran them all through what had happened the night before in the limo and they sat in silence.

'So, I don't know if it's any comfort, Carl, but he said your sandwich encounter was a mistake and it won't happen again.'

'Great,' said Carl his voice laced with sarcasm. 'And did

he offer to pay for the sandwich that got dropped?'

McQueen ignored the joke.

'So, I think we need to go back once more and talk to Mary, and—'

'No,' said Lia. 'My case. Not we, *I* am going to go back, but I'm not going to talk to Mary, I'm going straight to the root of the problem. I'm going to speak to Chris Bolton.'

Carl and McQueen exchanged a look and Carl shrugged.

The video entry buzzed from the other room and Dan gratefully went to answer it. Nothing about the things he'd just heard concerning a gangster in a limo had made him change his mind about finding another form of employment. When he went back into McQueen's room he said, 'There's a foreign woman, I think she said her name was Kowalski? She said she wants to speak to you, McQueen?'

'Ah, Mrs Kowalska, yes, please let her in.'

McQueen had cleared his office of the others and he and Sonia sat opposite each other and it was nice to see she was smiling.

'You have done me big favour,' she said and when he looked puzzled she added, 'By being expert witness you gave me power.'

'Well, we'll have to see how that goes when it gets to court, I know they are preparing to destroy my reputation, so we'll see how much my help really counts.'

'No, no,' she said shaking her head. 'It already has. No trial. I have settled. They have offered me money and I have

The McQueen Legacy

settled. I am not allowed to say how much, I am not allowed to speak about it, but it is much more than it was before they saw that you were the expert witness.'

McQueen was slightly shocked but also secretly relieved, he hadn't been looking forward to Tracey's hatchet job on him because he knew she could swing a mean hatchet.

'I think it's probably the right decision, but I thought you wanted to make them suffer a bit? Make it all public?'

'I realised nothing will bring Tomasz back. I am mother with three children and I have to do what's best for them. The money will help and when I prayed to God for help, he sent this offer. I have to be practical, my tears will solve nothing.'

'Okay, well congratulations sounds a bit crass given the circumstances but I'm glad you are satisfied.'

'And now you can sleep,' she said.

'What?'

'Now you don't need to think any more about what might have happened. What happened happened and we can't change it. I never blamed you.'

'But I blamed myself,' he said simply.

'So stop,' she said. 'Your tears will also solve nothing.'

When Tracey phoned later, McQueen could tell she was just as pleased as he was.

'I'll send you a copy of the report I did on you,' she said. 'You should take a good look at it there might be some pointers in there for you to improve your life.'

'Thanks,' he answered knowing full-well he was never

going to read it. 'But while you're on and we're on speaking terms again, I have a little favour to ask.'

'God,' she said exasperatedly, 'This is like point four of the report, McQueen. Your blurring of the lines and your entitlement.'

'I know, I know, it's a lot to ask, but it could lead to a murderer?'

She sighed heavily down the line.

'Go on then, what is it?'

Forty-Seven

McQueen had never been to Tania's flat before so he'd been surprised when she'd agreed to meet him there this time. He'd casually explained he had a few things he wanted to tell her that no other ears should overhear, so she'd reluctantly given him her address. Her place was out on the edge of Leeds and it was a beautiful flat, tastefully decorated and diligently clear of any clutter or mess. It was if it had been professionally dressed for a magazine shoot and McQueen had dutifully taken his shoes off at the door as requested. He wondered how it would look once the baby was born and running around creating toddler havoc. But maybe that wasn't going to be a problem anyway. Tania didn't offer him any refreshment and he was sure that was because she didn't trust him not to make a mess. She was probably right.

After they had been through the strained chit-chat and he'd asked her how her health was she asked, 'So what is it you want? You know you don't work for me anymore, right?'

'Technically, I never did, Tania. No business transaction

ever took place, no money changed hands.'

'Ah, well, none was earned. We've been through this already if that is what you've come about. You let me down badly and because of that my partner died, so don't be asking me for payment.'

'No, this is something else, it's to do with some information I've received.'

'Oh, good. Have you got news on Richard's murder because the police are telling me nothing, I think they've given up?'

The discussion between McQueen and Tracey had become quite heated. She'd wanted him to turn everything he knew over to them so they could do things officially, but McQueen had managed to convince her their best bet was to let him go in first.

'Tell me about Stanmore Woods?' he said, carefully gauging her reaction. She seemed emotionless.

'It's where they found Richard's body,' she answered flatly.

'Have you ever been there? To those woods?'

'To see where they found him? How ghoulish would that be?'

'No, I mean before. Was it somewhere you and Richard went regularly for walks together, perhaps? And then did you always stop at the cafe at the end, for instance?' She didn't answer and McQueen knew she was trying to calculate how many people might have been willing to testify it was their favourite Sunday walk. There were plenty of witnesses, the cafe owner even knew their names. She assumed correctly that McQueen had spoken to him.

The McQueen Legacy

'What difference does it make?'

'It's just you never mentioned it before. I'd have thought it would have been something that would have come up?' She fixed him with a cold stare, but didn't try to waffle her way out of it. 'Did you know the police can track your phone? Even when you aren't talking or texting it still pings the network masts. So they can pinpoint if a person is in a place and at what time they are there.'

She remained stone faced.

'So if a person was in the woods at a specific critical time and they had their phone with them, the police would be able to tell.' He let that sink in. He wanted to keep hitting her with difficult facts, to keep her off balance and overload her senses.

'Oh, and sorry to be gruesome, but they finally found the tree branch, by the way. The one that was used to bludgeon Richard from behind? The murder weapon?' Tania didn't react so McQueen pressed on. 'That fact hasn't been released by the police to the press for obvious reasons, but apparently it had been carried quite a distance away and partially buried.' She was still looking straight at him and her hand was slowly caressing her swollen belly but she was saying nothing.

'The thing about rough wood is that it's very hard to clean off. Too many crevasses and cracks. So if a person's DNA is on that wood, it is fairly easy to find.'

Her rhythmic stomach rubbing continued at the same comforting pace.

'Why are you telling me all this?' she asked at last. 'Why aren't the police telling me?'

'Because I'm very lucky. I have a close friend on the force and I get the heads up before anyone else. And that's good news for you, Tania, because I'm giving you a chance to get in first. If you go and turn yourself in now, before they come for you, which they certainly will, you can earn yourself a lot of credit with the court.'

'Credit?'

'A woman in your condition, with the stress that's on you, he takes you to the woods where you went on your first date and then he tells you he wants to leave you to join Zach Lindley's group? Brutal. No wonder you snapped.'

McQueen had been gambling on Tania's pragmatism, on her analytical mind being able to recognise the only escape route open to her. He'd also been taking a huge risk based on a guess. Tracey Bingham had refused to give him any confidential information from the phone records, he didn't know if there was any phone evidence placing her in the woods. All Tracey would give him was the information that a murder weapon had been found but the DNA testing was still to be done. It seemed there was a bit of a backlog of untested possible murder weapons at the lab.

It was time for hardest part of all now, it was time for McQueen to shut up and let the ball bounce around the roulette wheel of his gamble. He knitted his fingers and stared back at Tania, leaving the silent vacuum between them, hoping she would make the calculations and fill the void.

She looked down at her belly again and smoothed the material of her dress over it.

'I did snap,' she said. 'But it was because he threatened

me. It was self-defence. Do you know the statistics, Doctor McQueen, because I do? Did you know that homicide by partner is the leading cause of death for pregnant women in America? Yes, amazing isn't it? A pregnant woman is more likely to die at the hands of her partner than from medical complications. Weak, immature men who can't accept their responsibilities, just like Richard.'

'Is that why you decided to kill him first?' he coaxed gently.

'It's true he told me he was leaving me and his unborn child to join that ridiculous cult. Then he said he had taken all the money from the joint account. But it wasn't enough, he wanted half of my money, the money I had earned. Half the value of the flat. When I said no he got very angry and then he asked me if I realised that he could kill me right there in the woods and no one would ever know it was him and then he would get it all.'

'So, how did it actually happen? Did he attack you?'

'I didn't give him a chance, I had to protect my baby. There was a narrow path off the main track between some trees and he walked in front of me and told me to follow him, so I took my chance, I saw the big branch on the ground, it was fate, I grabbed it and smashed his stupid head in before he could do it to me. I wasn't thinking about trying to get away with it, it wasn't pre-meditated, it was a crime of passion, I was having an out of body experience.'

'You must have lost your temper, though, there were a lot of injuries, more than were needed to kill him.'

'He was on the ground, still moving, and I knew if he got up he would kill me so I kept hitting and hitting.'

Tania had said all of this without the slightest tear or sob, and McQueen was hoping that the recorder taped to the small of his back and the microphone at the second button of his shirt was picking it all up.

'And then you tried to bury him?'

'Not really, it was quite blowy that day and I think the wind must have blown leaves over him.'

'But you never reported it.'

'I called the police to tell them what had happened, I really did, but then I was distraught and I couldn't face it, so I just told them he hadn't come home. The next thing I knew he became a missing person and I sort of started thinking maybe no one would ever find him, which was a bit silly, I know, but I wasn't thinking straight.'

'But when they did find him, you could have come forward then?'

'It was too late by then. I did know about phone data and all of that, and I was waiting for them to come for me, but they never did. Every day it seemed more distant, I started to think I might be safe. Until now, when the man who I hired is the man to bring me the bad news.'

'I'm bringing you the opportunity to make the best of it, Tania. It's going to happen so this is your chance to control the narrative. A pregnant woman, tired and stressed defending her unborn child against an abusive partner.'

She snorted dismissively.

'It was your fault. If you had done what I asked in the first place, if you had told me it was a dangerous cult and they would brainwash Richard then I would have kicked him into touch much earlier and it would never have got this far. But no, you were brainwashed too, and now you've joined them, so I blame you, McQueen.'

'Yes, I've heard phrase that a lot lately.'

It was her final outburst and now her shoulders slumped, the fight had gone out of her. Tania seemed to have resigned herself to her fate and when McQueen suggested she go with him to the police station, she agreed without argument.

As he helped her to gather up a few of her things McQueen said, 'What's going to happen now is—' but she held up her palm to stop him.

'I know what's going to happen,' she said. 'I Googled it a while ago. Along with quite a few other related things.'

'Right, well, the police will seize your computer and see those searches.'

For the first time she smiled.

'Unfortunately, I lost my laptop. I accidentally left it on a bus. You get very scatty and forgetful sometimes when you are pregnant,' she said. 'Haven't you heard that?'

Forty-Eight

'We're dropping your mother's case.'

Lia had deliberately chosen a Starbucks to meet Chris because she wanted people around her, just in case. It wasn't hard to persuade him when she'd said she would be paying for whatever fancy, expensive coffee concoction he chose. Plus a toasted sandwich.

'Why?' he was munching his food, some of it dribbling down his chin and Lia could hardly bring herself to look at him. His aggressive attitude had been somewhat muted perhaps by the proximity of other people, and he looked slightly uncomfortable, his eyes flicking from left to right checking out everyone who approached. Lia wondered if this had something to do with habits learned eating in a Spanish prison canteen.

'I took this case against the better judgement of my boss because I desperately wanted to help your mother. I was convinced she was an innocent, and I still am.'

'And now you don't want to help her? Bit harsh, isn't it?'

'But now I realise there is only one person who can

help her and in fact save her life, and that is you.'

'What you talking about?'

'I don't think you are a man who appreciates bullshit, so I'll just say it. I think you bullied your mother into stealing the money for you when you were badly in debt. Maybe you just got her to give access to the system to some of your associates? That's why she was able to say she didn't actually steal the money, but in the eyes of the law it's not really the truth. I think your mum has been protecting you ever since.'

'Oh, is that what you think?' he said with studied indifference.

'Yes, and I think it was also your plan to stage the attempted attack on your mum to put the focus on Summertown. She went along with it because she's a mother and she loves her boy.'

He smirked and took a drink from the enormous cup he'd ordered.

'You think it was me who pushed you into the wall, do you?' he almost giggled.

'I've always known it was you, Chris, I didn't want to believe it, but I was pretty sure from that first time you came into your mother's front room.'

'Is that right? Can you prove it?'

'No, but I don't have to, you have much bigger problems, and so does your mother. Now, I don't know how much you care about your mum, you made a big show of pretending to care about her before but I trust you about as far as I could throw you.' He laughed in a display of how little he thought of Lia's trust. 'But

McQueen had a meeting with a guy called Mr Preston. Ever heard that name?' For the first time Chris looked as if Lia had hit a tender spot. 'He made it very clear the three choices you are facing are these: One, your mother, an aging vulnerable woman goes to jail where frankly the strain could mean she might die. Two, you, a young man who is tough and has thrived in the prison system before, goes inside. And let's face it, it will only be a couple of years, it's theft not murder.'

She had his attention now and he'd stopped messing around with his coffee cup.

'And what's three?'

'Three is we really go for it, your lawyer pulls out all the stops, we get lucky and no one goes to jail. Unfortunately, the downside is that to save Preston's reputation you both have to die.'

Chris started to speak, but Lia was already getting up. 'I'm not interested in your denials and lies, Chris, save your breath. You can check to see if I'm lying with your contacts, the ones who give you the buzz from the streets. Like I said, we're out, you're on your own and your life and your mother's is in your hands.'

She turned and left him sitting there. There was no point pleading or trying to appeal to the better nature of someone who doesn't have one so she wasn't going to try.

Forty-Nine

Saturday, the day of the big reveal and there was an expectant buzz circulating through the farm. Finally, they were going to find out what the great Zach Lindley had been planning for them all along. McQueen had got there with enough time to wander around soaking up the atmosphere like the time he'd been to a music festival before the bands had arrived. And it was very similar. There was an open area where a stage had been set up and an enormous screen was behind the microphone stand. McQueen hadn't seen Zach yet, he was locked inside the farm house with his two closest confidents, Brice and Joey.

The construction noises had stopped and everything had been tidied up, but the old farm buildings were still closed off. The men that were walking around all seemed to know him even though he didn't recognise them. He stopped one of the guys to ask what was going on and he said they had all been shown a film and briefed about how important he was. McQueen wasn't sure what to make of it but he carried on sauntering

He had no idea what was going to happen but he half

expected there would be a disappointing anti-climax. Maybe Zach would, once again, move the goal posts and delay the reveal to some point in the future. The shadow of the association with Richard's death had not been entirely erased now Tania had been formally arrested and charged. She would surely be trying to smear the group and its influence during her defence, but they would be able to dodge that now none of them were actual suspects.

McQueen was looking up at the giant screen when he felt a tap on his arm and turned to see Brice. He was smiling broadly.

'Zach wants to see you,' he said and led the way to the farm house. Once again, McQueen walked the scruffy corridor to the inner sanctuary where Zach was waiting for him. Zach had worn exactly the same outfit, understated white shirt and plain trousers every time McQueen had seen him, but today was different. He was dressed in a green robe. It was such a surprise that McQueen even said, 'Wow.'

'Did you bring the legal documents?' was Zach's first question.

'Unfortunately not, my lawyer seems to have mislaid them and I need to get some copies.'

'I thought not,' said Zach but he didn't appear too upset. 'No matter, we can work around that.'

'So, big reveal day,' said McQueen trying to change the subject in a jocular tone. 'Are we storming Parliament or setting up our own political party, what's the deal?'

'Do you remember I promised you a legacy, McQueen?'

'Yes.'

'Political parties are not a legacy, they do not endure.

The McQueen Legacy

Political movements are only fashions that change with the wind. There is only one thing which endures for centuries and that is religion. But we are in a modern age and it is time for a new religion, McQueen, one that does not place a non-existent god at its centre but one which embraces the harsh realities all those men out there have experienced. Whatever faith they come from, I guarantee none of their prayers have ever been answered.' He was pointing at the door behind McQueen. 'That is why they are here. That's how they were selected, people who are ready for something that will finally see who they are and provide for them. I am their new religion.' He had spread his arms wide, the sleeves of his robe hanging loosely. 'There will be resistance from the powers that are being usurped, but we are ready to fight fire with fire. We are ready for the battle.'

McQueen felt a wave of disappointment wash over him. So that was it, after all this Zach's big future was going to be another tin-pot pseudo religious cult, with him at the top, no doubt. He hadn't wanted to reveal it until he had established a big enough following for fear of putting them off, but now he was confident. Tania had been right all along. McQueen had allowed himself to think there might be something more, but he'd been fooled.

'And now I will tell you why you are so important to us, McQueen.' McQueen was trying to think of a tactful way to say it didn't matter how important he was and that at the end of this discussion, he was gone.

'You are well known and you are respected, you have a name, you fit the bill. Every religion needs a martyr to kick-start it, someone who is prepared to die for the cause and the more famous they are the better. In the case of Jesus, the genius stroke was they believed he rose again. And that's what they will believe of you. You will die tonight, on that big screen for everyone to see, and then through the power of artificial intelligence you will rise again.' McQueen wasn't really taking this in, it was a joke for sure and he wasn't taking it seriously.

'I thought A.I. was one of the modern big dangers you like to preach about?'

Zach laughed. 'We have to harness the power of our enemies for the greater good.'

'Okay, I think I'm done,' said McQueen standing up. 'I only ever wanted to know what you were up to and frankly I'm disappointed. Zach, you are just the latest in a very long line of men who want to play god.' He crossed to the door but when he opened it Joey was standing there with a gun pointing at his stomach. It wasn't the first time he had seen a gun and indeed it wasn't the first time one had been pointed at him. He still had the scars.

'Joey will take you to the room now,' he said. 'And later you will drink a delicious cocktail while being beamed live to the group outside. You will have already made a speech in which you pledge your eternal support to us and you will say you are sacrificing your life to show how much you believe in me. The ultimate sacrifice for the ultimate religion.' McQueen turned to Zach who was still sitting down. 'I know what you are thinking,' continued Zach. 'You think you won't do it, but that speech has already been generated and recorded in your voice. It's uncanny. Your dead body will be displayed to everyone and then in a few

The McQueen Legacy

days you will speak again.'

McQueen weighed up all his options. He could try to rush Joey but the gun was still pointed at him and he was far enough away to make it impossible without taking a bullet in the stomach.

'I know everything you are thinking, McQueen. I've told you before, I am the master of psychology. If you had truly committed to us and brought the legal documents this could have been voluntary, but you made that choice. Now you are wondering if you might overpower Joey, but if you die here it will make no difference to the plan but it might be more painful for you.'

McQueen allowed himself to be led away from the room. Joey opened the back door and pointed him across the yard to an outbuilding. As they were crossing Joey started to whisper.

'Slow down,' and suddenly bent over to pick up a half brick that was lying amongst the farm rubble. 'We haven't got much time,' he added passing the brick to McQueen. 'Try to make it convincing but don't kill me,' he said. 'You go through that gate at the end, then over a wall and you're away.'

McQueen was shocked but still suspicious, was this just a ploy to shoot him in the back?

'I don't get it,' he said.

'We haven't got time for this, I'm an undercover cop,' said Joey. 'I infiltrated this group months ago and we've been waiting for the right moment. There's going to be a huge raid tonight but if you hang around you'll be dead by then, so get on with it.' McQueen still hesitated. 'If you want a password, it's Tracey Bingham.'

McQueen had never hit anyone with a brick before but he didn't need another invitation. He tried to make it a glancing blow, but the blood looked real enough. Once Joey sank to his knees McQueen threw down the brick and made his break for it.

Fifty

Alone in his flat, McQueen was glad there was no wine in his cupboard, it had been an extraordinary couple of days and he might well have been tempted. He'd taken a call from Tracey and she told him the raid on the farm had gone well and a large cache of illegal weapons had been discovered. The police had been tracking the importation of arms for months. Zach's new religion had been preparing for their own kind of holy war. Joey was still undercover and to maintain the story, he'd been arrested along with the others. She said he had a sore head but he was okay.

McQueen rubbed his knee, he'd torn his trousers scrambling over the wall in a panic to get away and his knee had been scraped but it was a playground injury compared to what Zach had in mind for him. Come the time, McQueen would have to feature as a star witness in a charge of attempted murder and he was ready for it.

The intercom buzzed and, although it was late, he answered it.

'Hi, it's Lia.' The sound was crackly and McQueen made a mental note to ask the landlord when he was going to upgrade to a full-on video entry system for the flats, the extortionate ground-rent would surely cover that?

'Yeah, come up,' he answered, opened the door leaving it ajar while he went to get the bunch of flowers he had bought for her. He still hadn't had a chance to congratulate her on the brilliant job she had done with Chris Bolton. He wasn't sure what she'd said to him, but he had turned himself in, swearing that his mother had nothing to do with the theft of the money. He'd told the police he'd stolen the account details from her desk drawer. McQueen didn't believe him, but it didn't matter. The enigmatic but scary Mr Preston would get his man in jail and hopefully that would appease his bosses, especially as they already had the money back.

McQueen heard the door slam shut and he ducked out of the kitchen with the bouquet, but the "surprise" froze on his lips. Standing inside his door was Judy Greene. In her hand she was holding her mobile phone, she pressed the button and it played the recording of Lia's voice. *Hi, it's Lia*, and now McQueen recognised it from Lia's answerphone message.

'Dan told me about the entry phone but I thought you'd stop me at the door. I got lucky, I guess. Are those for me?' McQueen wasn't about to panic, he awkwardly put the flowers down on the coffee table. It was possible Judy had the blue handled knife in her bag but he was slightly more confident he had a chance against that than he had been about Joey's gun. But if she started slashing madly who knew what might happen?

'I know you know what I've been thinking about

The McQueen Legacy

because as soon as Dan changed his mind and said he would help me, I knew you'd got to him. I could tell from his clumsy questions and the way he was sweating that he was probably recording me and what he was trying to make me say. Entrapment, I think it's called?'

McQueen knew better than to try to deny it.

'Judy, don't you want to be happy now? It's been so long, don't you think there might be someone who could help you to be happy again? I know an excellent therapist called Maggie. She has helped me enormously and I would be glad to ask her to help you. I'd pay.'

'Out of guilt, McQueen, would that be from your own guilt?'

'I just want to help you, if I can, but I'm not the right person to do it.'

'Intrusive thoughts,' she said. 'I've been having these intrusive thoughts of killing you. That's why I went through that whole charade with Dan, so you could listen to it in the comfort of your own home. I wanted to scare you and I think I've done that tonight, but you know what, McQueen? I would never act on those thoughts. Not in a million years. It's not in me and I don't really want you to die. Your death wouldn't bring Katie back so it turns out you were right, intrusive thoughts don't mean a lot. Feelings aren't facts, they tell me. But I wanted to come to show you I could have done it if I had wanted to. To prove I am over that.'

'Will you speak to Maggie?'

'Maybe. I'm going to go now but I did bring you a couple of things.' She put her hand in her bag and for a split-second McQueen held his breath. She pulled out a bottle of red wine and put it on the coffee table and then she took out the framed photograph of Katie.

'It would be nice if you remembered her,' she said. 'It would mean a lot to me if you had a drink in her memory.'

An hour later McQueen was sitting nursing his aching knee. He'd put the flowers back in the kitchen sink. The picture of the baby was still on the coffee table, but he wasn't looking at it, a baby is a baby. Instead, he was transfixed by the unopened bottle of wine, lost in the ruby red colour of the thing that rather than a knife or a gun might well one day kill him.

But not today.

I'd like to thank every single person who reads this book, you are the reason it was written.

SRL Publishing don't just publish books, we also do our best in keeping this world sustainable. In the UK alone, over 77 million books are destroyed each year, unsold and unread, due to overproduction and bigger profit margins.

Our business model is inherently sustainable by only printing what we sell. While this means our cost price is much higher, it means we have minimum waste and zero returns. We made a public promise in 2020 to never overprint our books for the sake of profit.

We give back to our planet by calculating the number of trees used for our products so we can then replace them. We also calculate our carbon emissions and support projects which reduce CO2. These same projects also support the United Nations Sustainable Development Goals.

The way we operate means we knowingly waive our profit margins for the sake of the environment. Every book sold via the SRL website plants at least one tree.

To find out more, please visit
<u>*www.srlpublishing.co.uk/responsibility*</u>

Milton Keynes UK
Ingram Content Group UK Ltd.
UKHW021905061124
450796UK00001B/20

9 781915 073426